Kiss My AXE

R.M. NEILL

Contents

Chapter 1
Roman

"Tell me it was safe sex at least, Ro."

My sister groans as we clean up the kitchen after our family dinner.

"Of course it was! I'm not that irresponsible, Josie."

My sister, the oldest of the three of us, rolls her eyes towards her wife. "Says the man who also forgot to water my plants for two entire weeks because his eyes hurt."

"They did! Have you ever been on the water for twelve hours straight without sunglasses? And trying not to squint? It's hard."

"Cut him some slack." My sister-in-law, Violet, comes to my defence.

"Thank you, Vi. I always knew you were my favourite."

She shakes her head with a smile and leaves me and Josie alone again.

"Seriously, Roman. I worry about you. You shouldn't go off on these dates by yourself like that. People know your face."

She's right. Much like my best friend Sasha, I'm recognizable whether I like it or not. My name suits my looks, too. With my chiselled cheekbones and full lips, I do have a classic Roman look. I'm the prettiest of pretty boys and I know it.

And I also love it when men like to tell me the same.

Am I vain? Yes. But I don't aim to make it my entire personality. It's just one of those things I use to my advantage occasionally.

"It's fine, Jo. Really. Please stop worrying. And I wouldn't really refer to them as dates. They don't last long enough to know each other with clothes on."

With a huff, she turns to me and the same ocean blue eyes I see in the mirror every day look back.

"I'll never stop worrying, Ro. It's who I am. You know this."

Softening, I reach for my sister, who, at fifteen, became my mother overnight when our parents didn't come home. She shouldered every stress and worry for me. I was only seven, and I often slept with her for comfort until she gently explained it wasn't good for me to keep doing that. She loved her little brother, but not when he wrapped himself around her like an octopus every night.

She ate ice cream with me when I suffered my first broken heart and she bought me my very first lipstick after discovering I liked to wear hers. She's the best big sister a person could ever have. Well, one anyway. I have two big sisters, but Josie and I have a special bond.

I know she always walks this tight line of fear that it could happen to me, too. That I might not come home one night and she usually does a better job of hiding it.

"I'm sorry, sis. I promise I'll be better." Kissing her temple, I wrap her in my arms, squeezing her tight. "I can only do so much about the bears, though. They're wild and don't speak English."

"Roman! Would you stop!"

She wipes at her eyes with a smile. "I'm not worried about you being mauled by a bear."

"Well, not that kind anyway. Sasha tells me it's a veritable buffet of lumber-snacks at the lodge. I'd let that kind of bear do whatever he wants to me."

"Your mouth is going to get you in trouble, I swear."

"They like my mouth! No trouble at all."

"Okay, gross. I don't need to know that."

"Yet you questioned if I was having safe sex. Honestly, Jo, be consistent. Do you want details or not? Because the guy I met last night was—"

"Roman! Can you be serious for once?" She grabs me by the hand and pulls me out of the kitchen where our sister, Camryn, the middle child, sits with Violet. Camyrn is the quiet one of us three, but she's smart as a whip, and I know if I ever got into a fight with the meanest animal alive, Cam would be there risking her life for me. Even if it was my smart-ass mouth that put me in the position.

My sisters are fierce. They don't let me get away with much, but they love me and I know they'll have my back. Even if I do something stupid.

Camryn moves off the spot next to Violet so Josie can sit with her wife while Cam and I squish into the oversized chair, just like we did when we were kids. Jo and Vi live here in our family home and sometimes it's strange when we all gather here. I remember so many moments in this house, all of them happy, even after mom and dad died. We gather no less than once a month for a family Sunday. We have for as long as I can remember, and it's one of my favourite days.

Before Jo met Violet, it was just the three of us. We didn't allow any significant others until Josie admitted she really wanted Violet to be a part of our family. And for the last few years, it's been the four of us. Violet married us all, God bless her. And I love her like my biological sisters.

"Violet and I have something we want to tell you two. We haven't talked about it much because we didn't want to jinx it. With Roman moving away, we wanted to tell you in person before you go." Josie smiles at her wife and my chest tightens. There's no greater love I've seen between a couple than my sister and her wife.

"We're going to have a baby!" Josie bursts out and immediately starts crying. "They're happy tears and hormones. I'm sorry." She sniffles and both Camryn and I bounce out of the chair to our older sister.

Cam hugs her long and hard with quiet whispers, but she's smiling bigger than I've ever seen.

"Well? How does it feel to know you're going to be an uncle?"

I'm going to be an uncle. Oh, my god.

"Uncle Ro," I whisper. "Holy shit."

I hug my sister tight and feel the familiar prick of tears in my eyes. No. I'm not fucking crying over a baby. No.

"Roman...tears are okay."

Releasing her, I hug Violet too, and all four of us have tear-stained cheeks by the time the hugging is done.

"I'm coming back as often as you need me. I'm not that useful at the whole babysitting thing, but I could learn. And I don't want to miss a minute of this kid's life. You hear me?"

My sister just smiles that loopy, happy smile because she knows me the best. She knows I love my family and adore the stability, but a free spirit like me can't stay. I mean every word. If my sister needs me, I'll drop everything, just like she did for me and Camryn.

"I'm not even three months yet, but I wanted to tell you before you left and have Cam here. We all have lives, but another one is coming. Our family is growing and Violet and I would like to know if you two are okay with us renovating the bedrooms. We'll still have a place for you both when you visit, but we want the baby to have their own room."

"This is your home first," Camryn says, and I nod in agreement. "Make it the baby's home, too. We'll work it out, won't we, Ro?"

"Of course. I'm not changing diapers though. That's above my pay grade."

"We were hoping you could do something else for us, Roman." Violet takes Josie's hand. "Would you make a going home outfit for the baby? Something special they'd wear home from the hospital for their first car ride and arriving home?"

My family has never stopped being my cheerleader. I designed dresses for my sisters as soon as I discovered I liked to sew. They were there when I graduated with my bachelor's degree in design, and now they tug at my heart with this kind of request.

"If you were trying to see how much you could make me cry today, mission fucking accomplished. I'd love to."

The rest of my last family Sunday afternoon get-together before I move continues with the four of us, remembering things from our childhood that we want the baby to experience. Violet gazes at my sister like she hung the moon and I know this baby will have the best damn family it could ever ask for.

Leaving them is more difficult than I expected, but they're all a short plane ride away. I won't be completely alone either. My best friend Sasha is the whole reason for this move. I love him like a brother and our bond rivals that of my sisters. If you're in my circle,

I love hard. There's no other way I know. But the circle is small because, like my best friend, it's hard for me to trust.

When your entire world crumbles at the tender age of seven, you experience life with a different outlook than other kids.

But I still need to live the life I've carved for myself. I have an empire to build that my family supports. And it's waiting for me in the small town of Maple.

"It's a good thing I love you, Sasha."

The old pickup truck lurches along the dirt road and Sasha grins at me. He's so damn tiny behind the wheel he looks like a child playing at being an adult. Gone is the put-together friend I've known for half my life. No more fashionable clothes and perfect hair.

Nope, these days Sasha wears old clothes and ball caps and a smile you could see from space. The change from city fashion to country life with his lumberjack boyfriend, Leaf, has been good for Sasha. His spark is back, and he's moving forward in a new direction.

And here I am right beside him, just like I promised. I miss my sisters, but I can't work without Sasha. He's my friend and soulmate, and I'd follow him anywhere. He's also an amazing photographer.

He's the yin to my yang or some kind of shit like that. I just wish we had a more... refined mode of transportation. He advised me to leave my *Mercedes* roadster with my sisters. Now I understand why.

"Oh, you always talk such a big game, Ro. You're gonna love it here."

"I don't know, Sasha. There's still a lot of snow. And mud. Where's all the pretty stuff you kept texting me pics of?"

"Sitting right beside you." He snort laughs.

"That's my line!" I laugh along with him. "Seriously though, what the hell? You said this maple syrup thing is a festival. They do that in the mud?"

He's not that much further north of where I'm coming from. How is it possible for it to still be so... icky? The spring flowers are already starting back home.

"Well, sort of? I mean, the sugar shack is in the woods, and it gets muddy in the spring sometimes with the snowmelt and if it rains. But as long as you don't go there without your boots, you're fine."

"You're not exactly selling this to me, Sasha."

He laughs at me again and wrangles the big truck off the highway to a smaller dirt road.

"You'll be fine. You're free to move back or even into town if you don't like it out here. There's not much for entertainment that you'd like and it's a huge change and—"

"Sasha. I'll deal with it. You said the town has amazing coffee and a bar with lumberjacks. I'll find something to pass the time. Or someone. I'll make it work."

"I mean...I know you were concerned when I first came here for a month and you like to be social. I just don't want you unhappy."

And that's why Sasha is my best friend. He'd sacrifice his own happiness for me and, unlike myself, he often puts himself last.

"I'll be too busy working to go out. Since you left, all I've been doing is sketch after sketch. I'll need to make some samples and photographs and start planning how best to fulfill orders." Looking out the truck window, a man dressed in plaid on a bicycle waves at us. Sasha waves back. "It'll be fine, Sash."

When I came up with the crazy idea to branch out on my own and start a business designing bespoke lingerie for men, I didn't anticipate how quickly my designs would take off. What began as hand-making six to twelve orders a month in the corner of my bedroom quickly morphed to over a hundred a month and I called on friends to help.

Now I've paused them all to concentrate on the new line I've been playing with and revamp the online purchasing and catalogue. With Sasha's help, we're almost ready to get the company rolling again.

"Well, it can't be all work and no play, Ro."

"Oh, I'll play. Don't you worry about that. It just might not be as often."

I've already searched the area and there's a decent gay bar in the city ninety minutes away. Not to mention a handful of potential partners on the hookup apps nearby. Oh, and I can't forget the bar he told me about that's overflowing with beards and brawn. I have faith that I'll find a balance between work and... fun... easily enough.

"But I'll need to get another vehicle. Thanks for the heads up on leaving the car behind."

"Oh, about that. I know I said I'd take you to the dealership, but Leaf suggested he go with you. Would you mind? Leaf said he doesn't want you to be taken advantage of."

"Nobody takes advantage of me, Sasha. Do you even know me?"

His eyebrows scrunch together as he huffs.

"You know what I mean. You know nothing about cars except what kind you look good in." He raises an eyebrow when I protest. "Leaf can help you choose something more functional."

"I'm sure it will be fine. If you want me to go with Leaf, I will."

Sasha chatters away about his life at the lodge as we drive through the patchy snow-covered area. It's hard for me to visualize the beauty of the place with all the melting and general filth of spring, but Sasha seems to love it.

"Your delivery was supposed to show up today, too. So really, you just have to get unpacked and settled. Leaf expanded the suite to accommodate you and before you object, it was in his plans. He just never got to it. He wants to make it a two-bedroom rental."

"Your man sure is sweet, isn't he? You're sure I'm not imposing? I know we have a rental agreement, but if I'm in the way—"

"Absolutely not. Don't even think that."

He steers the mammoth truck onto another side road that's dirt and gravel and it's rather muddy the farther we go up. My friend pauses and pushes a button on the dash that says 4x4 high. He glances my way and laughs when I question him.

"It's so we don't get stuck. There was a washout earlier this spring and they haven't repaired the soft spot yet. It's usually fine, but I never want to take any chances with it."

"Listen to you. Did you ever think this would be you? Driving a giant truck in the bush, using a four-by-four and just... loving everything about it?"

Sasha steers the truck as the low growl of the engine fills the cab along with his contented sigh.

"Fuck, Ro...I've never been happier. Now that you're here, I hope you like it as much as I do. But don't be afraid to tell me if you don't!" He rushes on, "Because we'll make it work for both of us, okay? You try it like this and if it's a no-go, then we find something else."

"I'll be fine, Sasha. Don't worry."

He pulls up in front of the rustic lodge he sent me pictures of before and while it's still early spring, it's not as pretty and definitely more dirty. But I gingerly step out of his truck and avoid all the puddles to join him on the quaint wooden porch.

"Is there someone to get my bags? Like a porter or something? I don't want to keep walking through the mud."

Sasha snorts and loops his arm through mine.

"First, you're coming to the kitchen to meet Millie. I'll ask someone to help. There're no porters, Ro. It's a wilderness lodge, not the Ritz."

"Right." I'm not good at rustic... at all. "I'm still adjusting."

Perhaps it might be harder than I thought for this transition, but when my best friend is sunshine and happy to see me, pulling me into a kitchen that smells like maple heaven, I'm going to go along with it.

Chapter 2
Roman

"Oh my. You're the Roman that Sasha always talks about?"

The grey-haired woman in the kitchen just... hugs me. She doesn't wait for any kind of sign that I'm okay with it. She just does. And... I like it.

"I am. You must be the Millie he always talks about."

She smiles warmly at Sasha and a wave of nostalgia hits me so hard I have to blink it back. It's been over twenty years since I'd been in a kitchen with my mother, and that wave of emotion came out of nowhere.

"I am. Here, sit. I made Sasha's favourite cookies, and he said you like gingersnaps."

I settle on a stool at the large industrial stainless steel kitchen island. Millie places plates of cookies down and Sasha bounces with a laugh.

"Ah, yeah! How awesome! You're a peach Millie." Sasha reaches for his maple creme cookie with the boyish exuberance I love about him.

"All he ever eats is cookies, you know."

Millie chastises Sasha, but it's all in jest. She'd feed him cookies every day if he asked for it by the looks of things.

Sasha playfully sticks out his tongue as I reach for a gingersnap.

"It's not my fault you got me hooked on maple everything like it's heroin, Millie."

"I'm certain I'm not forcing you to eat them, my dear. Now, Roman, are you happy to join us? What did you think about the drive in?"

Pausing with a cookie at my mouth, my eyes dart to Sasha. He raises an eyebrow with pursed lips and I turn back to Millie.

"I bet it's really pretty when the snow melts."

"Oh, it is! But we need the snow and all the mess of the melt to make the syrup this boy loves." She ruffles the hair on Sasha's head and he smiles so big it's a pull on my heart. Sasha never had a family like I do. This is good for him. He's happy and thriving here and I couldn't be more thrilled to witness it.

"There's my beauty. I thought I heard you come in."

Leaf enters the kitchen and kisses Sasha, letting his warm gaze linger on his lover before turning to greet me.

"Nice to see you again, Roman. Welcome to the lodge. How did you like Sasha behind the wheel of a giant half-tonne? He's only taken out a few shrubs so far."

Leaf smiles at Sasha, and I have to look away. Leaf's gaze at my friend sets off an uncomfortable ache in my chest. One that keeps returning, and it's more annoying than heartburn. I have no desire to be all hearts and rainbows with one man forever, but sometimes the look on Sasha's face makes me want to change my mind. Almost.

"I wasn't in fear of my life, Leaf. Don't worry about that. But I'll need to get myself a 4x4 from what Sasha said. I was thinking about a *Land Rover*. Is there a dealer nearby?"

Millie sets a glass of milk in front of me, and I happily reach for another gingersnap. I could get used to this.

"Save your money and get a *GM*. If a Land Rover breaks, you're towing it two hours away for repair." A man wearing a pair of work overalls with no shirt underneath enters the kitchen and pulls a jug of orange juice from the fridge with a nod to Millie. He's all wide shoulders and muscles built with labour, not gym time. A swirl of dark chest hair peeks out from the front of his overalls and I wonder how the hell he's not cold without a shirt on. His hands look like he just dismantled a car engine. Covered in dirt or oil, it's almost too hard to tell the colour of his skin.

Although I can tell he still carries a tan from the previous summer. His chest is more pale than his arms.

I watch as he plucks a glass off a nearby tray and pours himself a glass of juice, touching the cap with his filthy hands. And something about that makes me snap.

"You're in a kitchen. You should wash your hands before touching stuff in the fridge. I hope that juice isn't for guests."

The man pauses and fixes his pale blue eyes on me. Along with everyone else.

"Are you the new kitchen police?"

"No."

"Then keep your opinions to yourself."

"Like you kept your opinion about a Land Rover to yourself?"

He nods with a condescending glance. "That wasn't an opinion. It's a fact. I'm doing you a favour."

"Well, *I'm* doing the guests of this lodge a favour asking you to wash before you paw everything with your filth."

"Ro, don't be so rude."

Sasha elbows me with a questioning stare.

"I'm not rude. He is."

The burly man pauses his drinking and smirks.

"Ah, so you're Roman. I should've guessed."

Standing straight, I glare at him. Words spoken to me with that tone are never good. And I won't let him think I have no backbone.

"What's that supposed to mean?"

Leaf claps his hand on the man's back. "Okay. Enough, you two. Roman, this is my brother Perry and I'm going to ask that you forgive his attitude today. We've been rushing to finish the renovations in your suite and we hit a snag. He's not usually like this."

"I fixed it." Perry grits and instead of flying off the handle, I breathe in and count to five.

"Is there a problem with the room?"

"Not anymore...Roman." He fake smiles at me. "Your palace is ready."

He makes a show of touching the juice cap again before kissing Millie on the head and leaving the way he came.

"Um, so I told you Leaf wanted to renovate, and this was the perfect time to do it, remember?" Sasha wrings his hands and I immediately let the anger go. I don't like him upset.

"I do. I'm sorry. But if I caused you any problems, I can help recoup the costs, Leaf."

"Oh, that's unnecessary. It's just..." Leaf rubs the back of his neck and Sasha smoothes a hand on his back.

"What he's trying to say is he got a little carried away in his quest to become the next great house flipper and fix past problems in an older building. There was a plumbing issue, and it took more work than he or Perry realized. They've put in some long hours and Perry is likely just overtired. But the good news is it's fixed!"

Leaf smiles with a nod. "Yeah, it's fixed. We hope you like it."

"Okay, great. Can I get my bags and settle in then?"

Sasha loops his arm through mine as we head to his truck for my substantial number of suitcases. Leaf comes with us and we catch up as the three of us struggle with the luggage through the lodge and up the short staircase to my suite. Well, Sasha and I struggle. Leaf seems to be fine carrying two enormous suitcases on his own.

When we reach the door, Leaf fishes out an old-fashioned key with a wooden maple leaf attached to it.

"Sorry, it's not a key card or *iPhone* or whatever." He smiles sheepishly. "I'm sure Sasha has told you I'm old school here. My guests don't particularly care, so it's still keys."

Sasha snorts. "Just a little old school, but I love you like that."

They do this cute, happy couple kiss thing in front of me while he turns the key to my room and I roll my eyes. Couples should reserve cuteness like that for puppies, not themselves.

The door swings open and I'm greeted with the smell of fresh paint and a room brimming with natural sunlight.

The room itself is bright and modern, which I wasn't expecting. New light fixtures and fresh carpet are obvious in the main room, and I smile when I notice the boxes piled up against the wall.

"Ah! Is that all my fabric?"

Rushing forward, I check the tags and it's indeed the shipment I was hoping for.

"They came two days ago. I just brought them up here but thought you'd like to wait to open them. And come see what we did in the bathroom."

Sasha pulls me into the oversized bathroom with a gorgeous shower.

"This is where the reno problems happened, so really it's my fault. I know you need to steam the fabric, so instead of constantly having to fill your steamer, the shower has an option for steam. I ordered a special rack to hold the fabric and you can just wheel it in and turn the steam on. Use an iron if needed on problem spots. It will decrease your work time, I hope."

Sasha, my bestest friend in the world, waits for my response and I'm truly touched by his thoughtfulness.

"This is amazing Sasha. I love it."

"I mean, you can use it for a steam room, too. It's not just for the fabric. I know you liked those Turkish steam baths that time in Montreal. I just...I want you to feel at home here, Ro."

"You're here. My fabric is here and we're about to work together...finally. This will be home, Sasha. Don't worry about me."

"Okay." His sunshine grin is hard not to return. "I'm so glad you're here. I can't wait for you to see the sugar bush and come to the Maple Festival. And feed you pancakes! You will die for the ones Millie makes."

Sasha once again loops his arm through mine and pulls me out of the bathroom to the main room.

"We should let him get settled, beauty. We thought you'd like to join us for dinner tonight in our apartment. This suite has no cooking facilities, unlike our cabins, so you'll need to use the lodge kitchen or join us when you like."

"I'm sure I'll figure it all out. I'd love to join you guys, though!"

"I'll come and get you around 6 P.M., if that's okay? I'll give you a full tour and show you where you can always find us."

"That's perfect."

After saying goodbye to Sasha and Leaf, I close the door with a sigh and survey the new space, done especially for me. It's small but functional and should do just fine while we get started. They set up one bedroom with two large tables for me to work on, and the other one is for sleeping.

Rolling one mammoth hard-sided Louis Vuitton suitcase into the bedroom, I'm pleased to see the king-size bed and an oversized wardrobe. It won't even contain my selection of business suits and corsets, but it will do for now. I have a feeling I may have to adjust my clothing choices here, anyway.

I've never been picky about the places I lay my head at night. When I moved out of my family home and away from my sisters, I preferred to share apartments with people who needed the help. As long as it wasn't some sketchy place where I'd get robbed, I was game. And it came with ample closet space, of course.

Where I called home wasn't something I ever concerned myself with. I'd rather drive a comfortable car and wear nice clothes than spend money on a fancy apartment or house I rarely spend time in. Not to mention my pesky hang-up about not being able to sleep unless someone else was in the house.

So this arrangement should do just fine. I hope.

After unpacking my largest suitcase, I grab the tote with my toiletries, strip down and head to the shower Sasha was so excited about.

For good reason.

After arranging all my hair and skin care products and placing my favourites in the shower, I fire it up and step inside. The water is hot and perfect and the steam releases the knots in my muscles as I plaster my favourite mud mask on and sink into the warmth.

Sasha isn't my best friend for nothing. This is amazing for me to sit and enjoy without leaving my room. I'll have to buy him one of those sappy romance books he loves as a thank-you. Maybe on my first visit to town after I get a vehicle. No, that will take too long. I'll ask for a ride in sooner and treat him. Hell, I should buy him the whole dang store for this.

With a low chime, the timer clicks, and the steam stops. Rinsing off, I step out and go through my moisturizing routine, humming and happy. Truly happy.

I might not like the mud and ick of spring here in the bush, but I love everything else. Mostly.

Until I arrive at Sasha and Leaf's place.

Chapter 3
Perry

"**I** did what you told me to, Ted. Maybe when you're up next, you can remove the panel and double-check."

My friend's voice booms over the phone's speaker while I trim my beard. I've let it get out of hand while helping Leaf with his renovations. I swear a bird could have nested in it, and I'd not even notice.

"I'm sure you did what you needed to, Perry. I'm not heading that way for a while yet, but you can send me some pics if you're worried."

Tapping my shaver on the sink, I toss it to the side and pile my damp towel on the counter.

"Yeah, I'll do that if it gives me any other issues. I checked damn near thirty feet of hose for leaks and nothing."

"And you're sure you didn't hit a water pipe on install? Some of those houses have shitty plumbing and when you renovate it disrupts their joints."

No, I'm not sure, but that's the part I'll keep to myself. We had already tiled the new shower, at Sasha's begging, and it completely slipped my mind. But the leak stopped, so I'm confident it was defective tubing. Mostly.

"I think it's good there. But if I hear anything on that construction project near Leaf, I'll let you know first thing."

"Thanks, buddy. You take care of yourself, okay? Call me anytime."

My throat closes a little, and I nod into the empty room.

"I will Ted. Thanks."

Ending the call, I walk naked to my bedroom and groan when I notice my basket of clean laundry is now empty. This rush to finish the renovation had me forget all about doing laundry. To be honest, I forget about most things these days. But I'm not out of clean clothes yet, so it's a win.

Sort of.

I have exactly three T-shirts left in my drawer and two aren't appropriate to wear out of the house.

"Maybe I should hire someone to help me out here."

I'm not sure who I'm talking to, but it's a thought that's crossed my mind a few times. But I always stuff it down because help means I can't do it myself. My therapist tells me it's an incorrect thought path and asking for help means you're strong, but I've yet to agree with him on that point.

After pulling on my last clean, appropriate shirt and mostly clean pair of jeans, I grab my keys and head off to my brother's place for dinner. Whenever Leaf invites me for food at his place, I never say no. Especially since he met Sasha and has rejoined society by coming out of his grief.

His life is finally back on track and every time I see him, I want to squeeze the ever-loving stuffing out of him because I'm so happy he's happy. Now, if I could get *my* life back on track, that would be great.

One thing at a time, as the saying goes.

Parking in the space next to Leaf's truck, I grab the wine bottle from the back seat. It's Sasha's favourite, and I let myself in their private entrance.

"I'm here! And since I'm late, you shouldn't be naked or anything."

I walked in on them once and it set off a fresh wave of nightmares. Nobody needs to see their brother's naked ass... ever.

"Coast is clear!" Leaf's voice carries down the small flight of steps. His apartment sits at the back of the lodge and over the lodge kitchen with an incredible view of the lake. While he has an entrance through the lodge kitchen, he has a private side entrance as well. Since Sasha moved here, there's been a conscious effort to use it more and make it feel more like home and less like work.

One of Sasha's ideas and I think it's a great one.

Bouncing up the stairs with my wine bottle, I step into his open-concept apartment and head straight to the kitchen island where Leaf chops something like a professional chef.

"Do you have to be good at everything?"

Leaf snorts as I place the wine in the fridge and help myself to a beer.

"Anything for me to help with?"

"It's under control. Sasha should be back soon."

"Where is he?"

"He's showing Roman around and bringing him here."

Closing my eyes, I breathe out through my nose. I should have known. Why am I so stupid sometimes? I don't think I've ever had someone get under my skin so instantly, like he did. Sasha has been so excited for this day to come and I had to go be an asshole in record time.

"Cool," I say, but Leaf gives me that look reserved for brothers who are only eleven months apart and know each other too well. "What?"

"Why were you so rude to him? He just got here and I know he's not a horrible person. Just like I know you're sometimes prickly, but Perry, it wasn't like you. He's Sasha's best friend. You need to get along."

"He started it."

Yes. I'm being childish and stubborn, but I don't have any other reason. At least not one that I want to dwell on with an empty stomach.

"Perry, come on. He's coming for dinner and I don't need you two at each other's throats like dogs." He raises an eyebrow as he tosses onions into the pan. "And you started it."

"Land Rovers are a waste of fucking money. He's just another uppity city boy coming here and thinking if he has all the big expensive toys, it will somehow make him immune to whatever the wilderness throws at him."

The lodge guests have been getting progressively worse with that attitude and it's been grating on me. I don't know if it's because people know a supermodel now lives here or they just suddenly feel like making a trip to a mosquito-laden lodge in northern Québec, but it's irritating as fuck. Especially since not a single one of them returned any of my flirting.

"He's not like that, and if you took the time to know him, you'd know that. Roman is Sasha's best friend and you know damn well he'll be crushed if the two of you can't get along." Leaf adds more onions to the pan with butter and flour before stealing a swallow from his nearby beer. "What's gotten into you? Are the nightmares picking up again?"

My brother has a knack for multi-tasking, and right now it's cooking and grilling me. He's always been able to notice when things bother me. Before his husband passed away–god I miss that guy–he always picked up on my moods before me. Now that he's enjoying life again with Sasha, it seems his superpowers are back.

"Your silence speaks for itself, brother. I can wait. When you want to talk, I'll be here."

"I —"

"Baby, we're here!"

Sasha's voice sounds and I watch as my brother's eyes light up as he rushes to meet his partner like they haven't seen each other in weeks. He kisses him soundly and I gulp the beer to drown the little voice that whispers it's what I want. To be kissed like that.

"Man, I need to leave the house more often." Sasha breathes.

Clearing my throat, I smile when Sasha turns my way.

"Perry! You're already here! Did Leaf offer the dip I made just for you?"

"No. Did you..." I can't help the smile as Sasha opens the fridge and sets a vegetable platter on the kitchen island. "Oh man, it's that dilly ranch stuff? The stuff you made before?"

"Yep. Made it just for you." He kisses my cheek before peeling the cover off of the platter.

Unbidden, my eyes water and I cover it up by pretending to choke on my beer.

"You remember Roman?"

Recovering from my fake coughing, I finally acknowledge the other man and immediately wish I hadn't.

Roman, the same mouthy asshole from earlier today, is here. And he sure knows how to make an entrance. Dressed in black leather pants, a crisp white dress shirt and a red corset with black details, he's fucking ravishing.

Until he opens his mouth.

"Oh. I didn't realize he'd be here too."

"Ro! Don't be so rude."

I smirk when Sasha comes to my defence and Roman scowls.

"Sorry. Hi. Are you going to share the dip or just hoard it for yourself?"

Sasha stares open-mouthed at his friend and, I have to admit, even I'm slightly offended.

"I had two carrots. I'd hardly call it hoarding. But I just lost my appetite, anyway."

Sasha cuffs Roman on the back of the head.

"What the fuck, Sasha?"

Roman rubs the spot Sasha smacked with a pout.

"Apologize for that right now. Perry is my friend and you're in my home. If your sisters knew you were acting like this, they'd be doing far more than cuffing you upside the head."

Roman's already alabaster skin pales at the mention of his sisters and he hangs his head.

"I'm sorry, Perry. That was uncalled for, and I didn't mean anything by it."

I nod in acceptance and Sasha claps his hands together.

"Great. Now we start over. Baby, what do you need me to do?"

Sasha and Leaf move into a comfortable rhythm in the kitchen and shoo us into the living room. It's open-concept, so Roman and I aren't removed from what they're doing. Avoiding speaking directly to each other, we watch Leaf and Sasha until it grows into an awkward silence.

"How was your flight?"

"Good."

He sips from the wineglass Sasha poured for him. Sasha's favourite wine I brought for him.

"Do you like the wine? It's Sasha's favourite."

"It's good."

This will be one painful evening if the level of conversation doesn't pick up. So, instead of trying for more conversation, I study him in between dunking broccoli in the dip and calculating how long is a polite time to pass before I eat and run.

Because fuck this.

The guy hates me and barely knows me. We're off to a horrible first meeting. But I'm not about to tolerate it for longer than I have to if he's not willing to start over. I'm also not ditching my brother's cooking for this guy. Ugh, or Sasha. How did this day get so damn complicated?

Roman turns his head to look around the apartment and I'm drawn to his profile. I admit, he's easy on the eyes. He is, hands down, one of the most beautiful men I've ever met. He's also the first one I've met who wears a corset to dinner as casually as one would a T-shirt from *Walmart*.

My gaze scans his torso without permission, drawn to the cinched waist and hips and back up to the delicate vine pattern at the shoulders.

"Did you have another question?" His cool blue eyes meet mine over his wineglass as he takes a sip. He caught me looking and knows it.

"No."

Yes. But now is not the time to ask.

"Dinner is ready!" Sasha interrupts and thank god for once his timing is impeccable because I'm still staring at Roman.

We all gather at the table and Leaf tells Roman how he loves cooking a roast for family dinner and it's his favourite meal to make.

"Reminds me of when we were kids," I say with a smile, and Leaf nods.

"Yeah, I loved the time in the kitchen helping mom. She taught me how to make the gravy."

Sunday family dinners like this were a highlight of our childhood. Our family was small but close and I cherish those times. When Leaf announced he bought property and was moving here permanently, even though our parents were already gone, I didn't want our traditions to fall away.

We tried our best with our careers to keep up some semblance of tradition, but our meetups were sparse. He was my big brother though and I couldn't just let him move away, so I did what was best. I moved here to be close to the only blood family I had left. By doing so, I also left the career I had made a priority in my life. But it had taken a toll on me and the move came at the best possible time.

"I'm glad you did. I love your onion gravy. It really is just like mom's."

I pour more of it on my roast beef. I'd put this stuff on everything if Leaf made it for me every day.

"Leaf has told me about learning to cook with your mom. I think that's why I enjoy being in the kitchen with Millie so much. I never had the home stability like that with my mom. She had us moving so often and she worked all the time with her art. Dinner was often whatever was frozen."

Sasha has mentioned many times to me how much he wished he had the idyllic suburban family life that Leaf and I enjoyed. But he still loves hearing our stories even if it makes him a little sad.

"I tried to cook with mom once, but it was a disaster." Laughing, I point to Leaf, who's trying not to laugh along with me and failing.

"The blender. Oh, my god. She was so mad at you."

Leaf wipes a tear from his eye as he laughs.

"She didn't tell me it needed a lid!"

"There was batter on the ceiling for years. Might even still be there." Leaf snorts.

Sasha sips his wine and smiles, basking in the memories Leaf and I sometimes get lost in. But Roman remains quiet. His blue eyes trained on his plate as he pushes food around rather than eating it.

Sasha whispers in his ear and Roman shakes his head before topping up his wine and joining the conversation with a fake smile.

"Your mom sounds wonderful, and it's an amazing meal, Leaf. Thank you so much for inviting me. I'd love to take you to a fantastic steak house this week when you take me to the Land Rover dealership to say thank you. It's not as good as you make, but I bet you'll love it."

Leaf closes his eyes with a groan.

"Shit. That was to be Wednesday, wasn't it?" He looks to Sasha for confirmation.

"Yes, but I can choose a different day if it's better."

"With all the renovations happening, I pushed off the meetings I have with supplying syrup to a grocery store and a restaurant chain. I could try the following week?"

Roman, to his credit, hides his disappointment well.

"Oh, it's okay. I don't want to bother more than I have. I can look for an *Uber* driver or something to take me."

I can't help the snort and Roman glares at me.

"Do you have something to say or just being rude again?"

With a sigh, I let the jab pass and attempt politeness.

"You can't get an Uber to take you to the city. Even if you can afford it, they likely won't wait while you buy a car. But people don't get Ubers here. I think the town has two taxis to it's name. If you don't mind going Tuesday, I'll take you."

His eyes widen while his mouth opens and closes and I keep eating. Because I honestly don't care if he takes my offer or not. I'm just trying to smooth shit over here for the sake of my brother and Sasha.

"Um, yeah, thanks. I'd appreciate that."

Sasha beams like I just gave him a new puppy and my brother, well... he's clearly got questions for me.

And I don't have a single answer.

Chapter 4
Roman

The sun peeks through the curtains of my room as I check the time on my phone.

8:30 A.M. is mighty late for me to sleep in.

But last night was literally hell. I travelled most of the day, unpacked in my new home and tried to enjoy the amazing home-cooked meal Leaf made. But it was a day with too much.

The talk of families and closeness turned my joyful mood into melancholy. I missed my sisters and parents. And it didn't help that Leaf's brother pissed me off with every clink of his fork, slurp of his wine, and word from his mouth as he laughed along with Leaf. I should enjoy time with friends laughing over memories, but last night I just couldn't.

Sasha should've warned me Leaf's brother was nothing like him. He was loud and opinionated on everything from cars to what colour the sky was. And yet I agreed to let him drive me to the city. Tomorrow.

Rolling out of bed, I make my way to the bathroom. A damp odour lingers, and I make a note to ask Sasha if that's normal here.

I'm so excited to get to work and bring our vision to life. I still need to set up my mannequins and sewing machine. And the lace.

Oh, my god I want to play with the lace I ordered and see if it's as amazing as the top designers say it is.

But first I need coffee and breakfast. While it's a minor inconvenience to get dressed and walk down to the kitchen instead of making it here, I like the vibe of this place. And I bet when it's teeming with people, it's actually a blast to be here.

Sasha can't stop talking about taking me hiking and out on the boat and as amazing as those things are for him, I'm more of a let's ride in an air-conditioned car and look at the sights through windows kind of guy.

Making sure I have my room key, I slip my short *UGG* slippers on and wander down to the kitchen. It's hard to believe that in two days time, this quiet space will be anything but as people flock to town for the Maple Festival and the grand opening of Leaf's sugar shack.

I pause at a series of photos in the dining room that Sasha took and framed. It's a history of the rebuild and shaping of Connor's Cabin and the whole maple syrup set up Leaf has. When his husband Connor passed away unexpectantly the poor man no longer had the heart to pursue his dream of producing maple syrup.

But in these pictures, he's smiling, and it's clear it's a passion for him. Just as much as his love for my friend is. And it warms my heart to know Sasha has finally put his past behind him to enjoy life again. His smile always lights up a room and when you're the source of that smile... it's truly something else.

And with my own big dopey smile on, I enter the kitchen to wrangle my coffee. It still smells like the cookies Millie baked yesterday and my mouth waters. Cookies and coffee sound like a hell of a way to start the day.

The coffee maker is a giant and meant for a restaurant. Millie, bless her heart, left me a note to remind me that the 'on' switch is at the back of the machine.

I chuckle under my breath because without coffee, that note came in handy.

After firing the monstrosity up, I wait for it to brew and poke around the kitchen to bring food up to my room. Sasha stocked some of my favourites, since he knows it will take a few days for me to get settled. He mentioned he bought my favourite banana yogurt and some strawberries. I won't attempt a smoothie today, but I'll take them separately. Only when I pull out the package of strawberries, there's two left.

With a sigh, I place it on the counter and opt to just eat them here and take my coffee upstairs.

The main lodge door opens and closes with a muffled thump and heavy steps approach the kitchen.

Perry steps into the doorway and stops short when he sees me. His eyes dart to the empty strawberry box.

Because of course he had to be the one to eat my strawberries. Guilt was never more transparent.

"I didn't think anyone was up."

"No one was when you raided the kitchen this morning." I raise the empty container and take a bite of the strawberry. "Did you even stop for a minute to think this wasn't for you? Or do you always make it a habit to take things that don't belong to you?"

"How do you know it was me?"

He strides to the coffee machine and reaches for the carafe.

"Excuse me! I made that for me and it just finished brewing. I haven't even poured a cup yet." Shaking my head, I bite the last part of strawberry and imagine it's his head.

"Sorry, your highness." he snarks, placing the carafe back with a shove and I smash my hand on the counter.

"Don't make me feel bad. It's my coffee! And you ate the strawberries!"

He throws his hands up and I mimic his reaction.

"I didn't know there was food police now. And I didn't know they were yours. I always just snack from the fridge, so don't make *me* feel bad!"

"For fuck's sake, all I wanted was breakfast and coffee, not a goddamn yelling match. You could at least apologize!"

I no longer even want the food. Just the coffee and to get away from Perry and his blazing blue eyes and pouty lips and... Jesus Christ. My brain has short-circuited.

Instead of making a coffee I storm out of the kitchen. He can have the coffee and I'll go back to my room. Because I'm not into fighting and I'm not into noticing someone's eyes -ice-washed blue—and their lips—perfect for biting- after they've eaten my breakfast and tried to steal my coffee.

Jamming the key into the lock, I enter the room with a rush and slam the door behind me.

"Get a fucking grip, Roman."

Sasha is going to kill me. I can't seem to stop running my mouth off with this guy. And I'll be seeing him every damn day. Not to mention stuck in a vehicle with him all day tomorrow. This is not good for any of us.

Stripping off my clothes, I toss them on the bed. A hot shower, then I'll send Sasha an SOS to bring me food and coffee. But on my way to the bathroom, there's a knock at the door.

"Who is it!?"

God, I just want to have a moment to settle myself and claw back some composure.

"Perry."

Oh, for the love of... "Just a minute."

Striding back to my bedroom, I pull on my sleep pants and robe before opening the door to find Perry waiting.

He wordlessly offers the mug that I left in the kitchen.

"You could have just left it there."

He shrugs. "You went there for coffee. It's the least I could do for eating your strawberries."

Taking the mug, I peer inside. It's a delightful light, creamy brown and despite my attitude, my traitorous lips smile.

"You left the cream and sugar on the counter. I guessed how you liked it, but you seem like a heavy sugar and light on the cream guy."

His voice is softer now that we're yelling at each other, and I don't hate it.

"Why would you say that?"

Is he some kind of coffee witch and reads people to make their coffee exactly how they want?

"Sugar takes away the bitterness and just a hint of cream makes it smooth. Makes coffee more palatable for people that way."

My gaze meets his, and for a moment he seems likeable. Perhaps I've been too harsh. Even if he is implying I'm bitter by the way I take my coffee.

Until he opens his mouth again.

"Anyway, next time just label the berries."

He doesn't even let me answer and just walks away. Like he owns the damn place, and I'm just... irrationally pissed off all over again.

Because he should've had the decency to make a shitty cup of coffee so I could justify my opinion of him and stay mad.

This time when a knock comes at the door, I know who it will be and I open it with a smile.

"Hey! Thank you for saving me."

Sasha steps inside with a bag he dumps on the tiny coffee table in my sitting area.

"I will always save you, Ro. But..." He raises an eyebrow. "You need to do me a favour and stop fighting with Perry. What happened this time?"

With a sigh, I sit on the couch and open the bag Sasha brought me. Does he know me well or what? A leftover roast beef sandwich from last night and veggies with dip.

Taking a moment to set the food out and gather my thoughts, I search Sasha's face.

"Don't look at me like that."

"Like what?"

"You're assuming I did something wrong. I didn't."

Sasha leans back with a sigh, and I tear into the sandwich.

"Is this homemade bread?"

His eyes light up. "Yeah! I made it with Millie. Good right?"

"Insanely good."

"She's the best. We're going to try sourdough next, but she needs to start the mix or something she said." He leans forward and snatches the rest of my sandwich off the table.

"Hey!"

"Tell me why you're at Perry's throat before you even give him a chance, Ro. It's not like you to be so rude. And I've heard his side. I want yours."

I should have known Sasha would look for answers right away. I'm a mellow guy and while I may be opinionated about certain things, I don't like to make people feel uncomfortable.

"I honestly don't know, Sasha. He just gets to me."

He cocks an eyebrow, not buying my explanation in the slightest.

"Try again."

Taking another bite of the sandwich, I look away. It's hard to hide from someone who knows you inside out. From someone who's seen you at your best and your worst and all points in between.

"I admit he's attractive in a very unkempt mountain man kind of way—"

"I knew it!"

Sasha sings as he shakes his head.

"Oh, stop it." With a sigh, I lean back and forget about the amazing sandwich. "I really don't know, Sasha. It's like everything out of his mouth annoys me and his presence is just..." Trailing off, I shrug. "Just something about him."

Sasha remains quiet, and I wait him out.

"Ro...he's Leaf's brother and a good friend of mine. He's not a bad guy. Honest."

"Of course, he's not. You wouldn't be friends if he was."

"See? So could you try to be a little less abrasive? It was my fault he ate the strawberries. This is just as much his home as mine. He didn't do anything unacceptable. He didn't know."

I'm not sure if it's possible to feel lower than a snake's belly, but hearing my best friend hurt over something I did sure makes me feel like it.

Sasha chews his lip and I motion for him to move closer. He hugs me, and I wrap my arms around him.

"I'll apologize to him."

"Thank you. Just give him a chance. You'll see he's not a bad guy. I mean, we didn't hit it off right away either. I thought he was an arrogant, judgemental prick."

Laughing, it's my turn to give him the gears.

"And you're telling me I'm being rude when you thought that!?"

"I kept it to myself! I didn't have yelling matches in the kitchen with him. Besides, he was worried I'd break his brother's heart, so he was being protective. I can't fault him for that."

"No, you can't. I'll talk to him. Promise."

Satisfied with the answer, Sasha walks over to the mannequin I set up and inspects the design I was piecing together.

"This looks promising. Tell me about it."

I abandon food, all thoughts now going to the latest project idea I can't shake.

"*Ohmygod*, Sasha, here. Look at my sketch." Passing him my sketch pad, he grins.

"I love it. Is this what the Italian lace is for? It's almost like a bridal garment for men, Roman. This will be so hot."

The intricate lace I had shipped from a factory in Milan has the tiniest flower pattern woven in. It's so pretty. Once I saw it, I made a rough sketch specifically with the lace in mind. What was to be a lacy pair of boy short manties morphed into something more sensual and intimate. And Sasha just nailed it.

"A wedding outfit for men is exactly what I was thinking. I sketched a top, too. The lace is expensive as hell, though. This won't be a pre-made item. Other than the one we use for pictures, it will be custom-made, like the corsets."

"Ohh...what about a corset with lace? Would that work?"

"I was thinking of a lace overlay, but a different pattern of lace." I flip to the page in my sketches. "Like this."

Sasha's jaw hangs open as he pulls the sketch closer to him.

"Jesus, Ro...that's incredible. If you're still pulling designs like this together, working out of a lodge room won't work for long. You're going to need way more space because this is going to take off."

"You think so?"

I know I'm a talented designer, but the thought of my stuff being worn all over the world or in high demand is such a crazy thought. Sewing a hundred orders a month in my bedroom seemed surreal. What will this be like if I need to rent a space and hire staff?

"I know so. Why don't I help you set up the sewing machine while you cut for this? You could finish one this afternoon." He smirks with a laugh. "It's not like you have a lot of pieces to sew together."

For the next little while, Sasha and I set up the sewing space to my specifications and I carefully cut pieces of lace and silk and pin where they need sewing. It'll be tricky because I don't want the seams to show and I'm attaching a very fine lace to an equally fine fabric underneath. The lace is gorgeous, but nobody needs this directly on their good parts. It would itch like crazy. I have a different lace in mind for that kind of design.

"Hey, Ro. Do you smell something funny in the bathroom?"

Setting my scissors down, I meet Sasha in the bathroom and the smell from before is definitely stronger.

"It's been there since I got here, but I thought maybe it was a smell from the renovations and it would fade. It's not fading."

Wrinkling his nose, Sasha pulls out his phone. "I'm going to ask Perry to come check it out."

"Can you at least ask him to come this evening? I don't want to be interrupted with this project. If I can finish, you can run for your camera and we can get some shots posted."

He finishes sending the text and squeals. "Oh yes! I'd love to shoot this! Something simple and sexy for now, plain black backdrop for the white to pop and you'll look so good against it, too."

"Okay then. Let's do it."

I'm so damn excited about getting this company started. We rebuilt the website and set up our social channels months ago, after Sasha moved here. I spent the last year finishing a modelling contract and lingering, so I didn't stiff my roommates while they found a renter to replace me.

I didn't have to, but they were solid dudes who I liked and became good friends. I suspect the jock was bi-curious, but I never pressed him when he asked me about what it was like modelling with naked men all the time. His fascination with men wearing little clothing had me raise an eyebrow a few times, but it wasn't up to me to say anything.

The timing ended up working perfectly and with the actual designing process only starting now, I'm high with excitement. I've been posting teasers on the website and our social accounts for months. Our *Instagram* page has a large following already. Most of them are likely people who drool over me in my corset pics more than anything, and I'm okay with that. It's part of the territory.

Besides, I know I look good in one, so why not flaunt it?

And I'm going to look good wearing this too.

Only this time I'll profit from my own designs and that's a feeling I can't even put into words.

Now I need to finish sewing this sweet creation and make it all happen.

Chapter 5
Perry

What a fucking way to start the morning.

Roman Auclair should not be allowed to stay at the lodge. It's throwing me off and now I've accidentally eaten his strawberries.

Channelling my pissy attitude into the axe and the wood, I swing the axe down and sigh with the crack of the splintered wood. Not that I'm wishing harm on Roman. I'm sure he's a nice guy. If he's a friend of Sasha's, he has to be. Sasha's just the sweetest guy ever. But I can't seem to do anything right when Roman's around and it's only been one damn day.

Taking a break from chopping, I walk to the nearby ATV for my water bottle. The cold liquid feels good going down, and the sensation gives me something else to focus on so I can settle my thoughts. It's been a rough week with the nightmares returning and if I don't address them soon, it's only going to get worse.

Chopping wood used to help. But it's clear that it's no longer the balm it used to be for me. The spring chickadees twitter and swoop and my anxiety isn't draining away as it normally does here.

With a sigh, I pull out my phone from my overalls and when it pings in my hand, I almost drop it.

Sasha: There's a weird smell in the bathroom of Roman's suite. Can you check it out?

Perry: Sure. I'm just at the sugar shack. I can be there in twenty.

Not that I'm in a rush to displease Roman simply by existing again.

Sasha: It's no rush. We're actually working. Could you wait until closer to suppertime?

Perry: Yep. No problem.

He replies with one of his cute smiley emoji animals and I feel my chest loosen a little. Sasha, while he's my brother's partner, always makes me feel lighter. Like there's nothing I can't conquer. He understands what it's like to carry heavy things. Other than Leaf and my friend Ted, Sasha is the only person who knows my heavy thing.

A pair of chipmunks race around the woodpile and I smile while at their antics. Their little striped bodies disappear in the bushes and I wonder what Roman will think of the wildlife here. Something tells me he's not a lover of nature. Which is unfortunate because nature soothes me. It always has.

Eating fucking strawberries should also soothe me.

Staring at my phone, I remember what I was doing before Sasha texted and I hit Ted's number.

"Hey, Perry. It's early." His voice softens from his brisk, 'get down to business' tone. "How long have you been up?"

"Since 4 A.M."

A low hum from Ted.

"Want to talk about it?"

"I'm, uh…" *Come on Perry, talk!* "My usual coping isn't working. I tried chopping wood. I've been on walks."

"Sometimes that happens to me, too. Are you medicating?"

My doctor gave me a prescription for a heavy-duty sleeping pill, but that scares me more than not sleeping. I don't want to be addicted and I'm terrified of taking too many by accident.

"Not the pills, but last time this happened, I forgot I accidentally discovered a great way to feel better." The heat flushes up my neck and I chuckle. I can't believe I forgot about this.

"Well, are you gonna share? Maybe I can try it, too."

I bark a laugh so loud it sends the chickadees off in a flurry. Ted and I are as close as anyone could be after sharing the job we did. But we've not talked about what I'm about to share before.

"Fuck, Ted." I pass a hand down my face and a laugh escapes. "I jerked off. I was surfing channels at some god-awful hour and that Android box has six hundred channels of porn. I stopped on one and rubbed one out. Ten minutes later, I was fast asleep."

Ted's laughter is immediate and I feel like a high school kid swapping stories in the locker room.

"Buddy, I love you, but I don't want to share stories about whacking off. Jesus, if you go through a really rough patch, you're gonna chafe if that's your go-to coping method."

We both start snort laughing and making jokes and the heavy weight on my chest lifts. Talking to Ted always helps when he's available.

"Have you been okay?"

"Yeah, I've been real good." The silence hangs and I swallow with his next words. "It's not your fault, Perry. We couldn't save him even if we had ten more minutes. He didn't want it."

Staring off in the distance, I nod to myself, not always convinced.

"I know. Tell that to my brain when it acts up."

"Are we still on for a visit soon?"

"Absolutely. You're coming to scout out the property for the rockstar's build, right?"

"I am and I can't wait to have a proper catch up, my friend."

We chat a bit more before Ted has to get to his next build site and I pocket the phone in my overalls.

Leaf's sugar shack is ready for its grand opening party. The Maple Festival kicks off in town tomorrow, but this place will swarm with its first visitors in almost ten years on Saturday. The sign to Connor's Cabin, a nod to my late brother-in-law, shines brightly in the sunlight. I'm so happy my brother is finally living his dream and I'm a part of it.

Stacking up the wood I chopped and making sure the grounds are still just as pristine as they were before I arrived, I hop into the ATV and travel the main road for a few hundred meters before turning off onto the trail down to Emerald Lake.

Behind the wheel of the ATV, I can let my mind zone out. I know the way like the back of my hand and muscle memory takes over while I soak in my surroundings. The beginnings of new grass and shrubbery fighting up through the last bit of snowmelt. The sun glinting off the ice on puddles that formed overnight. Soon, this trail will be as lush as any tropical jungle.

I've always loved the springtime and the new life. Perhaps because it meant the ice was gone off the lakes and rivers and I wouldn't have those calls at work. Not that people started behaving responsibly around water in the warmer weather. Because they didn't. I had my share of those rescue calls, too.

Slowing down to slosh through a large puddle, the water rushes over the floorboards and wets my feet before it drains out, leaving a trail of mud behind. Yeah, there's no way Roman would ever do this. And why the hell should I even want him to?

You know, coward.

Arriving at the clearing on the edge of Emerald Lake, I kill the ignition and walk to the water's edge. A light crust of ice covers the surface, easily broken if you throw a rock. In another week or two, this place should be ice free and the spring birds will be everywhere.

That's one thing Sasha and I have in common. He loves ducks mostly because they remind him of his mother, but I love all the birds that come here. The majestic herons who wait like blue sentinels to catch a frog for dinner. The bald eagle who swoops down with a gracefulness that takes your breath away. Even all the songbirds that nest in the forest here. I know all their calls and bird songs have a calming effect on me. Once I learned that, I started coming here when I could.

But I should really get back to the lodge and help Millie if she needs it before guests arrive. It's not high season yet, so it's a small crew and, while I'm usually given free rein to do what I want, I know I need to be more present for this. It's a big deal for Leaf, and I want to ease his burden if I can. He's carried too much for too long and it's the least I can do for him.

With a last glance at my favourite place, I return to the ATV and head back to the lodge to work.

"Is there anything else, Millie?"

Stacking the last pan in the sink to dry, I pull the plug to let the dishwater swirl down the drain. She's been baking and prepping pancake batter by the vat most of the day and tomorrow it will be much of the same, except Pete will help.

She sets her clipboard down with a tired sigh.

"I think it's okay for now. I've enough food for the continental breakfasts for lodge guests for the first two days. And I have pancake batter started to last several hours at the sugar shack Saturday." She pauses and scribbles on her board. "I'll make sure I have a staff to come in for help with room cleaning Sunday."

"Make sure you tell me what you need. I can help with that, too."

"Of course, darling. I'll need you for lots, I'm sure."

"Except tomorrow. I'm taking Roman to the city so he can buy a car."

She raises an eyebrow. "Oh?"

"Leaf is busy, so I offered to take it off his plate."

And to smooth things over, hopefully. It will either kill him or drive me insane, but it's only one day. I can handle it.

Millie pats my arm. "You're a good boy, like your brother. I think he needs a friend."

"Who? Roman? He has a great friend in Sasha already."

"True, but everyone could use more, right? Did Sasha tell you why he wanted him to stay here and not get an apartment?"

Placing the mixing bowl I finished drying on the table, I find Millie watching my every move.

"He said he wanted him close so they could work together. I just assumed it was a proximity thing. Why?"

She shakes her head. "I think there's more to it. It's a fashion business, Perry. They'll need more space than that suite can give them. And I know Sasha's studio is small, so that's not an option for the material and stuff, but…"

"But what, Millie? Is there something I need to know?"

Like maybe why the fuck he hates being in my presence, but I'll take anything right now.

"I just think it's odd they wouldn't have secured another business space is all."

"Maybe to save on costs?"

"I don't think cost is an option. Roman had bigger deals than Sasha for the last few years, including posing for *Calvin Klein* as their elite underwear model."

I level her with a look and she blushes.

"I googled him. Sasha said I could. If I was forty years younger and he was straight, I'd be banging on his door."

"Millie! God, you're like a mother to me. Please don't talk about banging the hot…"

Closing my eyes, I sigh with the slip. When I open them, her eyes sparkle with delight.

"Don't look at me like that. Anyone would think he's attractive. Especially if he's an underwear model. He's already shown most of the goods to half the world." Not to me, though. He barely wants to be in the same room.

"You two sure got off on the wrong foot. It's not like you."

I remain quiet and dry the pots and pans waiting. Millie puts them away without pressing me for more.

"You can always talk to me, you know. I know you keep it all inside, but my door is always open and I love you like my own."

"I know."

She nods, effectively ending the conversation and when I'm done drying, I kiss her on the head with a hug.

"I'm going to check on him now. Well, the suite. Sasha thinks there's something going on in the bathroom. Then I'm going home. But I'll call you if I need to. Promise."

She hugs me back and pats me when I leave.

"Thank you for your help. You're a good man."

That's debatable most days, but it's nice to hear, anyway.

Meandering through the lodge, I take the short flight of stairs to the hallway of Roman's suite. The melody of classical music floats into the hallway and I'm not sure why I was expecting techno or rock music, but I'm pleased it's something I recognize.

After knocking, I wait and hear movement inside, but he doesn't come to the door. I knock louder.

And suddenly the door flies open, and the air whooshes from my lungs.

Roman's pouty pink lips part in surprise and neither of us move. And I don't know where I should look, but it's not away from the man in front of me.

Mother of God.

First, I didn't know I liked a man in a corset when he showed up. Now it appears I might like a man in lace.

No. Scratch that. I do. That's not up for debate.

Roman stands before me in nothing but the tiniest scrap of lace that leaves little to the imagination. He's all smooth alabaster skin and ice-blue eyes. And he's the most beautiful creature I've laid eyes on.

"Sasha said you smell."

He snaps his head back. "The fuck?"

"The bathroom. He wants me to check you out."

I'm still fascinated with the pretty lace he's wearing, and he clears his throat.

"You're here about the smell in the bathroom, then?"

"That's what I said."

"No. No, that's certainly not what you said."

Playing back my words, it takes me far too long to process what I said, and he spins from the door leaving me with the back view and it's then I wonder what the hell I've done in my life to be punished so cruelly.

Good lord. That ass. That lace. The little fucking bows asking for a tug to unwrap the gift that's inside.

He turns again to find me still in the hallway.

"The bathroom is that way when you're done staring."

Finally coming to my senses, I rush through the room and into the bathroom, slamming the door behind me.

How do models just prance around like that in front of strangers? If I was his partner, I don't know how I'd hide my jealousy. Not that I'm jealous. That makes no sense. He doesn't even like me, so there's nothing for me to get all caveman over.

Get a fucking grip here, Perry!

Finally, my heart stops pumping blood away from my brain, and I focus on the bathroom. Roman must use vanilla-based products because it smells like someone spilled a bottle of extract. It's all my nose detects for several minutes. Until I open the doors under the sink and smell the wetness Sasha must have called me about. But there's no obvious leak here.

The only other place is behind the panel where all the plumbing is and I didn't bring my flashlight or tools. Which is... dumb. Why didn't I grab them before coming here?

And why am I stalling from leaving?

"Is everything okay in there, Perry?"

Sasha's voice—and I didn't even hear him come in or the music being turned down.

"Yep!"

I throw open the door and make a beeline to get out of there.

"I'll grab my tool tomorrow and come back."

"Are we still going to the dealership tomorrow?"

Right. I knew there was something else.

"I'll be here at 8 A.M."

"Are you okay, Perry?"

Sasha has every right to wonder why I'm so frazzled.

"Tell your friend not to make it a habit of answering the door half naked."

Risking a glance at Roman, I can't read his expression, but he's now wearing a short silk robe in a gorgeous blue that sets his eyes off.

And once that thought registers, I know I'm fucked. Since when do I notice a shade of blue making eyes pop? Who even talks like that?

Ugh.

Don't fantasize about the asshole who dislikes sharing the same air as you.

"Next time announce yourself and you won't have to see it." Roman steps in front of a backdrop I didn't notice earlier and unknots the tie at his waist. "I suggest you leave now if you didn't like the first free show. It's only going to get worse."

Before the door closes, his laughter rings out.

"Don't forget to use your tool tonight!"

Asshole.

Chapter 6
Roman

Dabbing more concealer under my eyes, I glare at my reflection in the mirror.

It's been my first restless sleep in months. Try as I might to convince my brain it's because I'm here alone, it kept drifting back to Perry's reaction when I answered the door. The parted lips and dilated pupils. The rake of his gaze down my body.

And I can't decide how I feel about it.

Sasha shared Perry was openly bisexual, so I knew he could be attracted to me. And I also knew that until Sasha arrived, Perry used to make it a habit to flirt with guests.

I thought it was rather creepy at first, but Leaf knew and didn't seem to mind. It was never anything more than flirting that sometimes turned into one night of fun. Just like those trips to Mexico where you have beach flings with the bartender, except here, it might be blowjobs in the bushes for all I knew.

And last night I felt irrationally angry that I wasn't a guest he hit on. I would've turned him down, anyway. It's funny. I've never judged the men I sleep with on their intellect or jobs. As long as they were attractive and let me fuck them, I really didn't care. But now I'm writing Perry off because he had dirty hands the first day I met him and hideous fashion sense.

Entertaining that shallow train of thought would horrify my sisters. Of course, I've not even convinced myself that's the real reason for my anger, either. No wonder I can't seem to get along with the guy. If I can't even decide how to feel about him, how is he supposed to react to my hot and cold demeanour without being an asshole in return?

Satisfied with my makeup application and the reduction of the dark circles, I glance at the clock. He's due in ten minutes and I'd like to meet him in the lodge lobby if possible. I grab my messenger bag and double check I have my phone and wallet and I add the room key with the wooden maple leaf attached, which makes me smile.

In my rush to leave the room, I rip the door open and step square into a hard, broad wall of flannel-clad Perry. He smells like cedar and I linger a beat too long with my face pressed into his chest. Who knew the scent of the cedar could be so appealing when mixed with flannel?

"Sorry," I mumble and turn around to ensure that I lock the door behind me. And to deny that I need a minute to compose myself. Cedar and flannel shouldn't rattle me that much.

"No problem. I'm just glad you're ready on time. I hate waiting."

He strides down the hallway, and I have to jog to catch up to him.

"Do you mind if we get a coffee on the way somewhere? I'm dying for my morning fix." Perry pauses at the door and looks over his shoulder at me.

"I have one for you already. Let's go. I want to make the city before lunch traffic gets too bad."

He waits with the door open for me and when I don't move he shrugs and lets it fall closed. It feels like I'm still dreaming. Why is he being so nice?

Finally coming to my senses, I walk outside to watch him climb into a huge *Ford* truck, similar to Sasha's. He starts the truck as I climb into the passenger seat and notice the one vast difference between Sasha's truck and Perry's.

"How long has it been since you cleaned in here?"

My nose wrinkles, taking in all the discarded garbage stuffed in the doors and the tiny garbage can in the back. You can't see the back seat because it's covered in all the… stuff. Literally just stuff. A bag of sand. An old parka. Three different snow scrapers. A bin of what I think is fake flowers and twinkle lights. And possibly tulle?

What the heck kind of hobbies does this man have?

"Does it really matter?"

"Don't you want to take care of it? Do you treat everything you own like this?"

He turns to me and for the first time since I slammed into his chest; I notice the dark circles under his eyes that are a lot like mine. And his pale blue eyes that usually glint with mischief are flat and dull. Not that I've paid attention to his eyes, but he has those laugh line crinkles I love. It just makes sense I'd notice that his eyes aren't smiling today.

"Has anyone ever told you it's impolite to point out obvious things to someone doing you a favour?" He points to a travel mug in the console between us. "Yours is the red one."

Perry throws the truck in gear, and without another word, we're driving. It's not until we're off the country road and onto the pavement that I reach for the cup and take a drink. And it's heaven.

"Wow. This is good. I was expecting the usual watered-down homemade brew."

He shakes his head with a snort and drinks from his own cup with a mutter I can't make out.

"Excuse me?"

After placing his cup back, he inhales and risks a quick glance my way.

"I said you're unbelievable. Was that clear enough for you?"

My spine straightens, and I inhale.

Don't snap, Roman.

"I don't like your tone."

"You're not supposed to. That's the point."

"The point? What point?"

He blows a breath, puffing his cheeks out.

"Jesus Christ Roman. I don't want to spend the next two hours fighting with you in my truck."

"Then maybe you should stop using such an insolent tone."

"Maybe you should stop insulting me with every damn word out of your mouth. That would probably help."

His fingers flex on the steering wheel and I think back to what's happened in the last seventeen minutes because it was enough to make him bitchy.

"Is it the coffee comment? I'm sorry. It was just a statement. Not that you always make shitty coffee. It was..." With a sigh, I stop talking. There's no use. His jaw clenches so hard I worry for his teeth.

"Just forget it."

There's a sag to his shoulders and I feel a pang in my chest for whatever is bothering him. But I'm only staying quiet for now because he *is* doing me a favour and if my talking is pissing him off, I'll just stay quiet.

The truck tires hum along the pavement and I turn my attention out the window at the countryside rolling by. It's still horribly dreary, with all the patches of dirty snow melting and the lack of grass in most places along the highway. Not that the city didn't get snow, but it felt more civilized than this.

More... people-y.

Perry continues to stare straight out the windshield, likely wishing he hadn't offered to do this, and for the first time since I moved out from my sisters, I feel alone.

Pulling out my phone, I find Josie's contact and send her a text, hoping she's awake and well.

Roman: Hey sis. Just thinking of you. I hope you're well and I miss you.

There's only a brief pause before the dots dance with a reply.

Josie: Hey, Ro. Puking like a champion. This baby is kicking my ass. I miss you too.

Roman: Shit. I'm sorry. Can I do anything to help?

Josie: *picture of her pale and tired with a can of ginger ale and crackers*

Josie: This is my life for the next while. Send crackers.

A small sound escapes my lips as I both laugh at her photo and miss her terribly. I fire off a reply and send her a selfie of me in the truck.

Josie: You look tired, my sweet. I know you haven't been gone long but are you ok?

Roman: Mostly. It's harder than I thought, not having someone in the same room, you know? Like it's a lodge and people will eventually be across the hall, but that's different. There are a lot of doors between me and Sasha's place.

Josie: Can you stay with Sasha until you find a better place?With a loud sigh, I shake my head as I reply.

Roman: He has Leaf and no extra room. I won't impose. I hoped our being in the same building would help. It still might. I'll give it more time.

Josie: Put yourself first, Ro. You don't need to consider every single outcome to do that. Promise me.

Roman: I'll try.

Josie: I'm gonna try to have a nap but keep in touch, okay? I love you.

Roman: Love you too.

With no one else to talk to, I sip the coffee and stare out the window some more. And then I sit forward and bash my head on the window in my excitement.

"Oh my god! Are those wild turkeys?"

Perry grunts a yes, and to my surprise, slows down.

"Do you want to watch them for a bit? They're far enough away. They shouldn't scatter immediately."

He pulls onto the gravel shoulder and backs up to where we first spotted the turkeys amongst the decaying crop of whatever was planted here. Seven of them just peck around, and I've never seen a real one in the wild before. I thought they'd be bigger.

"Did you know they can fly up to 60 miles per hour? I'd have never thought a bird that looks like that could fly that fast."

"I didn't know that, but I've seen them fly." Perry clears his throat after a moment and adds, "Did you know they sleep in trees?"

The birds spook and move from the field into the tree line. They're crazy fast and disappear in an instant. Perry pulls us back onto the road and a giant grin fills my face.

"That would be so cool to see them fly."

He glances my way before returning his attention to the road.

"I didn't peg you as a wildlife person."

There's a hint of disbelief in his voice, and I prickle over his tone. My excitement from a moment ago disappears as fast as the turkeys in the trees.

"I'm not just a pretty face. I have interests other than fashion."

"Are you always so full of yourself?"

Once again, I'm going to battle with Perry and I can't help it.

"It's confidence in how I look. I'm not conceited. I'm aware of it and I was born with it, so I embrace it."

Perry snorts and drinks from his coffee, which infuriates me more. Reaching forward, I switch on the radio and I don't even ask him for permission because fuck him for trying to take me down a peg.

"You should have satellite radio. You'd not have to listen to all this talk radio bullshit."

"Is there anything else you'd like to tell me how to do properly? Am I breathing correctly or is that wrong too?"

Perry's voice doesn't raise. It's deathly quiet and I swallow the response, waiting. Instead, I shut off the radio and stare out the window again. Two more hours in the truck with him and uncomfortable silence. Great.

Why can't I seem to do anything right with this guy?

"Would you like to take a test drive?"

The salesperson approached me right away. Perry leaned against his truck, scrolling through his phone and feigning interest. I was happy about the distance between us and I wanted him to just leave me here, but he insisted he wouldn't do that.

From the corner of my eye, I see him approach while I ask the salesperson questions.

"What's the difference between models for features and price?"

Carl, the salesperson, knew his stuff and cited the major differences between all the models and I asked to see the super-loaded one. With leather seats and all the bells and whistles you could ever want, it was an amazing vehicle. I was in love with it based on looks alone.

Perry still hovered at the vehicle next to us, and just as I was about to tell the man to do up the paperwork, he pipes up.

"There are reports the new model of SLE has an issue with the drive train and the four-wheel shift. What can you tell us about that?"

Carl stutters and pauses. "There are a few bugs with the shifter, but I'm told it's on its way to being resolved."

"And how would we know if this one has an issue or not?"

"Well, the comprehensive warranty would cover any repairs."

"Even if he lives somewhere without a dealership? What if he gets stuck because it doesn't work and it causes other damage? He's living in a rural area and his vehicle needs to be trustworthy, Carl."

Perry continues to grill Carl over things I've never heard of, but I can tell they're things I should have brushed up on by the way Perry argues his point. And Carl is rapidly losing brownie points from me.

"If the luxury model has so many issues, I'll take the first trim package down, then."

"It's really not that big of a deal. There's only been a few complaints from people with the four-wheel drive."

Perry sniffs, clearly not impressed with that answer.

"Roman, you need that to work properly. If he's going to fuck you around, pick another vehicle you like and I'll take you there instead."

"Carl, could you give us a minute, please?"

After Carl walks away, I stand close to Perry and ask him to bend closer so I can whisper. That cedar scent hasn't faded.

"I admit I don't know half of the stuff you were asking this guy about. Do you really think I should buy something else? I was told Land Rovers are top in class for off-roading."

"You won't be off-roading. You're just driving with it, but you could do just as well with something domestic. Why are you opposed to a half tonne?"

"Well, I...I guess they feel like too much for me and if I'm shipping packages or picking up fabric, I don't want it in a truck bed. That's why I like SUVs better."

He nods along and purses his lips in thought. "Okay, that makes sense. So why don't you look at a *Mitsubishi Outlander*? They have a great reputation and the higher model has loads of room for that and you'd still have a decent four-by-four for the lodge road. It's only bad in the springtime but if you're still here in the winter it comes in handy then, too."

Perry's gaze stays on me and I can tell this means a lot to him for me to not only listen but also to take his advice. And oddly enough, I want to please him.

"Okay. Can we go to Mitsubishi instead? You don't mind?"

A smile appears on his lips as he shakes his head.

"Not at all. I want you to drive safe." He takes me by the elbow and guides me back to the truck with a wave to Carl that we're not buying today. I want to snap at him to let me go, that I'm perfectly capable of walking to the truck. But he opens the door and genuinely smiles at me. Whoa.

And in the three seconds I have to collect myself before he slides into the driver's side, I know there's more to Perry than plaid, scuffed work boots, and stealing strawberries.

I'm just not sure how much I want to know.

Chapter 7
Perry

After taking Roman to the Mitsubishi dealer and finding a much better salesperson, he decides on the loaded Outlander.

It's far more bells and whistles than he'll ever need, but from what I've observed so far with Roman, is that he likes to look good. And when he looks good, he's confident. I'm no expert on human behaviour, but I think his clothing choices and prickly demeanour are a mask. For what, I don't know and I doubt I'll find out.

When I picked him up today, I expected a casual dress like me. Maybe jeans and a dress shirt, but I was wrong. Roman dressed to kill a business deal. At first, I thought he was foolish and shallow for wearing yet another heart-stopping corset and dress pants.

But when he approached the salesperson with his questions on warranties and four-by-four performance, I noticed the transformation. His confidence, beautiful features and hot-as-fuck attire—seriously, when did I become obsessed with corsets and tight pants?—made him a proverbial force and I was in awe watching him come to life with the information I fed him.

He excused himself from the salesperson and walked over to me. A ghost of a smile on his lips.

"Okay, it's not the first time I've purchased a car, but I usually just buy them for leather seats and how I look in them." I raised an eyebrow as if to say I'm not shocked and he surprises me with a laugh. "Yeah, yeah I know. Bug me later. But you're sure this car will be adequate where we live?"

"It's very adequate for where we live, yes. It's a smart purchase."

"Okay. I guess I'll go sign the papers then."

"What did you negotiate?"

His smile disappears as he focuses those ice blues on me.

"What do you mean?"

"Any extras? Free tires or oil changes?"

"I just agreed to the sticker price. You can ask for more?"

He can't be serious.

"How are you a businessman to even ask that? Do you just pay full price when you order fabric?"

"Yes?"

I stare at this man who could literally use his face to save thousands off of a purchase price and I wonder why he never has.

"Do you trust me to talk for you?"

He bristles and pulls his shoulders back. I see I've found another sore spot. "I can do it myself," he snaps. The lightness from a moment ago dissolved and the arrogance back.

I raise my hands in surrender and he returns to the salesperson inside. My stomach growls and I'm surprised to see it's almost 3 P.M. He won't be able to drive this car home today, but hopefully the delivery is reasonably fast. I hope he at least negotiates that.

While I wait outside in the lot, my phone chimes with a message from Leaf.

Leaf: You two still alive and not ripping each other's head off?

Perry: We had a rough start but surprisingly it's going okay.

Leaf: Did you check out the smell in the bathroom? Sasha said you showed up but didn't have tools. You want me to go have a look?

Of course, Leaf's mention of the bathroom only conjures the image of Roman wearing nothing but a scrap of lace, and I don't want my brother in there. It's stupid. He owns the place, but I'm irrationally protective of the room and the job.

Perry: No, I'm going to check it out tonight when I drop him off. I think it's just leftover from our first leak, but I need to send the camera down the wall to check.

Leaf: Okay. Let me know what you find. We might not be home when you get back, but I'll see you at check-in Thursday afternoon for sure.

My finger hovers over the button to call Sasha, but I decide against it. I know he loves Roman dearly and they have a friendship different from the one I have with Sasha, but part of me wants to know what I've done for Roman to be so pissy with me. I know I don't always make the best first impressions, but I've tried to smooth things over and Roman just keeps being, well, an asshole. Although we seem to be getting along fine right now.

But I know that will change soon as we head home. On cue, the doors open and out walks Roman with the most blinding smile in place, and I wish I wasn't as drawn to him as I am.

"I just bought a car!" He points to the black one he was looking at earlier. "That one, actually."

"Congratulations! Did you negotiate for any extras?"

"A half-price winter tire package and delivery to Maple on Monday."

He puffs out his chest, swagger kicked up, and it's actually kind of cute. Pride blooms in my chest for my part in this.

"Good for you! Are you hungry? I need to eat and then get back home so I can check you out in the bathroom."

Roman smirks and heads to the passenger side of my truck while I desperately wish for a sinkhole to swallow me whole. This time I know damn well what I said. There's nowhere to hide, either.

"Pick your favourite place and it's my treat for your help today."

I think he's going to let that little verbal slip slide, but nope. After I buckle in behind the wheel, he turns to me. "You don't need to check me out in the bathroom, Perry. Right now is fine."

My cheeks burn. He's a bold motherfucker.

"Jesus Christ," I mutter as I pull us out of the lot. "Could your ego get any bigger?"

"Only time will tell."

He laughs, but at least he's smiling and not griping at me for something.

"Are you almost done? I'd really like a shower and to get to bed."

The whine in Roman's voice grates like nails on a chalkboard, and I back out from under the bathroom sink.

"I'm trying to be thorough, so I don't have to keep coming back here. And stop hovering."

This time when I turn to go back to the panel that opens to the hot water tank, Roman stands there in the same blue robe he wore yesterday with his scrap of lace for panties. It cuts off mid-thigh and if he steps just right —

"Seriously Perry?"

"What?"

"Just hurry up. I'm tired and bitchy."

"And that's different from other days how?"

"Oh, fuck off. You've known me for two days."

"I could say the same for you, yet you never stop with your insults. Now let me do my job."

He raises his hands and lets them flop back to his sides with a huff. His robe slides up and I look away. Christ. I think I saw dick.

I definitely did.

"You know what? On second thought, I think we've had enough of each other today. I'll come back tomorrow to finish. Do you mind if I leave my tools here?"

"Fine. It's not like I'm going to touch them. I just want to shower."

I brush past him towards the door and even after all day driving and at dealerships, he still smells like fresh vanilla.

"Have at it then. I'll come back tomorrow."

He's about to close the bathroom door, but I bark at him.

"Roman! Come turn the deadbolt first. Just because nobody is in the lodge doesn't mean you should be lax with your safety."

He stares at me with a blank look before moving toward the door. I let it close behind me and wait until the deadbolt turns before leaving.

Then I linger a beat longer.

"Don't let go!"

My throat is raw from the scream as I bolt upright from a dead sleep. Sweat sticks to my brow and with a shaky sigh, I fumble for my phone to check the time.

It's barely 3 A.M. and I've been asleep for roughly seventy-six minutes.

Of course, the nightmares had to ramp up right before the Maple Festival, when I need to work my ass off.

Flinging the covers back, I walk naked to the living room and stare into the dark black of my backyard. Like my brain, it offers no explanation for why I keep reliving this single memory.

When the nightmares come back, there's no sense trying to fall asleep right away. The surge of adrenaline is too great and I need to work it off. It's why my basement is littered with gym equipment and I'm as fit as I am. Manic-like workouts, while not a fitness regime I'd recommend, usually do the job of taking the edge off.

Filling a water bottle from the kitchen, I trot down the stairs to my workout area and snag a pair of running shorts off the treadmill. They smell a bit, and I glance over at my laundry area. It's overflowing, reminding me again that I've not done any laundry in recent memory.

Sorting through the pile, I quickly throw a load into the washer before returning to my treadmill. Sliding my shoes on, I step up and hit my saved programs on the treadmill. Then I run.

Away from my nightmares, my anxiety, and sleep. My failures. I run until my legs shake to keep me upright and the lactic acid builds until I can barely walk. And it's only then I stop the treadmill and collapse on the chair in the corner.

The washing machine cycle ends, and I throw the items into the dryer. One bonus of being down here is attacking the laundry pile, at least. Chugging my water, I start another load and strip out of my shorts, leaving them in the pile. Sweat sheens on my body and after a quick shower, I settle on the couch to watch some mind-numbing show until it's time to work.

The Android box I bought usually has cool shows. I'm always finding *National Geographic* or nature shows to binge. The channel selection is almost too much, but my thumb stops on the remote when the adult channels appear. Porn. I remember telling Ted about jerking off to get back to sleep.

It's already past 5 A.M. and I'll need to be at work soon but… my dick plumps with the idea now that I've entertained it. Since my first stop this morning is back to Roman's with my wall camera, I can't show up with my dick half-hard. He'd notice right away and I'll probably say something stupid. He'd laugh, and I'd feel like a giant loser. It's honestly not how I want to start the day.

So... rubbing one out wins.

And there's like six hundred channels of porn on this thing. Who needs that kind of variety? There's only so many ways to fuck, no matter what your kink or preference. Okay, maybe you get more creative with multiple partners, but that's still a lot of options.

Scrolling along the thumbnails with movie titles and their cover shots, one immediately catches my eye. A younger man wearing lace and garters. Clicking on it, I'm immediately thrown into the movie with a couple arguing. Over what to eat and, ironically, it makes me laugh and think of Roman.

But I'm not here for the setup. Nobody watches this stuff for the cinematic performances. I fast forward and piece the "plot" together until they're in the bedroom and the young man appears in his lingerie as an apology. And you know, I'm a fan of lace-clad apologies when they drop to their knees for you like this guy.

Real big fan.

My hand works my dick in long pulls and it leaks so much I don't even need to search for lube. Not that I'd need to go far. There's usually a bottle in the drawer under my coffee table. The advantages of living alone, I guess. Or disadvantages since I'm naked on my couch with my dick in my hand fantasizing about a certain lacy model.

And that's the lucky spark.

The scene playing out on the TV isn't nameless people anymore. It's Roman with my cock shoved down his throat and my balls draw up before I can even process I'm about to blow. My toes curl into the floor and I fucking explode across my belly and chest, the biggest cum dump of my life.

"Jesus Christ." Panting, I reach for the tissues nearby and mop most of myself off. "This is not good."

Even though it is because my eyelids are already drooping and I feel like I could sleep for a week.

But I just jerked off to the mouthy model who so far only tolerates me at the best of times.

To Sasha's other best friend, Roman.

Fuck.

I'll deal with this small bit of self-discovery and unpack what it all means later. Right now, the exhaustion sits like lead on my eyelids and I can't fight it.

I lean my head back and close my eyes.

And get the best sleep I've had in weeks.

Chapter 8
Roman

Somehow I've managed to work the check-in desk at the lodge this morning since Perry didn't show up.

Millie graciously supplied me with never-ending coffee and a plate of gingersnaps in the office. I fired up the now computerized check-in system and had it figured out pretty quickly. It also helps I used to work at the front desk of a hotel when I was in high school so it's not completely foreign to me.

But also, where the hell is Perry? This was his job today, and he didn't even call.

Sasha planned this entire package for anyone wanting to stay at the lodge in the spring and enjoy a real sugar bush experience. Not my ideal vacation but whatever works for the nature lovers of the world. He's a natural planner and has the lodge booked to capacity for three nights. Which, in the off-season, is a big deal.

The Maple Festival offered guests a shuttle into the festival, tickets to the dinner on Saturday and, of course, the accommodation which comes with an amazing continental breakfast spread by Millie. And I can't forget the special gift for guests because they sit next to me at the desk.

Each guest receives a small bottle of Leaf's maple syrup and a package of maple cream cookies Millie baked. And of course, an invitation-only code to book their next stay at a discount. Next to me, the syrup and cookies sit wrapped in a pretty cellophane bag. Each one has a tag with a photo of Leaf and Sasha smiling outside the lodge and the caption, '*Your hosts, Leaf and Sasha.*'

It's so domestic and so very Sasha that I can't help but smile. But I also wonder where the hell Perry is and why he didn't call. I had plans to finish my next lace design this morning so we could get it photographed. I couldn't say no when Millie asked if I could help. Sasha and Leaf were in town for a business breakfast and final arrangements for Saturday. Pete was picking up guests, and Millie had to keep her kitchen running.

The lodge door opens and the next set of arrivals tumble in to check in.

"Well, hello handsome."

The tall brunet man leans against the counter with a flirty grin. "We're here to check-in. I'm Bruce Bishop and this is my partner Avery."

Bruce's voice has a silky salesman quality to it. He's probably never heard the word no.

"Welcome to the Maple Mountain Lodge. Is this your first visit?"

Locating their reservation, I ask for their credit card and Bruce hands me a platinum visa.

"It is. We're here for a bit of fun and to celebrate our anniversary. Maybe go a little wild." I glance over the top of the computer screen to find them both aiming a lust-filled gaze my way.

"Well, I hope you can find something to make it memorable." I hand them the room keys with the cute wooden maple leaves and explain where to find their room.

"And since you know our room number, don't be shy to come by to say hello when you're free."

Bruce licks his lips, his intent clear, and when Avery shifts closer to him, I know I didn't read the encounter wrong. It's been a long time since I've been in this kind of situation and they're both attractive men. They're even staying here. No need for me to search in town. But the vibe is all wrong and for once, it's not the type of connection I want.

I want to reply in a way that doesn't give a promise, but perhaps says I'd keep it in mind, but a deep rumbling voice doesn't let me get that far.

"He won't be free this weekend. Enjoy your stay."

Bruce glances between Perry and me with a salacious grin. "He's got the burly lumberjack thing down to a tee. Well done with that fantasy, my friend. I'll see you around."

He waves as he and Avery turn back to the lobby to get their bags and find their rooms.

"Oh, crap. I didn't give them their gift. I'll deliver it later."

Perry takes one of the wrapped gifts and sears me with a look. "You most certainly will not." He jogs out to the lobby with the maple gift and calls out to Bruce. I watch as he accepts it with a smile, and Bruce's gaze drifts my way. He winks and I drop my gaze to the computer and immediately greet the next people in line.

Perry eventually returns to help, and together we process everyone who's waiting quickly. But with the line gone and quiet returning to the lodge, I finally turn to him.

"Where were you? I wasn't even supposed to help with this."

"Were you thinking of going to that couple's room later?"

He completely ignores my question, and I stand tall.

"Answer me first."

Perry's jaw clenches, and he drops his gaze briefly.

"I slept in. Now answer *my* question."

Perry's in my space more than before. His blue eyes blaze as he waits and I'm pissed that he's angry about me possibly visiting a guest's room.

"Am I on your turf? Is that it? You mad at me for getting the invitation before you?"

His head snaps back and his brows furrow.

"What the fuck does that mean?"

My temper flares, and my mouth engages before I can think.

"I know you make it a habit of flirting with guests here and sometimes hooking up. If I've crossed some kind of line, just say so. But I don't think it's any of your business what I do."

He steps away from me with a frown. "Is that what Sasha told you?"

Oh shit. I probably shouldn't have said that. Instead, I shrug, noncommittal. The flash of hurt across his face makes my gut drop.

He says nothing more and stalks away. Leaving me standing to stare after him as he disappears somewhere in the lodge. The longer I stand there and think about what just happened, the lower I feel.

Pulling out my phone, I text Sasha.

> **Roman:** Call me when you're free, please? I fucked up.

It's not the first time I've said things I shouldn't and it likely won't be the last. But I can't create friction between my best friend and someone he cares about. Even if it wasn't intentional.

After reviewing all the reservations, I confirm there's no one left to check in. I don't need to linger here, but I don't know what to do. For the first time, I'm scared I fucked up with someone I care about.

When the phone rings, and it's Sasha, I answer with a squeaked greeting.

"Ro? What's wrong?"

"I think I've made a problem for you with Perry, and I'm sorry. I didn't mean it. It just slipped out."

"What did you do?"

"I was checking a couple in who were flirting and clearly wanted to invite me to their bed. Perry overheard and got all judgy about it. Then I sort of threw it at him that you told me he did it all the time."

Sasha stays silent and I shuffle the paper clips on the counter around.

"That's not what I said, and that was in confidence, Ro. Now he's gonna think I don't respect him."

"I know, and I'm sorry. He was just...he was all up in my space about it and didn't want me to talk to them when it's not his business! And you know how I can be when someone tries to do shit like that."

"Where is he now?"

"I'm not sure. I think—" There's an engine roar and I peek out the window to see Perry peel out of the yard in an ATV. "He just left on the four-wheel thing."

Sasha blows out a breath. "I'll talk to him when we're done here."

He sounds defeated and maybe even a little disappointed.

"Are we okay?"

"Yeah, Ro. We're okay. I love you and I know how you can snap. You've been doing it since I met you, but listen...you need to back off with Perry a little, okay? He's...there's stuff you don't know, and I'd hate for you to say something you can't take back."

"I'm sorry. Fuck. I've been here a few days and I'm already causing problems."

"Ro, it's gonna be okay. I'll find you later, okay?"

"Okay."

Shoving my phone in my pocket, I head to the kitchen in search of Millie because the thought of being alone in my room right now isn't something I can bear. When I see her moving around the kitchen and the mountain of pots and pans piled high, I know I made the right choice.

"Oh, it's nice to see you, Roman. How did you make out at registration?"

"Smooth as silk. Can I help you with the dishes?"

"Oh, that would be lovely. I've called one of our part-time girls to come, but she's babysitting and can't be here until late. But I've at least got her scheduled to help for the next few mornings. I think Leaf underestimated how busy we'd be."

Finding an apron hanging in the corner, I put it on to protect my clothes. I didn't dress for dish duty, but I'm not about to go change either.

"I think he's just excited by what Sasha has told me."

Millie smiles at me once I mention Sasha. "He's excited about everything again. Sasha is to thank for that."

Smiling right along with Millie, I run the dishwater and squirt in the soap. "Sasha has that effect on people. When we met, I was determined to not make new friends. I didn't want anyone to be close to me, but he just sort of stuck to me and I couldn't tell him to stay away if I wanted to."

Which is true. He just kept attaching himself to me at shoots, and he was so damn sunny and beautiful on the inside that I couldn't turn him away. It was like he knew I needed him.

"Do you have any family, Roman?"

Smiling, I think of my sisters, sister-in-law, and the new addition on the way.

"I'm going to be an uncle! My oldest sister Josie is pregnant and due in six months. She has a wife, Violet, who is the sweetest person ever. And I have a middle sister, Camryn. She's a cancer researcher and super smart."

Just talking about my sisters makes me feel lighter. Even though I miss them, I love talking about them.

"That sounds like a wonderful crew. So you'll have a baby in the family by Christmas then. It's so special that first Christmas."

Millie keeps talking about her grown daughter who lives out of town, and I nod and answer as I wash the dishes. It's what I needed to pull me back from the cliff that I thought I was teetering on. The possibility I fucked everything up. The mundane tasks and conversation with a real person, especially Millie, ground me.

When we're finished, that familiar vise around my chest has lost its grip and there's still no sign of Perry or Sasha. But I want to work on my designs today. Design has always been my outlet, no matter what my life is like. The conversation with Millie set me at ease. Now my work will soothe the wounded soul I never let anyone see.

With the first lace mantie now complete, I want to create a top piece. My sketch is so close to being what I want. With my classical music on low, I fall into my calm space. The notes of Vivaldi wrap around me and I'm lost to my muse. Sketching on paper and adjusting pieces of lace and material on a mannequin until it clicks, then I scramble to get the details right on paper to recreate it later.

It's a lot of trial and error. But it's the discovery that thrills me. How a material hangs or bunches, how a certain cut flatters a body part and even how the material feels against your skin. All of it I love and get lost in.

When the heavy knock sounds at the door, my heart jumps, hoping it's Sasha or Perry and I almost throw the door open without looking. But Perry's message of staying safe still lingers, and I check the peephole.

"What the fuck?" I mutter before opening the door.

"Hi, handsome. Care for some company?"

Chapter 9
Perry

Killing the engine of the ATV at the edge of the lake, I grip the wheel and stare out at the water's surface. Not much has changed since the last time I was here. But more open water peeks through with a promise that warmer weather is on the way.

The clicks of the cooling engine overpower the bird chatter, and for the first time in a very long time, I feel the crack inside me open. And it hurts to know Sasha spoke so ill of me to a person I never met. To a man who has captivated me since the moment I walked into the kitchen and saw him laughing with a gingersnap cookie in his hand.

Isn't that a double kick in the teeth?

So what am I supposed to do now? It's my brother's big weekend coming up and there's no way I'll allow it to be anything but perfect. He doesn't need a moping little brother to worry about. Which means there's only one thing I can really do, and that's just pretend until it's over.

I never thought Sasha of all people would hurt me like that, though. There's no way I can be that wrong about someone... is there? My gut feelings are always on point. Sasha is a good egg. So what did I miss here?

Cocking my head, I focus on the low hum of an engine in the distance and it's drawing closer. Walking down to the lake, I pick some rocks from the ground and throw them at the water. If it's flat, I try to skip it across the ice. If it's a round rock, I try to aim it to land in the open water with a solid sploosh. A mindless activity, but it sometimes helps.

With the crush of tires on gravel, the engine I heard arrives and comes to a stop. There are only two people who would come here looking for me and I should feel better knowing that one of them did. But a bruised ego and hurt heart don't comfort that easily.

"Can I join you?"

Sasha stands next to me. A giant pair of green rubber boots over his dress pants.

"You should be with my brother."

"The meeting was over. It was just socializing when I left."

"Why did you leave?"

He picks up a few rocks from the ground and tosses them at the water.

"Because one of my best friends called me to confess he fucked up."

And the hurt stabs more when I face my friend.

"Is that what you really think of me, Sasha? I'm just the lodge gigolo and fuck anything that moves?"

My voice bites and Sasha's shoulders droop.

"That's not what I told him and no, I don't think that." He places his hand on my arm, but I shrug it off. "Will you let me explain? Please?"

"It's what you came here for. Go ahead."

He has this little growl of frustration, and despite being angry with him, my lips try to smile.

"I'm sorry I said anything to Roman at all. That was wrong of me. But what I said was that you like to flirt with the guests. That's all. I never implied you were sleeping around with everyone. That was Roman making assumptions on his own."

"Well, I have slept with a few, so it's not wrong."

Sasha kicks at the ground with one giant boot.

"That's not the point, Perry. Sure you like casual sex. Who doesn't when you have a busy life and things to hide?"

"Things to hide?" I stare back out at the water and throw another rock. "Are you my therapist now?"

"I'm your friend and I know you." He whips a rock into the lake with more force than expected, and I turn to face him again.

"What is it you think you know so well, Sasha?"

I'm scared to hear his response, but I suppose I need to hear it, too.

"I know you let no one get close because of your former job. Just because you were always away from home and your previous partners left doesn't mean you're not worthy. It means they weren't strong enough to accept you as you are." He drops his remaining rocks and pokes a slim finger into my chest. "Which is a truly selfless man with a giant heart that's too tender for most of the world. And I'm sorry that I might have hurt you." Tears well in his eyes. "Not because you're like a brother I never had, but because you saw the real me when I needed a kick in the pants. And I don't want to let you down."

He sniffs and pokes me again. "And I don't want you out of my life, okay? I'm sorry and I love you."

"Don't cry, Sasha. I'm not going anywhere." Shaking my head, I stare back out at the lake. "It hurt. I won't lie. He made it sound like you were talking shit about me."

"I wasn't. I promise. He didn't tell you the rest of the conversation."

"And what's that?"

"That you remind me of him."

"Of Roman?" I snort. "In what way could I possibly remind you of your gorgeous model best friend with a sharp tongue who dislikes every molecule of my being and merely tolerates my existence?"

"He *is* gorgeous, isn't he?"

I sigh and stuff my hands in my pockets.

"Anybody with eyes can see that."

"True. I'll let that slide. But nobody sees past that Perry. He's like you in the way he guards his heart for literally everyone. He flirts and has casual hookups because he's afraid."

"Afraid of heartbreak? It happens to everyone at some time."

Sasha sighs and I feel bad that he's caught in the middle of this spat with his two closest friends.

"I've already said too much to you about him. I guess I really am a gossipy bitch." He laughs, but it's humourless. "It's not for me to tell, but if he ever shares with you about his losses...he trusts you. And he feels safe with you. Which is a huge thing for him."

"You both had some shitty pasts, didn't you?"

Sasha shakes his head. "No. I had a shitty past. Roman had unfortunate events. There's a difference. But the outcome is still the same." He touches my arm again. "Do you forgive me?"

His soft voice carries hope and I can never not forgive him. He's my ball of sunshine on cloudy days.

"Only because I love you and my brother. I don't want to believe you could ever be cruel like that."

"I can't. He wanted to make you angry and twisted my words."

"Why though?"

Sasha chuckles. "Because you're getting too close, Perry. He likes something about you and that scares him. It's what he does."

My heart shouldn't thump faster when Sasha says Roman likes something about me. It really shouldn't. Right now, he's still a prickly asshole who I'm attracted to on the physical level only. There's absolutely nothing about me he's indicated he likes. He hates the way I dress, drive, and talk. Fuck, I'm pretty sure he just hates the fact I breathe the same air in the room.

"What could he possibly like about me?"

"I think the better question is what's not to like about you."

"Please, Sasha. Be serious."

"I am! You're thoughtful and kind. You have this whole mountain man vibe going on that's ultra sexy. You have a sexy laugh and smile when you think nobody is watching and you're pretty buff, Perry. I don't know if you're aware, but you wear the plaid well." He chuckles again. "Not as good as your brother, though, in case you're wondering."

Sasha's laugh and twinkling eyes are infectious and the previous weight on my chest with the potential loss or damage to our friendship lifts.

Offering my hand to him to shake, he swats it away and instead wraps his arms around me in a hug.

"Thank you. Now I have a very important question for you."

"What's that?"

"Have you read book two in that rockstar series yet? I'm dying for it and you said we'd buddy read."

"I haven't. But when I'm in the mood to read again, I'll text you?"

"Deal. I'll read other books until then." He checks his phone with a grimace. "And I need to get back. Leaf wants to celebrate that he got the supply deal with the grocery store."

"Oh my god! Why didn't you start with that!? That's amazing."

Sasha beams with pride.

"It was more important to me to make sure we were still okay first." He grabs my hand again. "He knows I'm happy for him and excited already. I couldn't let you think bad things for too long. You don't need to go there."

And with a soft smile, I drop a kiss to the top of his head.

"We're okay, and thank you. Now let's go celebrate."

He blushes and bites his lip.

"Uh...well...the first one is a naked celebration. For two. But we'll call you?"

I shake with laughter and push him toward his ride.

"Please don't talk about my brother and you naked. It's not right."

"Sorry." He walks up to his ATV and grabs the flame helmet I bought him when he proved he could drive on his own. "Can I ask you a favour?"

"Sure."

"If anything comes up or you sense something off with Roman, would you...could you offer to help him?"

It's what I do even when I know my hand will get bit. Which will probably happen again with Roman. But Sasha knows I'm a caregiver. I can't help it.

"You don't even have to ask. Of course, I will. It's important to you. I can put our differences aside for you."

He snorts as he fires up the ride he arrived with.

"Differences. Sure. Right. Thanks, Perry!"

With a wave, he reverses and, after a few attempts, he has the vehicle turned and he speeds off. With a final rock toss at the lake, I do the same.

After parking the ATV in the shed and cleaning up, I've stalled long enough. After much internal debate and thinking about what Sasha said, I'm offering the olive branch to Roman. It might not get me anywhere with him, but at least it's a good faith action to keep the peace for Sasha and Leaf.

I get along with everyone and it won't interfere with my brother's business. Ever. End of story.

Ducking into the guest bathroom quickly, I wash up before walking to Roman's room. But turns out I don't need to go that far to find him.

He's sitting with the flirty man from earlier in the common area. Two open bottles of wine sit between them and Roman has his head thrown back in pure, unfiltered laughter. His smile is like an arrow to my heart, but when he leans forward and touches the other man's knee, that arrow twists. And I want to rip it out and stab the man with it.

Roman notices me first. His cool blue gaze drinks me in and he leans back, removing his hand from the other man. The man twists to see what has Roman's attention and when he notices me, he smiles like I'm the buffet for dinner.

"Well, hello. I wasn't sure I'd see you again." He pats the chair next to him. "Come and join us."

Roman shifts, angling himself away from me, so I accept the man's invitation and take the chair.

"I'm Perry. Nice to meet you."

He grips my hand tightly. "Bruce. It's my pleasure."

His words are a flirty purr, and my gaze flicks to Roman. He says nothing but sips from his glass.

"I was just telling Roman here that my partner and I will be at the big event Saturday night and we'd love to have Roman join us. The more the merrier, right?"

Bruce holds my gaze and only now lets my hand slip from his and while I read his intentions loud and clear, I can't read Roman.

"I'm not sure I agree. Sometimes it's nice to keep gatherings small. You know, just two people."

Bruce smirks and leans towards me. His wine sloshes in his glass and I instinctively reach out to prevent him from spilling the whole thing on the floor.

"I've always had a thing for the burly woodsmen type."

"Is that right?" Bruce licks his lips and I shift away. "Well, you should visit The Log Jam downtown tomorrow. After the woodsman competitions, it will burst with all kinds of them."

"But not you?"

"No."

"Well…" He leaves my personal space and sips his wine. The man is pure sex and if I wasn't interested in attention from the man across from us, I might flirt back. "Do you still want to come and meet Avery then Roman?"

Roman drains his wine in one gulp. "Sure. Lead the way."

Bruce takes the bottles from the table and smiles far too friendly at Roman. He heads to the hallway where most of the rooms are and Roman takes a step to follow, but I grab his arm.

"What do you think you're doing?" I hiss.

"None of your damn business." He wrenches his elbow from my grip. "I'll see you at the party, Perry."

As he walks away, I can't fucking keep the words inside me.

"Enjoy being sloppy seconds, Roman."

His steps falter, but he doesn't stop or look back.

And I storm out.

In a jealous rage over someone who's not even mine.

Chapter 10
Roman

The dinner celebrating Leaf's reopening of his maple syrup business is a success. A delicious one too. The foodie scene here is on point and I can't wait to discover it all when the weather is warmer.

People from the small town of Maple truly support Leaf, and it's wonderful to witness how they've also taken Sasha in. This town loves them both and they keep giving back in amazing ways.

When Sasha gifted Leaf maple trees to plant in Connor's memorial park downtown, there wasn't a dry eye in the room. Even Perry wiped a tear when he bothered to look my way.

It shouldn't bother me that Perry's avoiding me. I'm the one who said mean things and implied he was the lodge slut. Which was wrong, I know that. But the thing is, Perry is different. The kind of different that makes me want what Sasha has. But so far all we've done is ignite each other's tempers. Especially his comment to me last night while I was with Bruce.

If he wants to think I'm sleeping my way through the guests, fine. Go ahead. Nothing happened, but if it keeps him away from me and out of my business, then perhaps it's a good thing. Yes, Bruce knocked on my door with an invitation to join him and his partner for some no-strings-attached fun. They have an open relationship and I have no problem with that, but it's not my style. I thanked him for being forward. When he saw the mannequin and lace in my room, he told me he was a buyer for a major clothing chain. We went to the common area for drinks and to talk business after that.

Our conversation eventually turned to Perry, and that's when things took a turn.

Bruce has it in his head that Perry wants me, and the only reason he's behaving like an ass is because I scare him. Which is funny because it's the other way around.

Perry himself doesn't scare me. Not all his manliness and sometimes scowly face. Not his barbed words or caustic comments. But it's his almost casual declarations for me to protect myself, to negotiate for a damn car, and even his quick apology for eating my food and bringing me a coffee without asking. Those are the things that terrify me because he wants nothing in return. Underneath all that attitude is a kind man. A man who wants the best for those in his life.

It's just the way he is. Even with my best friend. He dotes on him like a little brother and understands Sasha in ways others don't. When he caught me in my lace panties, it wasn't just a desire for my body he projected. That would be too easy to deal with. Perry was like a neon sign flashing, '*I will worship you until the end of your days and you shall want for nothing.*'

So yeah, I'm scared of Perry. Because he has the power to undo me.

The couples I joined after dinner have amped up their drinking and shot glasses litter the table. I excuse myself and wander the room for a place to people-watch and perhaps just give myself space to think. Finding a semi-private space in the corner, I lean against the wall with a sigh.

"That sounds like a troubled sigh."

My hand jerks, sloshing my drink over the side of the cup.

"I'm so sorry. I thought I was alone."

The man points to the floor. "I was tying my shoe and I probably blend into the scenery down there."

He's attractive in a clean-cut way. Very boy next door vibe and he offers his hand.

"I'm Brad."

I accept his hand with a smile.

"Roman. Nice to meet you."

He blushes and I bite back a laugh.

"I'm not good at meeting people or saying things, but um...would you like to dance?"

It's not what I left the table for, but it might be fun.

"I'd love to."

Downing my drink, I place the glass on a table as we walk by. Brad holds me like I'm made of glass and the faint aroma of hotel soap lingers on his skin. His hands hold me away from him with exactly enough room for another body to squeeze between us, and I feel like I'm back in grade school with too many chaperones.

"Did you go to Catholic school, Brad?"

His eyes open wide.

"Y-yes. How did you know?"

"Call it a hunch."

He blushes some more, and he's a nice guy. Possibly a bit too plain for me, but he's nice. He's safe. He tells me how this is his first trip away from home and I'm trying really hard to listen, but I keep searching for Perry. And when I finally find him, he's watching me. His icy gaze meets mine as he sips from his glass. Perched on a stool at the bar, with one elbow leaning behind him, he appears calm. But there's a flicker, a small one, as he watches me. Is he actually jealous?

And I'm not proud of what I do next, but I have a theory to test.

"Brad. I need to visit the men's room. Would you like to follow me?"

"Oh, I don't need to go, but thank you."

With a sigh, I lean in closer to his ear. "You don't have to go. But I need you to follow me. Please?"

He nods then, eager to do as I ask.

"Of course. Yeah."

"Give me a head start and come find me in there."

Leaving Brad on the dance floor, I head to the men's room and Perry tracks my movements like a hawk.

Once in the bathroom, my nerves kick up and I regret using Brad the moment he comes through the door.

"Is everything okay?"

His kind brown eyes spread more guilt over me.

"Listen, I'm sorry, but I only asked you here to make someone...think I'm into hooking up with people in bathroom stalls." I cringe at how shitty that sounds. "Which is fine if it's your thing, but it's not mine. I prefer less public places."

He nods along, taking it in stride better than I hoped.

"Oh. Okay. I was hoping you'd let me suck your dick, but I get it."

His response makes me choke on my saliva, and he pats me on the back. It's always the quiet ones, isn't it?

"Brad! I didn't think you even knew what I wanted."

This time, his grin is downright sinful.

"Don't let the 'aw shucks' act fool you. Just because it's my first trip away from home doesn't mean I'm naïve. Just means I don't have to be as careful about seeing someone I know."

My heart aches for him to be in that position. God, when did I turn into such an ass?

"Hey, I'm sorry. Maybe I'll just go. I shouldn't have asked you here."

"Oh no. I'm all in if you need me to pretend." He bounces on his toes, more excited about the prospect of pretending now. "What do you need?"

"Um...well, could you maybe let me muss up your hair and come out looking like you just had the best orgasm of your life?"

He chuckles and reaches for my arm.

"Sure, on one condition."

"Okay?"

"Kiss me once, for real." He taps his cheek. "Just right here is fine."

I press my lips to his cheek with a short laugh. He smiles and runs his hands through his hair until we're happy with the sexed-up look.

"Thanks, Brad. I'm...I'm sorry if I led you on or was rude, but I appreciate this. You're a good guy."

He cocks his head as his warm gaze assesses me.

"It's the big dude near the bar, isn't it? Plaid shirt, kind of menacing with beautiful blue eyes?"

My mouth gapes open as I stare at Brad.

"Yeah. How did you know that?"

"He's been staring at you since we started dancing. I got the feeling if I tried anything more than that, he might rush over and punch me in the face. So make sure he doesn't come after me." He laughs a little. "Although what a story that would be when I get home."

"God, this is a horrible mess. I'm really not an asshole and he won't hurt you."

As I walk to the door, Brad stops me.

"He won't hurt you, will he?"

"Not the way you think. I'm probably hurting myself more by doing this."

With a nod to Brad, I exit the bathroom and march up to Perry at the bar.

Chapter 11
Perry

Babysitting Roman for Sasha is not my idea of a fun night.

The tension between us since I caught him drinking with the hotel guest—the very attractive hotel guest—has been so high I need to learn how to mountain climb just to scale over it. Which is so stupid.

I've been in his shoes. If the guy wants to have fun, he should be able to, and I shouldn't give a single fuck. But tell that to my jealous brain. Every time I see Roman, it's a reminder that he's out of my league and looks down his nose at me. Which is a mind fuck because I don't give those kinds of people a second glance. I never have.

But I can't let it go. Not with him.

I don't know what he's trying to pull tonight. He did shots with a group of couples, including the pair from the lodge. He's cruised the dance floor and, when I thought he might finally slow down for the night, he ends up dancing with a guy who stares me down every time we make eye contact.

And now he's in the men's room with the same guy and I'm so fucking over this.

Turning my back to the area, he and the mystery man vanished into, I signal to the bartender for another water.

When more time passes and Roman still hasn't appeared a stroke of worry flashes. Should I make sure he's okay? Maple is a fairly safe place, but there are so many people here visiting. What if the mystery man wasn't as clean-cut as he appeared? You'd think I'd be more aware of these things after being in law enforcement for so long, but I spent most of my time talking to dead people. You lose some of that sharpness when the other person has no response to read.

Mind made up to go search that he's okay, Roman appears and struts up to me.

"You ready to go?"

Still snappy. Glad nothing has changed.

"I've been ready for at least an hour. You said you had to finish your drink."

I pointedly look at his empty hands.

"Oh, right. Well, I'm *definitely* finished."

He glances behind him and the man from the dance floor exits the men's room. His dishevelled hair pairs well with the lust-drunk gaze of a man who just emptied his balls with a pretty face.

Roman shrugs with a smirk and heads to the coat check. Hips swaying as he walks like a man on a mission.

Sliding off the bar stool, I stalk after him.

"Did you really need to be that cliché? If you wanted to get laid again, you could have done it in the privacy of your room."

His steps falter and I feel a little bad about the comment.

"You're a fucking cliché, Perry. I didn't want to go to a room." His judgy gaze roams over me. "Do you own anything *not* plaid?"

"I like plaid."

"I like sex."

The lady at the coat check passes him his giant, puffy white coat and I shake my head. Roman couldn't be a wallflower if he tried. He shrugs into his oversized marshmallow-looking coat and covers his corset, which is white flecked with red and gold. He rolled the arms of his white dress shirt up hours ago and it's a good look on him. Really fucking good. Pity he has to cover the only thing I enjoy about him right now for the ride home.

That damn coat, though. A snort laugh escapes.

"What's so funny?"

"You look like a fucking marshmallow."

He shrugs into his coat with an annoyed huff.

"I don't expect you to understand fashion when you're a walking billboard for an *LL Bean* ad."

"If fashion involves looking like an oversized cotton ball, then I'm happy to emulate LL Bean. They make great hats."

"Emulate. Such big words tonight."

We've reached my truck, and I don't bother opening the door for him. If he can blow a man in the restroom on his own, he can sure as fuck open his own door.

"I used to play *Scrabble* a lot. I know some words. But if it's too much for you to keep up, just say so and I'll dumb it down for you."

Starting the truck, we buckle in and I just want to drop him off and go home. Maybe even find someone to call over for once. It's been a long time since I risked someone coming to my place, but right now, I wouldn't mind having someone to hug.

"Your truck is filthy. I'm wearing white. If I have to get this dry cleaned, I'm giving you the bill."

"You could walk if it's that big of a problem. Trust me. I won't mind."

I think he's finally shut up, but he opens his mouth again.

"I could've asked anyone to give me a ride. If it's such an inconvenience to you, drop me off and I'll go back."

"I'm not fucking dropping you off here. Do you even have bear spray with you?"

"What!? Aren't they sleeping still?"

I shrug, totally willing to scare him because he's been nothing but a thorn tonight.

"Maybe. The weather has been warm, so you never know." His complexion matches his coat, and it's really hard to not laugh at him. "You know what to do if you come across a bear, right?"

The truck's headlights cut through the inky black of the night as we leave the streetlights of town behind. I shouldn't be winding him up, but... it passes the time.

"You should play dead, right?"

The quiver in his voice shocks me. I thought he'd not be afraid of a single thing. Man or animal. Maybe I'm wrong about him.

"Well, not really. That only works for grizzly bears and mothers protecting cubs. If it's a predatory bear, you just served yourself as dinner. For the bears around here, it's best to make noise and be big. Never turn your back on it, though. Bear spray can send a curious bear off easily, but when it's springtime and they have cubs, that doesn't always work. It buys you time, but it's not a solution. The best thing you can do is to prevent an encounter. Make a lot of noise out in the bush. Carry a horn or bells. Let them know you're coming, so they get out of the way and you never have to see it."

In the dim light of the truck cabin, I notice how he rubs his palms against his pants and part of me wants to keep egging him on. But I know what it's like to be terrified of something out of your control. I don't want him to feel like that.

"If there are bears around the lodge, we let guests know." I soften my voice. "Don't worry. The odds of you meeting a bear and being injured are pretty low."

"But not zero."

"Nothing is ever zero."

The rest of our drive home is in silence and when I park at the front of the lodge, Roman hesitates to leave the truck.

"You still scared of bears?"

"Are you going to mock me about it if I say yes?"

We stare across the seat at each other and there's a wounded look in his eyes. It's fleeting, but I see it and I recognize it. Because I often see it in myself for different reasons. With a sigh, I do the right thing.

"I'll walk you in."

His breath whooshes out. "Thank you."

The lodge is literally twelve steps away, but if it helps him relax, I'll walk him inside. Besides, I can hit the kitchen for a snack, so it's a win-win.

He exits the passenger side and rushes around the front of the truck, gluing himself to my side as we walk up the steps. It's not until he steps into the lobby that his shoulders drop.

"Do you want me to walk you to your door, or can you manage that?"

"I can manage."

No thank you or good night. He stalks across the lobby, puffy coat swishing, and disappears down the hall to his room.

Poking my head into the kitchen, I smile when I spot the small plate of cookies off to the side with my name on it. Millie really is the best. Unwrapping the plastic cover, I pop a maple cream cookie in my mouth and grab a glass for milk.

I've barely poured the milk when the sound of feet running carries into the kitchen. The main door opens and closes with a thud before opening and closing a second time.

"Perry!" Roman whisper-yells and reluctantly I abandon my snack to see what's going on.

"What is it this time, Roman?"

His eyes are wild and huge. Without thinking, I clamp my hands on his biceps.

"What happened? Are you okay?"

"There's water everywhere in my room! The floor is soaking and my fabric is still there!"

"Shit."

Without waiting for him, I jog up to his suite while he trails behind. He left the door open and when I step in on my way to the bathroom, the carpet squishes under my feet. Not just a little squish, either. It's like walking on a saturated kitchen sponge.

"Fucking hell. Leaf is gonna kill me."

There's water in the bathroom, pooling along the base of the wall from the hot water supply and when that water hits the carpet, it's like a giant straw, sucking up all the water in a fast draw.

Fumbling under the sink, I shut-off the water to the taps, then find the shut-off valve for the toilet before jamming my body into the tiny space with the hot water on demand and turning off the main water there. Thankfully, this room is the only one with this system since Leaf hasn't renovated elsewhere yet. It's also a good thing that this part of the lodge is raised with only storage underneath because there are no spare rooms to allocate to misplaced guests from a flood.

Oh no.

Roman hovers behind me with a scowl and I'm just as unhappy as he is.

"What happened?"

"There's a plumbing leak probably caused by our renovation. You can't stay here."

"What? Where am I supposed to go right now? The town is booked up for this festival and I just got settled here." He runs back into the main room, water squishing as he goes. "My fabric!"

"Roman."

"And I mostly unpacked my things. What if —"

"Roman!"

He snaps his mouth shut and focuses his blue eyes on me.

"Pack a bag. You'll stay with me until we can sort this out."

It's not ideal, but I can't leave him here. It's not safe and he needs water.

"Stay with you!? No. No way."

"You just said you don't have any other options. I have a guest room. You'll have privacy. Hell, we don't even need to talk."

He disappears into his bedroom, and I glance around the bathroom again. He really has moved in here. And how many bottles of lotions and cremes does one person need? Picking one up, I read the label—antioxidant serum.

"Do you mind?"

Roman carries a tiny case and sets it on the counter before filling it with most of what I see. Including snatching the bottle from my hand.

"Do you need all of that for a night? We can come back tomorrow after some sleep and sort this out."

"Yes." He snaps and marches out of the bathroom.

He returns to his bedroom and there's a lot of slamming and muttered curses, which only pisses me off because I'm not sure if he's mad at the water leak or because he has to come home with me.

Finally, he emerges with a giant suitcase and his case full of lotions.

"Okay. Let's go."

"Would you like me to help with that?"

"I'm more than capable of pulling a suitcase behind me."

With a shrug, I hold the door open and make sure it locks behind us. Roman stalks ahead of me, pulling the suitcase along and the smaller case dangling from his hand. He still wears that ridiculous coat, though.

Once outside, I let him carry his giant suitcase to the truck and wonder what his plan is once he reaches it.

"Need help now?"

"Please."

"At least you still have manners."

I open the backseat door and push over some of the clutter there to make room and swing his suitcase up. He slides into the front seat, clutching the small makeup case like a lifeline, and stares straight ahead.

Not the way I was hoping to end the evening. But I'm sure as hell not going to bother my brother and Sasha while they take a much-needed break together. I might not be good at the whole relationship thing, but I know when you make time to step away from work and life stress to wrap yourselves up together and shut out the world, it should be respected.

"Do you have *Wi-Fi*?"

"Yep. As long as you don't bite my head off, I'll even share the password."

"Any pets?"

"Do dust bunnies count?"

He huffs a small breath.

"Can we call a truce while I'm here? I...I'm actually not that bad, you know."

His quiet voice makes me pause.

"Yeah. Truce."

We change one darkened roadway for another and the headlights cut across the dark road on the way up to my house.

"Where do you live? This seems more remote than the lodge."

"Give it a minute and you'll see."

At the crest of the long climb, we round the corner, where a few streetlights dot the small neighbourhood of exactly three houses. Mine sits off in the corner away from the other two and when I pull into the driveway, Roman turns to me.

"You actually live here?"

"Were you expecting a cave in the forest? Yes, I live here."

"It's gorgeous."

"Wait until you see it in the daylight."

This time on autopilot, I round the truck to get his suitcase and he doesn't complain about the help. Instead, he trails behind as we walk the brick path to the front door.

Opening the door, I motion for him to go ahead of me.

"Hey *Google*, turn on the lights."

Roman snort laughs, and it's the cutest thing I've ever heard.

"You have Google Home?"

"I'm not a dinosaur like my brother. I have a few things to make life easier."

"Finding a light switch is hard for you?"

It's in jest, I know, but it's all we seem to do. I cock my head.

"I thought we were calling a truce?"

"Right. Sorry. Can you just show me where I'm sleeping and where the bathroom is? It's been a long night."

You're telling me. And it's about to get longer knowing I have to fall asleep in *my* house with him under the same roof.

Leading him down the hallway, I push open the spare room and flick on the light.

Thank god this room is somewhat decent. Ted is the only one who ever stays here, and he's a neat freak.

"The bed is clean, and the bathroom is across the hall. My bedroom has an ensuite so don't worry about running into me. It's on the other side of the great room. Do you need anything?"

"Um, no, this is good."

With a nod, I turn to leave, and he stops me.

"Perry...thank you."

Roman's voice is quiet and genuine.

I acknowledge with a nod and close the door behind me.

Chapter 12
Roman

Perry's guest bed is heaven. The duvet is a dream and the pillows are masterpieces. His guest bedroom gave me the best sleep I've had in a long time. It's easily one of the most decadent bedrooms I've ever spent the night in.

But I still haven't slept in. A quick peek out the window shows no sign of the sun and my phone says it's 5:07 A.M.

Gross.

I pad across the hall to the bathroom for my morning business and pause when I hear voices. But not Perry's. I bolt back into my room and pull on a pair of lounge pants and a loose T-shirt before venturing down the hall to what Perry called the great room. It's still dark in the house, but there's a muted glow spilling around the corner to guide me.

Just as I'm about to round the corner, a loud moan sounds and I freeze. Dear God, is he fucking someone out there? I'm both angry and... hurt. Mostly angry though. How could he when I'm sleeping down the hall?

Stepping around the corner, intent on giving him a piece of my mind, once again I'm frozen. Perry isn't here with someone. Well, no one in the flesh, that is.

The TV plays a porn which makes me shake my head.

Again with the clichés, Perry.

Until I pay attention to the movie because the actor is wearing a gorgeous corset and nothing else. It's stunning, really. Perry still sits on the couch, head dropped back, lightly snoring and legs spread wide, wearing nothing but his underwear. The remote sits on the arm of the couch and a pile of tissues sits next to him. At least he had a happy ending, I suppose, but why would he do this when I was here?

The action picks up on the screen and I turn my head to watch. The bearded man could be Perry if you give him a plaid shirt and blue eyes. I bet his beard feels amazing. I've never been with a man who keeps his beard short like Perry.

Oh! Be careful with the corset, you monster! That one looks like it's quality!

There's a groan, and it sounds an awful like Perry. Which is weird because my dick kinda notices and likes it. Then it sounds again, and it sounds like... oh God.

Perry shifts and I bolt back around the corner and down to my room, closing the door behind me as softly as I can.

What the hell just happened? Holy shit. Ho-ly shit.

Pacing around the small space, I tug at my hair and wonder if my sister is awake. Or Sasha. Shit. I don't want to interrupt Sasha this early and I can't talk about it over text with him. He's supposed to be enjoying a night away with Leaf, anyway.

My phone hums with a notification and I lunge at it, hoping it will be someone who understands my dilemma.

> Sasha: Hey, Ro! Are you okay? We just heard about your room and Leaf is going to check

it out, but I wanted to make sure you're okay with it.

Roman: Can I call you?

He doesn't answer, but instead my phone rings and I breathe a shaky sigh.

"Ro, what's wrong?"

"Good morning to you too, Sash."

"Sorry, good morning. I just spoke to Millie when I went to the kitchen and heard about the flood in your room."

"You're up early."

"Leaf promised me pancakes, and we ran out of milk. I ran down to the kitchen for some and got the story from Millie. So...you're at Perry's place?"

"Yep. I didn't have much choice, you know. The lodge is full and everything in town is booked. It was after midnight and I grabbed what I could and he took me here."

Truthfully, I mindlessly shoved things in my suitcase because I needed to distract myself.

"You're not okay, Ro. What's wrong?"

He picks up on everything. Even over the phone.

"I had the best sleep here," I whisper. "I've not slept that well for a very long time."

Sasha hums. "That's wonderful, Roman. But I know when something is up."

Still pacing, I take a moment to figure out how to say what I saw without making it weird for Sasha. Perry is his other best friend, after all.

"I don't want to say exactly but I...um, sort of found Perry in a compromising situation, okay?"

"Did he say something to upset you? You gotta give me something here, Ro."

"No, he doesn't know I saw him and maybe I'll share it later, but the freak out I'm having is..." Fuck, I can't even bring myself to say it out loud. But acknowledgement is better, right? Something about admitting you have a problem is the first step to dealing with it? "I think I'm attracted to him."

Sasha barks a laugh and then can't stop laughing, which only pisses me off more.

"Are you done laughing?"

"Maybe." He sniffs and snorts before returning to his mostly usual tone. "As an observer, I'd say you're definitely into him. But I'm happy you realized it early."

"Are you insane? Now I need to be here 24/7 with him! What if...what if something happens?"

"Well, if something were to happen, how about you enjoy it and see where it leads? You already said you had a great sleep for the first time in forever. I know how hard it is for you to be comfortable in a new place."

"Don't be logical when I'm freaking out."

Sasha sighs and I know if he were here right now, he'd be pulling me into a hug.

"Is it really that horrible to let someone in, Ro? To let another person know how fucking amazing you are under that snark and armour?"

Closing my eyes, the only thing I can latch onto is the pain of losing people. The death of my parents and the way the news was delivered is still a scar that never fades. I've tried for years. The only man I allowed to get close, I pushed away in a panic because I knew I wouldn't survive if something happened to him. He tried to plead with me, but I wouldn't listen.

It's why I've only allowed myself mostly anonymous hookups and nothing more. But Perry gets under my skin. His taunts, I admit, just spur me on, but he's still been kind. Even after I insinuated he was the lodge slut. Not my proudest moment to throw that jab. But I let him have his own jab in return because I deserved it.

"He's your other best friend. I wouldn't want it to be awkward."

Sasha huffs a small laugh. "It would only be awkward if you made it that way. I have no issue with it. You only get one life and if you meet someone to join you on the adventure, you should take it."

"He's rude. No fashion sense."

"He's rude because you dish it out and he gives it back. He won't let you walk over him. And nobody will ever meet your fashion standards. Nobody."

"He probably hates puppies."

Sashas laughs some more and I have to hold the phone away from my ear. I scowl the whole time he laughs. Some best friend, laughing at me in my hour of need.

"Do you have anymore excuses? Or are you done?"

"I don't know why you're my friend. This was entirely unhelpful."

"Do you remember when I first came here, and I texted you about how scared I was that I met this amazing man? Do you?"

"Yeah, I do."

"You told me I was special and deserved love. And that I should grab the man if I felt he was worth having in my life."

"That's different. You were all hearts and mooning about the hot lumberjack and I'm…I'm just horny because I saw him almost naked. There's no special love or whatever bullshit you're talking about."

"Ro, I love you like a brother. And I say this with the best intentions, but the fact you're freaking out over whatever it is you're not completely telling me actually tells me more. So my advice is this. Look forward and not back. Keep an open mind."

There's a muffle in the background and some mumbling before he returns.

"Listen, my breakfast is ready. Perry will bring you back later today and I'll help you pack and move, and we can get down to work again. I want to post the pics I took of you. Will you be okay?"

"I will. For now. Love you, Sash."

"Love you, too. See you soon."

Well, that call didn't help at all. There's no way I can just forget I saw Perry in his underwear post-wank while watching porn with a character who dressed like me. There's literally no way to scrub that from my mind.

My stomach growls, reminding me I'm still human and need food. With a breath, I push back my shoulders and stroll down the hall again towards the great room. There's no moaning to greet me this time. Just Perry, in the kitchen, wearing an apron and a pair of the shortest running shorts I've ever seen. Holy shit, he's got a great ass. And legs!

When I clear my throat, he turns and smiles. One side of his mouth tips up and his hair pokes up in places. He holds a spatula in one hand and I don't know why, but seeing Perry like this is... different. Like... a bunch of bees woke up in my gut and told the butterflies to fuck off. No fluttering will be happening. Nope.

"Hey. Sorry if I woke you up. I don't sleep much, so I'm up before the sun most days. Do you like omelettes?"

I know he's speaking to me. I hear the words but I'm still trying to reconcile the Perry I've met previously to the Perry standing before me with a sunny smile.

"Um, yeah. Whatever you make will be fine. Would you like help?"

"You could make me another coffee and one for yourself. The creamer is in the fridge."

Nodding, I move to the fridge and try not to notice the flex of his muscles as he whisks the eggs. Or the fact he's wearing stupid *Crocs* in the house. But that one is hard to ignore.

"You could at least dress the Crocs with charms, so they're less atrocious to the eye. I can't believe people still wear those things."

Locating the cream, I set it by the coffeepot and reach for his mug.

Instead of snarking right back, he wears a tiny smile.

"They were a gift from Sasha, so take it up with your best friend."

"You're kidding. I'll need to have a talk with him about that." I mix his coffee and set it back down near him. He takes a sip with a sigh and my whole body warms.

"Perfect. Thank you. And nope, not kidding." He pours the omelette into a frying pan before popping it into the oven and setting a timer. "My old ones floated away one night when the river rose." He sticks out a foot and wiggles it, silly grin still in place.

"These babies stay inside now and don't leave. I can't risk losing them."

His blue eyes dance as he peers over his mug at me. I try to take a sip of my coffee and choke, sputtering all over.

"Shit. Do you need help?" He whacks me on the back several times as I cough, wheeze, and sputter. "I know first aid if you need it."

"I'm okay." I croak and clutch the kitchen counter.

One large and very capable hand rubs circles on my back while I catch my breath and my brain feels as scrambled as the eggs. "If you're talking, then you're okay." But he still rubs small circles on my back and I have to fight the urge to purr like a cat and climb in his lap.

The timer dings and he moves back to the oven. First, he removes a tray of bacon, then sprinkles cheese on the omelette and places it back in the oven. He moves with a confidence in the kitchen I didn't expect. When we had dinner with Leaf and Sasha, he said he never cooked.

"You seem to do okay in the kitchen. I thought Leaf was the one with the skills."

He smiles again as he butters toast, and I pour another cup of coffee for myself.

"This is the only thing I can make half decent. And lasagna. That's it. He has all the kitchen talent."

"I wouldn't call this no talent, though, Perry." I snag a slice of bacon and take a bite. "Fuck, this is good bacon."

His neck flushes, and he ducks his head and for a moment, I can only stand and stare. As much as I hate to admit it, it's then I realize I've made far too many assumptions about Perry. There's way more to him than the abrasive lumberjack wannabe I thought he was.

"I made it." He points to the slice of bacon in my hand. "I made the bacon."

"Like...you raised the pig, or?"

"I bought the pork belly from a butcher. I smoked it and flavoured it myself."

"Perry Attwater, you are full of surprises. Seriously? You made it?" I swipe another piece. "I'm a slut for bacon. This is amazing. I can't believe people just go around making bacon. How cool is that?"

Perry removes the omelette from the oven and plates up two servings along with dividing the bacon between us and it doesn't escape me that he gives me the extra piece when I'd already taken two.

We eat in silence until Perry breaks it.

"So, did you sleep okay?"

"Like a stone. It's unusual for me to sleep that well in a new place."

"Oh?"

In a rare moment, I tell him something I don't normally share.

"My parents died when I was seven. It was unexpected. After that, I developed separation anxiety. My sisters helped me cope with it, but when I moved out, it was a struggle. Still is. I only had roommates who I was comfortable with. I could never sleep in an apartment by myself because I need to have someone else there."

"I'm sorry for you loss." I nod to acknowledge him. "But you slept here. You were comfortable here with me?"

I shrug. Trying to play it off, but that's the truth.

I'm comfortable here with him.

And I just admitted it.

Chapter 13
Perry

"Well, that's the last of it."

Heaving the soaked piece of carpet into the garbage bin, I wipe my brow and turn to Leaf. He tosses over the last chunk of drywall with a grunt.

"Thank god. Now that the clean-up crew is here, it should go a lot faster. Hallelujah for insurance."

Leaf is casual and I know he knows I fucked up, but he'll never make me feel guilty about it. Still doesn't mean I don't feel guilty.

"I said I'd cover what you're out of pocket. I know it's my fault."

He shakes his head. "No. It's mine too. I let Sasha win and pushed you to finish the shower when we should have investigated that leak further. We needed more time and we should have told him no."

I chuckle at my brother's straight face.

"You can never tell him no, so don't even go there."

"True." He laughs and motions towards the lodge. "Want to come up for a beer? Sasha said he'd be home later. Roman is on some kind of streak, he said?"

"Beer would be great." We traipse through the kitchen, which is now empty and quiet. The only good thing about the leaking pipe is that it's still the lodge's down season. It was full for the maple festival as a trial, but bookings won't start up again until mid-May. He occasionally gets a one-off call to book and he'll take it, but the guests have no food services if they stay.

"How's it going with the house guest, anyway?"

Leaf leads us into his place, and we leave our boots at the door. He passes me a beer from the fridge and we both collapse onto the sofa with a sigh.

"Well...it's been...different."

"Is that good or bad?"

"I'd like to say good, but I'm not sure." I run my finger around the edge of the can before finally just saying it. "Uh, I haven't told you, but the nightmares started again a few weeks ago. I haven't been sleeping very well."

"I thought something was off with you. How come you never said anything? You know that just because Sasha is here doesn't mean I'm not here for you."

"I know, but they usually go away on their own. I discovered a rather, uh, unconventional way to deal with them last time. So I've been trying it again."

"Okay..."

"I can't believe I'm telling you this. But the last time this happened, and the exercise stopped working, I found something else by accident that put me to sleep. Something I maybe enjoy...a lot."

Leaf still stares blankly at me, and I just blurt it out.

"I jack off, Leaf. It's like as soon as I come someone shoves a sleeping pill down my throat and I fall asleep in minutes. It doesn't always last long, but at least it's sleep. That's why I wasn't here on time for the check-in before the festival. I actually slept that morning after I ah... that.”

Leaf clears his throat before taking a drink.

“Well, I don’t think that’s uncommon, Perry. Lots of people do it. Hell, I fall asleep sometimes before I even pull out.” He snorts and I shudder.

“Please don’t share that much again. Sasha is my friend and I can’t have a visual of him shagging my brother.”

Leaf just shrugs like he does these days. It’s already in the past.

“Fine. But what’s this have to do with Roman at your place?”

The heat travels up my chest and neck and I look away from my brother. My cheeks must be fire engine red because it feels like I’m bathing in hot coals.

“Oh my god, bro. Are you two screwing?”

“What? No! And who even says that word anymore?”

He shrugs and sips his beer. “So he’s cramping your style with the right hand or what?”

“Leaf...do not repeat this. Especially to Sasha.”

“Of course.”

“He caught me.” Puffing out a breath, I lean forward and rest my elbows on my knees. “I passed out on the couch and still had the porn playing. Porn with men in corsets, Leaf. And my spunk-filled tissues next to me.”

“Dude...” Leaf leans forward. “You’re serious? What did he say?”

“Well, that’s the odd thing. I moaned in my sleep and saw him there watching the screen, so I closed my eyes and hoped he’d go away. Which he did when I made more noise and he thought I was waking up. Neither of us said anything. We had a nice breakfast about an hour after that, like nothing happened."

He raises a finger with a quirked eyebrow.

"Can we back up to the corset thing?"

Groaning, I drop my head. "What about it?"

"Perry…"

I raise my head to meet my brother's gaze.

"Do you want something to happen? You two didn't get along very well and now he's in your house. He saw you with your dick in your hand whacking to men like him. That's hella awkward. Should we try to find him an apartment or a room for rent?"

"No!" With a sigh, I realize I sort of want him to stay. "He's comfortable sleeping there. He told me that. Since his parents died, he has some anxiety and he can't sleep in a place without other people."

"The lodge would be empty most of the time. Sasha told me he had some sleep issues, but I thought the lodge guests would be enough. Or the fact he didn't have to leave the building to find us." He slides his fingers up the beer can. "Maybe the plumbing was a blessing in disguise then."

We sit in silence as I let that fact settle. Roman still pushes all my damn buttons, and he's not said anything about what he saw. Yet he still sleeps well under my roof with me in the house. I'd be lying if I said I didn't like that. It brings me comfort to know I help when he told me about his anxiety. It doesn't bring me sleep, but it makes me feel like I'm redeemed in a way.

For the one I couldn't rescue.

"Anyway, other than that, it's been okay. And Sasha said the walk-out basement is the perfect space. He loves the lighting for photos and Roman mentioned he'd be open to a rental agreement if I want." I shake my head. "Which is absurd. How could my walk-out basement be the perfect place for designing lacy men's underwear and photographing them?"

"I'm willing to bet there's a lineup of men who wished they were in your shoes right now." He throws his arm across the back of the couch. "So...corsets, huh? Gotta say I didn't see that coming."

We both laugh and the mood lightens.

"Nope. Me neither, but I guess I have a type. That type is a mouthy, blond, corset-wearing lingerie designer who both infuriates and excites me in equal measure. So if you have any brotherly tips on dealing with that, now would be a good time to share."

He whistles long and low and reaches for his phone when it chimes.

"Sasha is on his way home. Do you want to stay for supper?"

"No, it's okay. I should get home anyway. I still have laundry to catch up on and a million other things I've been avoiding. Call me when you're ready to redo the suite. This time no rushing."

Walking to the kitchen, I leave my can on the counter and slip into my boots. "Ted will come before we finish to inspect if I ask him."

"We'll see how it goes. I trust you, Perry. We both made a mistake, is all." He pauses before I leave. "I don't have much advice for you about whatever this is you feel for Roman, but I know you're a good man. Don't forget that."

"Thanks, Leaf. I appreciate that."

We do the back-slapping bro hug thing before I leave and it always lifts me when Leaf supports me. Not that I need constant coddling, but he's my big brother. I've admired him since I was old enough to say his name.

The air outside is unseasonably warm for March and I consider visiting Emerald Lake, but instead I end up driving home with an odd feeling of anticipation. Of what I don't know, but like him or not, having Roman at my house isn't as awful as I thought it would be. Minus the being caught watching porn bit, which maybe we should talk about? That's what roommates do, isn't it?

God, are we roommates? I don't even know, but it seems like we should have a conversation about how long he wants to stay here, if nothing else.

After parking in the driveway, instead of heading to the front door, I take the path to the back of the house where the back yard slopes towards the river. You'd think after being a police rescue and recovery diver for ten years that I'd want to get away from the water. But even with all the lives water took away...I love the peace it can bring me.

The spring thaw is well on its way, and most of the ice has finished floating downstream. Soon, the ducks and geese will randomly show up on my lawn and, while I hate how they make a mess of the place, I love watching them raise their babies.

Lights blaze inside the house, and I turn to gaze at my little slice of paradise. My home sits on the hill overlooking the river. The walkout basement is a wall of cathedral windows. I've never installed shades of any kind since nobody can ever peep at me here. It's woods and a river. It's private unless you mind the odd duck or goose sometimes looking through the window.

And right now I've never been so happy to not have window coverings.

Inside, Roman moves around his half of the space. I can't tell what he's doing, but his silhouette is unmistakable and I lick my lips, watching the corset-clad man move confidently around my home. And that feeling I couldn't put my finger on before flares up again.

My skin feels tight and rather than going back around and entering the front door, I slide the patio door open and step inside. Loud classical music greets me as Roman, with his back to me, pins fabric on a mannequin. My lips curl into a warm smile. He works from my home, but still dresses for a high-powered business meeting. A navy blue corset with a white shirt and the sleeves rolled up, paired with a pair of black dress pants. But his feet are bare. Another juxtaposed image.

He hums under his breath and when I glance around, it's odd seeing my gym equipment on one side of the enormous area with his perfectly set up sewing area on the other.

Roman pauses, one hand in the air as he conducts the symphony and he's a picture of content. There's no uptight, mouthy man. No shoulders tight with defence. He's at home and has zero guards up. This is the real Roman. He's beautiful.

He finally turns and freezes when he sees me. His blue eyes turn hard, clouding in an instant.

"Do you always make it a habit to sneak up on people?"

"I wasn't sneaking. It's my house. You have the music up fairly loud."

He steps over to his *iPad* and smashes the button, filling the room with silence.

"Is there something you need? I'm in the middle of a design here and don't want to be interrupted."

"I was going to ask you if you've eaten today? But if I'm just an inconvenience to you, I'll let you starve."

My light mood dissolves with the harsh exchange.

Turning, I stalk to my laundry room off the gym, intent on stripping out of my clothes from the day instead of doing it upstairs, but I remember I'm not here alone anymore. After a nanosecond, I say fuck it and strip down to my underwear, leaving the pile of clothes on the floor before stalking back out to take the stairs to the main floor.

"You're just leaving your clothes in a pile like that?"

"Yep."

I don't care. It's my house. I'm not changing my entire routine to fit his. He already took over my basement. Would it kill the guy to show some manners for once?

Once in my ensuite I strip out of my boxers and step into the shower. I scrub at my skin like it offends me while inside the simmer turns to a low boil. Why does he turn everything in to a fight? I don't even bother to dry completely. Instead, I dab myself off and yank on a pair of lounge pants, tossing my towel on the floor.

I'm intent on giving him a piece of my mind. Instead, he's in the kitchen heating something in the microwave.

"What the hell are you making? It smells like milk left out in the sun for a week."

"Mac and cheese."

"I'm too vile to join for dinner? Is that it?"

He cocks his hip and rests a hand there. That shouldn't be sexy.

"You didn't invite me to dinner."

"Does everything need to be spelled out to the letter with you? I asked if you wanted to have dinner with me."

"No, you did not. You barked at me like a rabid dog that the music was loud and if I'd eaten. You most certainly didn't invite me to dinner."

"Roman. Jesus Christ. You're a guest in my home. I'm going to make sure you're fed. Have you not been comfortable here?" Throwing my arms in the air, I heave out a breath. "What have I done to offend you this time?"

He nods and presses his lips together.

"Offend me? Where do I start? Since you asked and I apparently have no manners, here goes. You leave your laundry all over the place when you could either wash it, put it away or, at the very least, contain it in a hamper. You stripped in front of me while I was trying to work!" He swallows hard, but keeps going. "And you cook practically naked. It's not right."

His eyes blaze as he steps forward and pokes me in the chest with a strong finger.

"You got off to porn when I was sleeping down the hall and you weren't even ashamed to do it. And don't even get me started on the filth of your ensuite bathroom."

"What were you doing in my bathroom? You have your own."

"Looking for more toilet paper. I didn't...I wasn't snooping, but honestly Perry, what is your problem with cleanliness? Towels piled all over, and when's the last time you bothered to clean the sink?"

The microwave beeps and both of us stare each other down. His throat bobs as he swallows, and I let all his comments slide—except the one thing I can't stop thinking about.

"I was awake, you know. I know you saw me."

He swallows again, but never breaks eye contact.

"Were you going to keep that from me forever?"

"Which part? The part that when I can't sleep I sometimes jack off on my sofa to porn so I can finally get some rest? Or the part that I seem to enjoy watching men in corsets that look an awful lot like you?"

Roman's nostrils flare, and he straightens his shoulders. I can't believe I put that out there like that and I can't believe I'm holding my breath waiting for his answer.

"Are you trying to make me uncomfortable on purpose?" His voice wavers and I refuse to back down.

"No. But you didn't answer the question."

"The second part, then." He whispers. "I thought people were here, and I came out and you...you were..." He puffs a breath. "You made me confused."

I wasn't expecting that and soften my voice.

"What? How?"

"Because you were under my skin since I met you and then I saw you mostly naked and I thought it was such a pity that you had to watch poor acting with someone who only looks like me when the real deal was down the hall. I should still dislike you, but you made me wonder if I was wrong."

A shift in the air. There's a sharp spark, like an electrical storm, and my entire body feels lit up.

"About what?"

Roman inhales and licks his lips.

"About if you're someone I could take a chance with. How your lips would feel on mine. How you'd taste."

My chest feels heavy as I struggle to breathe. Is he yanking my chain?

"Don't you dare tease me by saying shit like that."

He shakes his head.

"I'm not. I really am confused. Every damn hour of every damn day, I swing between wanting to kiss you and wanting to slap you."

"And where are you right now on that scale?"

His lips turn up in a small smile.

"Well, my hands are in my pockets and you're still talking, so...pick up the clues, Perry."

Taking a step forward, I back him into the kitchen counter and bend closer. His hands grip my hips.

"I'm not fucking Sherlock. I don't do clues, Roman."

"Jesus Christ, you're annoying. Kiss me. I want to know if I'm right."

My lips brush over his. "You sure about this?"

"No, but I want to do it, anyway."

His hands reach up and pull my head the rest of the way to his lips. His fingers curl into my hair and his nails scratch across my scalp. And there's no more time to hesitate.

Roman's lips are soft and his tongue meets mine. The taste of something fruity lingers, maybe from the gum he chews, but it's forgotten as soon as it's discovered because my brain is officially offline.

Roman presses against me and snakes a foot around my leg, pulling me closer. Pushing back, I pin him against the counter and a small gasp escapes from his lips. His hands move to my ass and I've torn myself from his lips. Desperate to lay them on his skin. He tilts his head and I kiss down his neck, biting and sucking along his collarbone. His urgent moans and fingers gripping my ass urge me on. Our lips meet again and he's putty, letting me shape his body to me and his mouth to mine.

He's ambrosia and I can't stop.

Until his hands press against my chest, shoving me away.

Stepping back, panting and brow furrowed, Roman gazes back. His lips are puffy and parted, pale skin flushed a strawberry pink. But his eyes aren't wild and lust-filled. There's no kindness there and my stomach plummets.

"I was right," he rasps.

"About?"

"How you would taste."

His voice cracks with a pain I don't understand.

"This sounds like an answer I don't want to hear."

He wraps his arms around his middle and shakes his head.

"Probably not."

Giving him further space, I step away before turning and leaving him in my kitchen.

Chapter 14
Roman

It's hard to concentrate while you work when all you can think of is a kiss.

Not just any kiss. That would be easy to forget. Like the peck on the cheek I gave Brad. Over and done with no second thought.

Of course, Perry had to kiss me so good I still taste it. Feel it.

It's a permanent tattoo on my brain on constant replay.

His kiss lit up everything I thought was dead inside me. I loved it. But it didn't clarify my thoughts the slightest bit. Not about letting someone in, that is. It did, however, cause a burst of creativity. One of the side effects of the best kiss of my life was sketching up a storm and having so many creative ideas I was bursting to get them out.

I kept going and skipped sleep. Perry's kiss seemed to do more than just make me question my life choices. It seemed to be what I needed to jumpstart my designs even further.

It even got my butt in gear to think about the baby outfit my sister requested.

It also had me wearing a collared shirt. Not that the collared shirt was unusual for me. Buttoned all the way to the top with a tie was. Perry gave me a hickey in a one minute make-out session and I didn't want to answer questions about it. My best friend has done well with not asking me about my change in wardrobe... until now.

"It's a gorgeous day out, Ro. Summer is just around the corner! Dress down a bit for once and be casual. Oh! I know! Let's go into town and take a break. We can get a coffee and wander the bookstore."

My best friend stares out the window at the beautiful weather with a smile. Sometimes I wish I could be as carefree and joyful as him.

"I don't know, Sash. I really want to get this last piece finished so I can go live with the complete collection next month. Just in time for the wedding season to really heat up."

He spins from the window and bounces over to me.

"Exactly! And you'll be busy filling orders after that. Let's take a break." He playfully tugs at my tie. "Why so formal? You never button all the way with a tie." He loops his arm through mine and pulls me up the stairs towards my room. "We're going out to get sunshine and watch ducks. No argument."

He all but pushes me into my room and starts rummaging through my closet.

"Are you still okay here? I'm sorry it didn't work out at the lodge. Once the suite is finished, you're welcome to come back again. But...I feel like being at Perry's has opened up something in you. Given you a new creative outlet."

If only he knew how close to the truth he was.

"I am. I mean...we avoid each other mostly, but I can't ignore the fact I feel comfortable here." Except when I lay awake thinking of that damn kiss. I'm not at all comfortable then.

Sasha holds out a pair of jeans and a long-sleeved Henley.

"I want to take you to the park. No suits and corsets allowed. Be casual."

Eyeballing the Henley, I know the neckline won't come close to covering the love bite. Sasha waits with a look I know too well. Removing my corset, I carefully hang it in the closet while Sasha sits without a word. My tie comes off next, and I unbutton my dress shirt from the bottom up.

"How are you and Perry getting along?"

Sasha's face gives nothing away, and I wonder if Perry confided in him already.

"Good. We have our routines and stay out of each other's way."

"Oh. Well, that's good though. He likes to smoke bacon sometimes. Did you know that?"

My fingers pause at the top button. "Yeah, he made some for me the first morning I was here."

"And? Amazing right?"

When I first arrived, I wouldn't have used the word amazing to describe Perry. I still might not. But he's definitely something. With a sigh, I remove the dress shirt and turn to take the henley Sasha picked off the bed.

"I fucking knew it!"

He launches off the bed and inspects my neck like it's an incurable disease and not a hickey.

"It's Perry, right? You haven't moonlighted without telling me, have you? OMG...he's a great kisser, I bet. No. Don't answer that. I sleep with his brother and that's weird. But seriously, Ro. What the hell is going on?" He sits back on the bed and tilts his head, finally out of breath, after spewing all that on me. "And how do I get Leaf to do that to me?"

Slipping the Henley over my head, I check where it sits in the mirror. It's not as bad as I thought, but it still peeks out like a forgotten cherry in the fruit salad. Still a beacon on my pale skin.

"I'm pretty sure if you asked Leaf he'd do it."

"Yeah, but that's not the same as a passionate kiss in the heat of the moment that leads to...well, that."

Tugging on the jeans, I struggle to find words to express my mixed-up feelings to my best friend.

"Yes, it's Perry. And...has he talked to you about it at all? Or said anything?"

Why do I hope he has?

"No, but I know something is up with him. He's been unusually quiet, and he cancelled our book club meeting."

"You two have a book club?"

He nods his head, smile in full force, and I internally groan. Once he talks about books, it's sometimes hard to get him to stop.

"Yeah. It's just us. We sit around and moon over the swoony romantic guys in the book while we eat junk food and wonder if those kinds of characters exist for real." He laughs softly. "Well, I love Leaf. He's pretty dreamy, you know? But sometimes it's fun to escape into the fantasy of a romance novel."

Thinking of him and Sasha talking books and romance brings a smile to my face. I don't know why, but it's so perfectly them. And it makes me see Perry in a different light. Perhaps I've been too harsh.

"Did he say why he cancelled? What day was that?"

"No. He just said he wasn't feeling up to it and wanted to skip this one. That was on Wednesday. So just a few days ago."

That would be the day after we finally collided like two tanker trucks loaded with gasoline in an explosion that rocked me to my soul. It's nice to know it affected him too on some level. Although, I wouldn't know if it had. The level of avoidance I've reached is Olympic calibre.

"I don't want to put you between us. If I confide in you, it might make it awkward with you and Perry later."

Sasha shakes his head.

"Ro...let me worry about that part. If either of you were to say something confidential, I'd never share it with the other one. I love you both. And you have nobody in town. Perry can also talk to Leaf if he needs."

I hear what Sasha isn't saying, and I'm incredibly grateful for his friendship right now.

"How about we get that coffee and I'll spill my guts? Maybe even buy you dinner."

Sasha's lip quivers and I reach for him as his sunny smile vanishes. "What's wrong?"

"Nothing." He smiles before wrapping me in a hug. "It's just that we've been apart for so long and now that you've been back, I still haven't spent much time with you. I miss you."

Holding him close, I agree. "I've missed you too. Let's ditch work and catch up properly, yeah?"

Sasha beams his sunshine on me again, and I know this is the right thing to do.

"Yes. Let's go. And let's take your fancy new car, too."

Our first stop is the coffee shop, Ragged Chutes, where Sasha introduces me to his friend Caleb and the most amazing brownie in the galaxy.

"This is probably the most incredible thing I've ever put in my mouth." I moan while inhaling all the chocolate goodness.

Caleb, the man who owns the shop, chuckles. "That's not the first time I've heard that. Although the boyfriend doesn't enjoy hearing it." He wiggles his eyebrows with a smirk and he and Sasha laugh.

"Do you want me to make a dash across the street for you? Deliver a secret love treat?"

Caleb pauses. "Would you?"

Sasha agrees, and Caleb disappears in the back.

"Caleb dates the guy who owns the bookshop across the street. My friend, Malcolm. They have the cutest meet-cute."

He steals a brownie crumb from my napkin, and I slap at his hand.

"The cutest meet-*what*?"

"The cute way they met! Seriously, Roman. You really should read more."

Caleb appears and hands Sasha a single paper flower. A raggedy coffee filter forms the petals and the stem is a plastic straw. The straw has several bend lines on it and looks like it was fished from the bottom of a box. It's fugly. Sasha seems to think it's the sweetest, cutest thing on the planet aside from baby ducks and drags me out the door across the street.

"Why doesn't Caleb just do this himself?"

"Roman! It's sweeter this way. They work across the street from each other. They get to share lunches most days, but they work a lot. It's a gesture to show he's always on his mind. And he *made* it." He sighs with hearts in his eyes and I note how my friend is giddy over a paper flower and wonder if it's something Perry might like. Not that I'd ever make him a flower. He needs something practical.

The bells on the door to the bookshop jingle and an attractive older man smiles warmly at Sasha.

"It's not Saturday. What brings you by, Sasha?"

"I bring you a message." He hands the paper rose to the man. "From Caleb."

The man's face softens as he takes the rose. His fingertips brush over the petals as he smiles. "That man. He always surprises me. You know, when we went on our first date, he showed up with a whole bouquet of these and inside each one was a *Hershey's Kiss*."

"I know. You've told me, and I still love hearing it." Sasha turns to me. "This is Malcolm. He owns this magnificent store that I spend a lot of money in. Malcolm, meet my best friend Roman."

"Nice to meet you. Sasha talks about books and this store non-stop."

"He's one of my favourite customers."

"What do you mean, '*one of*'? Aren't I the only favourite?"

Sasha has drifted down a row, leaving me with Malcolm, and I shake my head with a laugh. "He's not one to share anything. Even the title of favourite."

Malcolm twirls the rose between his fingers, and I notice the petals have bits of writing inside. I pick out an 'I love you' and a few hearts as he spins it. If anyone asks, I won't admit that writing inside a handmade rose might be kind of romantic.

I'm also not ready to admit that I like it. And maybe I might even wish I had thought of it.

"You just got a set of demon romances in!?" Sasha returns, aglow with excitement. "I'm trying those next."

I drift over to the end of a row while they chat about books and demons and shit I've never even heard of. A row of cookbooks sits on display and while I can't cook, I can relate to that more than swoony romance. I don't even know what that means.

"Are you ready to keep walking, Ro?"

"Absolutely. Nice to meet you, Malcolm. I'm sure we'll see more of you."

"I'm sure we will. Welcome to Maple."

The sun is bright and warm on our faces as we stroll around the small downtown. Sasha guides me to the park that's dedicated to Leaf's late husband and the way my friend is so caught up in the meaning behind every gesture for Leaf has me pause my steps.

"So when you did the calendar shoot of lumberjacks for your last college project, this is what you used the funds raised from it for? This park?"

Sasha smiles in that way he has. The way that makes you feel wrapped in the snuggliest of blankets on the coldest of days.

"Yeah. At first, I thought I'd put all of it towards his maple syrup start-up, but that didn't feel right. It was so important to Leaf to keep Connor's memory alive that I felt it was a better fit to donate to the park fund. When we get enough money raised, we're building a concrete pad in the backfield for a skating rink in the winter and basketball in the summer."

Sasha points out the field and keeps talking about his project and how Leaf is friends with a man who manages his favourite rock band. His next calendar project will be the band and even though he fangirls over them in the hardest of ways, he's more fixated on how Leaf will react when the rink vision comes to life.

"You're an amazing human. You know that, right? And I'm so damn proud of you."

He smiles at me and loops his arm through mine.

"Thank you, Ro. I'm proud of me too. But you know, this didn't come easy. And if you want to talk about anything, I'm here. It doesn't go back to Perry."

We stroll through the park in comfortable silence while I gather the thoughts that keep floating through my head.

"Sash...I'm not boyfriend material. I'm...opinionated—"

He snort laughs. "You don't say."

I silence him with a look, and he tightens the squeeze on my arm.

"I don't allow men into my heart because I'm too much. I've never had a grip on the separation anxiety, you know that. Few know. You and my sisters, really. And if I..." I puff out a breath with a harsh laugh. "If I were to try and they left because they couldn't accept that, I don't think I'd like how that feels. And I don't think I'd be able to give someone else what they need because I'm always so self-conscious of it."

Sasha shakes his head with a sad smile.

"I know you struggle with that, Ro. You dress to project the confidence you don't feel. I get you. You know I do, but let me share something with you?"

With a nod, he leads us to a bench and we sit, looking out on the creek that flows through the park.

"When I came here, I was healing. I needed to find, well, me. For years, I didn't know who I really was. You entered the model scene knowing full well you'd be recognized everywhere with that gorgeous face. I didn't understand that Sasha *the model* was someone different from *actual* Sasha." He swallows and pauses, and I find his hand to squeeze. "The men that hurt me weren't good people. It took me a long time to understand it wasn't me. It was them. And I still struggle to remember that sometimes. But Leaf...he never lets me forget that I'm amazing, just as I am. That it's me with all my insecurities and issues that he loves."

"You think someone is out there to love me for my flaws? Is that it?"

"I know there is. If it happened for me, it can happen for you. But you need to want it."

My mind drifts back to how I felt when Perry walked out of the kitchen after that kiss. I was relieved I didn't need to tackle all the emotions it brought up, but I was disappointed he walked away so easily.

"He just walked away. Not a word since. We've been avoiding each other and I don't know how to talk to him. All we've done is snark and snap at each other until that fucking amazing kiss in the kitchen. Now it's just silence."

"Perry is...he has his own issues that are for him to share with you, Ro. And I promise you, he will understand. You're more alike than you know."

"So you think he's avoiding me because he doesn't know what to say, either?"

"Something like that. Roman, if you like even a tiny bit of Perry, if he's stirring up that pot of butterflies in your gut, find the courage to put yourself out there."

"I wish it was that easy."

"Nothing worth it is, Ro. Leaf and I work to keep what we have so amazing. Some days are a breeze and some days he's holding me while I cry because I think I shouldn't be here and have this." I look at him with shock and he nods. "It's happened a few times. But he doesn't turn me away. That's love, Ro. Sticking through the good and bad. And Perry knows all about that kind of thing."

There's no one I trust more than my sisters and Sasha. Without even speaking to Josie, I knew she'd echo Sasha's thoughts.

"I said I'd buy you dinner. How about you take me to this lumberjack dream place you told me about? All this talk makes me want to eat my feelings."

"You'll love it, Ro. Big, burly bearded guys wall-to-wall. But there's a lot of plaid there, so try to keep the opinions to yourself."

Genuinely laughing, I playfully push his shoulder.

"I don't know. Plaid might grow on me. They wear it well around here."

"Maybe it's your next design?"

"I don't like it that much." I deadpan. "Let's go."

"I bet you're wearing plaid jackets in a month."

Sasha cackles as he jumps away from my swat.

"Bite your tongue! It's like a gateway drug. Once I wear plaid, what's next? Sweat pants and shopping at Walmart?"

Sasha only laughs more at me while he shakes his head.

"Be careful what you say out loud, Roman. It just might come true."

Not in my lifetime.

Chapter 15
Roman

Sasha and I stayed out late. We ate and drank and laughed.

We played darts, and I was happy to spend time with my friend. I fucking missed him more than I thought I did. It lightened my heart to talk to him like we used to. Even surrounded by a sea of plaid-clad and bearded men, just my type, I could only think about one of them.

Perry.

After driving home, Sasha slipped into his vehicle and left, promising a text once he arrived. Thank god we switched to tonic water and lime early. Hangovers are not my thing, and if I wanted to talk to Perry tonight, I didn't want alcohol to cloud my mind.

The lights are off in the house, but Perry's truck is in the driveway. I stay quiet and don't turn on the lights, instead using the glow of my phone. I admit, I sort of hoped he'd be on the couch again with his corset porn. But he isn't and I hesitate before taking the hallway to my room.

Would he come out later? God, what do I plan to do? Wait and ambush him and offer to do the stroking myself? This isn't as easy to do now that I'm here, but I should at least talk to Perry about the kiss.

A shout comes from his hallway, and I freeze.

"Don't! Hold on! No! No!"

On autopilot, I jog to his bedroom door. More random shouts and a rustling of blankets. His voice is so hoarse and painful that I make a split decision to open the door and go in.

Moonlight shines through the high dorm-style window and bathes the room in a muted glow. The sheets wind around Perry like a cotton constrictor and even in the low light, the sheen of sweat on his skin is visible.

I've been there a time or two after my parents died and I know he's having a nightmare. His chest heaves and he cries out again, breaking my heart that I can't remove the memory that steals his sleep from him. But I can soothe it.

Just as my sister did for me, I peel off my jeans and slide into bed behind him, untangling his sheets and recovering both of us. Wrapping my arms around him, he tenses, but soon relaxes with a mumble.

"Roman? I can smell your vanilla." I smile at his sleep-slurred voice and his big hand pulls my arm tighter across his chest as he snuggles back into my body.

I'm paralyzed with fear. Being this close to him, in his bed, has me second-guessing my decision, but his breathing evens out and the grip on my arm relaxes.

"Yeah," I whisper. "It's me. I got you."

The room is heavy with silence. My blood pounds through my ears, but Perry sleeps on. And he doesn't let go of my hand.

And against the fear that rages inside me, I like this.

I don't know what this means for me, though.

Sleep overtakes my worry, and I hold on tight.

Blinking my eyes open, I jolt with the late morning sun bathing the room.

Not my room. Perry's.

I don't know what time it is, but it's later than I've ever slept. And tangled up with me is Perry. Still holding my arm across his chest, my leg is trapped between his, so if I wanted to sneak out without waking him, I couldn't.

There's a low buzz followed by the ping of a text notification. It's muffled by my pants, but it happens three more times before Perry groans and releases his hold on me.

"You should get that."

His gravelly morning voice is possibly the sexiest sound, and I drop a kiss on the back of his neck without thinking.

"It's probably just Sasha, but I should make sure."

Sliding out from behind Perry, I find my jeans and fish out my phone, which is filled with messages from Sasha.

His last one is genuinely wondering if I'm okay, so I send him a quick message with a promise to talk to him soon.

"It's 9 A.M. I can't remember the last time I've slept all night. Let alone this late. It's been...years."

The blankets rustle, and Perry turns onto his back. The muscles in his arms flex as he tucks his hands behind his head.

"It's been nine years and three months since I slept this well. A few times I've slept through the night. It comes and goes, but even when I *do* sleep, it's never this late." His blue eyes, still foggy with sleep, fix on me. "What made you come check on me? Did I wake you?"

Avoiding his questions, I first ask him my own. "What happened nine years ago to give you nightmares like that?"

He rubs a hand down his face with a sigh.

"Roman, are you asking for curiosity or because you care?"

"Well, I'd like to think it's not because I enjoy listening to you in pain."

Perry runs a finger over the same place on his neck where the hickey is on mine.

"Did I leave that mark on you? Is that why you've been wearing your collars up all week?"

"Well, I haven't been out with anyone since I've been here and you're the only one I've made out with in the kitchen. So...yes to both questions."

He remains quiet and my skin feels too tight. My hands wring together and I remember I'm only in my underwear. Not sure where my shyness came from, but I reach for the edge of the blanket to cover myself with.

"I used to be a search and rescue diver for the provincial police. Sadly, it was more often the recovery I did. Rescue was rarely part of the job by the time I was called. Most of the time, I could keep it locked away inside and it wouldn't bother me."

My eyes fly to his and my breath hitches.

"Roman?" Perry swings his legs over the bed and reaches for me. "What's wrong?"

The memory of the police officer at the door telling my aunt that they found my parents' snow machines, but needed to call in divers, rips the breath from my lungs. The other officer didn't make sure the kids were out of earshot as they told her their bodies were recovered under the ice. My aunt sobbing. My sisters pulling me into them, relieved they could say goodbye while all I could do was panic that it could happen to any of them.

It all plays back in my mind like an HD movie on an *IMAX* screen. Still tearing me apart the same as it did on that day over twenty years ago.

"Hey, babe...it's okay. Take a breath."

Perry holds me against him and my whole body shakes.

What are the fucking odds this man can connect with me over such a tragic event? This must be what Sasha hinted at. That we might be more alike than I think.

"M-my parents were...they drowned when I was a kid." My voice is barely a whisper. "They had to be recovered from under the ice by a diver."

"Roman..." He squeezes me tighter and his words aren't empty. "I'm so sorry."

"Is that what gives you nightmares? All the people you had to tell their family died?"

His giant hand is soft despite the calluses as he caresses my cheek.

"No. Recovery actually made me feel useful. Because I could give families like yours closure. They could know their loved ones were at rest and not still missing." He hesitates and I lean into his hand. "My nightmares come from a rescue that went wrong."

His thumb wipes at my wet cheek. I've never cried in front of anyone. His phone chimes but he doesn't move, focused on me only.

"This is going to sound weird, but...would you be open to spending today with me somewhere? I think it would do both of us good."

This new and tentative connection between us scares me. But I can't ignore the pull or the relief that someone else who isn't a therapist might understand why I'm like the way I am.

His phone beeps again, and I nod.

"You should get that and tell them you're busy today. I'll go get changed."

His smile is warm, and he reluctantly moves away to get his phone.

"Dress down Roman. Wear something you don't mind getting dirty in." He chuckles. "Not that kind of dirty. The muddy kind."

"Um, I don't really have anything like that?"

He pauses from his texting and his blue eyes seem... hopeful.

"Do you plan to stay in Maple? Like you and Sasha planned to base your business here and to live?"

"Yes, of course. I know I'm still staying here and the lodge probably can't be a long-term arrangement, but...yeah, I intend to stay here. This is my choice. My plan with Sasha."

He holds up a finger while he finishes his text.

"Then you're going to need some things and if you'll let me, I'd like to help."

Chewing my lip, I stare at the naked chest of Perry before bringing my gaze back to his. His sincerity is there. I have no reason not to trust him. Sasha's words echo in my head about opening up to people, and maybe this is my first sign.

"Okay. I'll, ah, find something to wear then."

A tentative smile flits on Perry's lips.

"I'll be ready in a few. Meet you in the kitchen."

"I fucking trusted you, Perry! What is this bullshit?"

"Quit bitching for once. This bullshit is what will keep you warm and dry in the spring when you're in the bush."

"You know what else keeps me warm and dry? A fucking house. With warm blankets and not in this hideous green."

It's not Walmart in sweatpants, but it's damn close. After a quiet breakfast together, Perry dragged me down to some kind of outdoor store. There are animal heads and dead fish on the walls, an aquarium bubbling away with tiny bait fish called minnows and the whole place stinks like... well, what I imagine the place he wants to take me smells like. Fucking vile with a side of sadness.

He's currently fussing over the right boots for me. They're all ugly and I swear if anyone sees me like this, I will die of embarrassment. The boots paired with the neon-yellow lined rain jacket make me feel like a lemon with feet.

And I'm about as sour as a lemon right now too if he dares to laugh one more time.

"Try these. If they don't fit you right, you'll have cold feet."

He opens the box and sets the pair of rubber boots in front of me. With a sigh, I slip them on and stand up.

"They feel fine. Can we go now?"

"You're sure they aren't too big?"

"Yes. They're fine. Let's just get out of here so you can show me the purpose of this misery."

Perry grins as he re-boxes the boots and piles the coat and gloves on top of the box.

"Okay, fine. This should do for now."

"I'm never coming back to this place. Just so you know."

It's a version of hell for anyone who appreciates high fashion. People need to learn comfort doesn't have to equate to flannel and felt-lined boots. Options are out there!

He places the items on the counter at the cash register and a woman who seems absolutely thrilled to be working today smiles at Perry with a wee bit more than friendliness in her greeting.

"Hey, doll. It's nice to see you again." She peruses Perry slowly instead of ringing through our purchases, and I'm irrationally irritated that he smiles back.

"Nice to see you too, Linda."

She scans one item before speaking to Perry again. Multi-tasking is not in her skill set.

"You know...my address is still the same and I don't work on the weekends."

Wow, honey, you need to work on your subtlety.

Perry just smiles and nods and darts a glance my way.

"You'll have more time to visit the lake then. That's great."

"It's better with company, though." She winks at him! Fucking winks at him, and I bite my tongue so hard I taste blood.

"You know, Linda. We're on our way to the lake right now and if you could hurry this up, I'd appreciate it. Keep the flirting to the coffee breaks, yeah?"

I'll cut a bitch. Don't test me, Linda.

Linda glances between Perry and me, and I raise an eyebrow in defiance. She scans the rest of our things and when I present my card to pay, Perry smacks my hand away.

"No, I'm buying. This is my treat."

"Hideous boots and ugly rubber jackets are your treat? *Wow.* Can't wait to see what you do for my birthday."

"You could say thank you, you know. You'll be thankful once we get there that you have these."

Thankfully, Linda has stopped flirting and I'm not sure why I smile victoriously at her as I follow Perry out of the store with all this stuff. But damn girl, pick another man to flirt with and not the one I'm with.

Not that we're together or anything. It's just rude to flirt when the person is with someone.

"So where to now?"

Perry pulls out of the store's lot and the earlier playfulness has faded from his expression.

"To the lodge. Then you'll put on the things we just bought and I'm taking you somewhere that..." He pauses and runs a hand over his face. "To a place that often brings me peace when things are rough."

What am I supposed to say to that?

"I'm honestly wondering if I was drunk when I agreed to this!"

My words whip away on the wind as we speed down the dirt road on what I can only describe as a death trap on wheels.

After changing into the rubber boots and rain jacket, Perry handed me a helmet of questionable origin and told me to get in. After fumbling with the strap under my chin, his large fingers batted mine away, and he secured my helmet with practiced ease. He lulled me into a false sense of security. His confidence blinded me and now I'm strapped into a machine on four wheels with no doors and an impossibly loud engine as we barrel along a skinny path that he assures me is a road.

I've never been more terrified.

But Perry laughs and squeezes my knee as he slows down some. Not enough, but some.

"You're safe Roman. Relax and enjoy the ride."

He zigs to miss a pothole, jerking to the right, and I scream with surprise.

"Please tell me we're almost there!"

And no sooner are the words out of my mouth, we turn a corner and descend a hill towards a clearing and a lake.

Now, I'm not a nature lover by any means. I enjoy looking at the photos Sasha takes and I like to watch the sunset. I prefer to experience nature through a window. Not dressed up in various shades of rubber and swatting bugs off my skin.

But this place is something you could never capture in a photograph and do it justice.

Perry pulls to a stop a few meters from the lake's edge and kills the engine.

"C'mere." He gently turns my head and undoes my helmet. I remove it as he does the same, and the heavy silence here is deafening. After all the noise from the machine getting here, the pure silence at the lake is harsh. But in a good way.

It's focused and lets you gather your thoughts.

After setting our helmets on the seat, Perry leads me to the water's edge. My boots squish into the mud and now I understand why he made me get these.

"When you asked me how I can still like water after everything I've seen as a rescue diver, I couldn't explain it in words. I thought it might be easier to show you." He stuffs his hands in his pockets and stares across the smooth green surface of the lake. "The amount of life I can see here on any given day far outweighs the amount of lives lost. Water brings life to everything. It only takes life from a few."

My heart beats double time and I blink tears that threaten. My parents are in the category of the few. Gone before they even had a chance to really live. I don't hate the water because of it. I hate the thought that the one time you might step off the known path, it can end in disaster. My remaining childhood had me afraid to do anything with even an ounce of bodily risk attached. Afraid of stepping off the known path and leaving safety.

"At first I hated the water. Then I hated my parents. Then I hated the cards I was dealt." Swallowing, I avoid looking at Perry. His gaze is heavy on me and knowing he might understand me more than anyone I've ever met has me gulping in lungfuls of air. "Then I realized I couldn't stay shut up in a house for the rest of my life. My sisters were going on with their lives and I was still this scared seven-year-old boy. I got better about always clinging to them. It took a long time, though, to be out on my own."

We stand together on the shore staring at the water. Sharing burdens in the silence of nature.

"I was called to a rescue one spring. A group of teenagers were fooling around on the thin ice and a few fell through. It was a place with a powerful undertow." Perry exhales a shaky breath. "All but one boy had pulled themselves out of the water and were sliding to safety when my team arrived. My teammates looked after the kids out of danger while I rushed into my dive gear to go for the remaining kid."

I've drifted closer to Perry as he speaks, the shaky lilt to his voice not at all representative of the larger-than-life man. "My buddy kept throwing him a line to grab while I made my way out to him. Even where I was and knowing how long he'd been in the water, I knew the clock was ticking. If I didn't get to him soon..." He licks his lips. A hard swallow clicks in the silence and I touch his arm. "He finally grabbed the line, and I was so close to him. He just had to hang on for a minute more and I'd have him safe in my arms."

Perry doesn't have to finish the story. His cries from his nightmare spell the rest of that out.

"It took me thirty minutes to recover him after that. And I've never been able to box that one up like other stuff I've seen. That boy haunts me. Sometimes for weeks. Sometimes for a day. I never know."

Oh, Perry.

"I don't sleep because sometimes I think if I do, I'll miss my sisters in distress. It's more a fear for me that someone I love might be gone when I wake up. Even when Sasha moved here without me, I kept myself overly busy, so I couldn't think about that. I know it's irrational, but..." I shrug with a sigh. "That's just how it is."

He clears his throat.

"So, now you know I'm actually human, after all."

"Well, that remains to be seen."

"Oh yeah? What exactly do you need to see, Roman?"

"I don't really know yet. Maybe it's you in lace."

Oh, okay. I guess my mouth is working without a brain filter today.

Perry's eyes are saucer wide and I think I've struck him speechless.

"Not gonna happen."

"If I had to wear this ridiculous get up to come out here with you, why can't you wear a little lace so we're even?"

His brow scrunches as he studies me.

"Are you even serious right now?"

"There's only one way to find out, isn't there?"

After several minutes of silence, each of us just standing on the shoreline lost in our thoughts, I realize that I'm serious.

I want to have Perry.

Chapter 16
Perry

"**I**'m not letting you dress me like some kind of doll."

When he said he wanted me in lace, I didn't think I'd be a fucking mannequin.

"You said I could have you in lace."

Roman arches one perfectly sculpted brow, daring me to say otherwise. Calling me on a damn technicality.

"Next time, I'll be more specific."

"Next time? So sure of yourself, aren't you?"

"Would you just shut up and get this over with?"

I said he could have me in lace. But this is a little too... uncomfortable. Standing half naked in front of the first man who's ever raised my dick to attention for longer than an hour and made me feel things. Big *emotional* things.

I spilled my guts to him a few days ago when we went to Emerald Lake. It was both freeing and scary as hell to tell him about my nightmares and why I have them. But he shared right back, and I wasn't expecting Roman to open up so much. Especially after all the bitching he gave me just to make sure he had proper boots and a coat.

There's more to Roman than the attractive model-turned-businessman with his nose in the air. Those sexy as fuck corsets aren't the only thing about him that draws me in, and I'd be lying to myself if I didn't admit I want more of him. To see more of what makes him so Roman. One shared kiss, a snuggled sleep, and a day of me showing him a little of our life here isn't enough.

But Roman waits, arms crossed over his chest with his haughty, judgy stare aimed at me. I should hate that look, but I don't. His corset today is black with blue trim and silver roses for buttons. Each one would make a lovely bouquet and that's a rose garden I'd love to spend more time in.

"I'm waiting, Perry. Are you in or not?"

Ah, there's the thorny side of the rose. And yet... I still want to prick my finger.

"Fine. Where do you want me?"

Roman stares at me. His throat bobs and he shifts on his feet. His bare fucking feet when he works with pins and needles. He needs to be more careful and wear shoes.

"Just...next to the mannequin." I do as I'm told, and he shakes his head. "Without clothes. How am I supposed to use you as a model when you're covered up more than a Buddhist monk?" He snaps his fingers. "Naked. Now."

Okay. So here's the thing. I know from Sasha that it's no big deal in the model world. They see each other naked all the time back stage. There's a level of comfort. It's expected that you'll see your co workers naked.

Roman views this as business.

He's not asking me to wear lace for his own enjoyment. He wants a real person to drape fabric on and visualize. That's all. I'm merely a canvas for the artist.

But I'll be standing naked in front of him. If he drops to his knees for measuring or pinning or whatever the hell clothing designers do, I can't be responsible for my actions. Or my body's reactions. It could go either way.

With a huff, I peel off my shirt. Roman smirks, pleased that I'm doing what he asked. God, he's irritating. I'm a man of my word and only following orders because I promised. Not because he snapped his fingers.

I hesitate for a moment at my boxers, but what the fuck, in for a penny, in for a pound, right?

Once the material hits the floor, I kick it to the side and my boxers land on the pile of clothes. Now I'm buck naked next to his mannequin and it's weird. Not just standing next to the fake human form, but what do I do with my hands?

There's a clatter, and Roman grips his cutting table with his head down.

"You okay over there?"

He's the one who asked for me naked. Deal with it, buddy.

Roman mutters to himself and if I didn't know any better, I'd think me standing here in the buff may have rattled him. I hope so because if I'm going to be uncomfortable, so is he.

"Yep. Peachy."

He clears his throat and grabs a measuring tape, walking my way with eyes to the ground.

"I'm ah, I have to measure your hips before I cut the fabric."

Roman's voice is thick and inside I'm pumping my fist in victory.

"Should I raise my arms then?"

I don't wait for him to reply and stretch my arms over my head before resting my hands behind my head. His cool blue eyes stare right at my face as his hands move. The smooth slide of the measuring tape snaps against my skin and he deliberately brushes his hand across my belly as he moves the end of the tape.

"42.5 inches. In case you were wondering."

"I wasn't. But thanks."

He spins and walks back to his table and I lower my arms, still feeling awkward as hell. I mean, who stands around naked for long periods like this? When you take a shower, your hands are washing. You get dressed and your hands are pulling on clothes. You go to bed and your hands are pulling up covers or flipping pages of a book.

Or...

No. I won't stand here with my hand on my dick, even if Roman is into that sort of thing. I side eye the mannequin next to me. Especially not with that thing right next to me. Ever notice how vacant a mannequin's face is? It's creepy.

Roman marches back with a piece of material in his hand and a pincushion in the other.

"Are you hitting on Ken? Don't be offended if he turns you down. Hold this, please."

He hands me the pincushion and before I can respond to his comment, he wraps a piece of fabric around me that pulls an involuntary purr from my throat.

Roman chuckles. "This is quality fabric against the skin, Perry." He plucks a pin from the cushion and licks his lips. "You like it?"

"What is it? It doesn't feel like lace."

"It's not." He leaves me there with his pins and walks back to his table. "This is lace." He holds up the very dainty fabric for me to inspect. "See the little flowers and the flecks of the gold in there? This stuff is $250 a meter and is some of the finest lace on the planet. But even fine lace you want to protect." He plucks a pin from the cushion and secures the lace to the other material draped across my groin.

"At that price, I'd expect it to come with a bodyguard."

"You don't strike me as someone tight in the wallet, Perry. You know quality comes at a cost."

I'm sure the way he's smoothing the material and dusting his fingers over my package is just him looking to get a rise out of me. In a few more minutes, something will definitely rise and it's not my fault.

"Of course. Sometimes the cost isn't monetary, though."

Sometimes the cost is driving myself insane waiting for the attention of a man who deserves the world on a platter.

"No? What else then?"

His throat clicks and there's a distinct waver in his hand as he reaches for the pincushion. After placing it on the table, he motions for me to turn around. So I do, moving slowing and feeling the slippery fabric slide against my dick. It's excruciating and blissful all at once and when I face forward again, Roman steps closer.

"Take it off and be careful of the pins."

His creamy skin is pinkish, and he bites his lip. Feeling brave, I reach out and grab his hand.

"You'd better help me. I'd hate to fuck something up."

He nods, relief clear. "You're right. Let me help."

His slender fingers, digging into my skin, manage to gently slide the pinned fabric pieces off my hips.

"Do you mind if I...um, I need your..."

He's gonna be all shy now that he's deliberately teased me and has my thickening dick to deal with? Nope. I'm not playing that game.

"Do I mind what, Roman? Is there an issue?" His eyes narrow as I lean forward and whisper next to his ear. "Do you need to touch my dick?"

"Y-yes."

The word is a breathless hiss and I'm here for it.

"I won't stop you."

His smooth hand grips the base of my cock, angling it down so he can shimmy the pinned fabric over it. I deserve a medal for not reacting to his touch. My breathing remains controlled and bonus, found a place to put my hands.

They rest on Roman's hips and I let them rest on his shoulders when he bends slightly. He taps my leg to step out of the garment and all too quickly I'm standing naked next to the mannequin named Ken and staring at Roman's back as he walks away.

He lays the pinned item out on the table and fidgets with scissors and measuring tapes. He's avoiding me. Do I force him to admit he's just as turned as I am right now? Or do I get dressed and leave like the man I desire didn't just see me naked and touch my dick?

I know he's skittish about opening up to people, but he's never been shy about sex from what he's shown me so far. And that hurts. That he'd give his body to these other men on such a casual basis, but shares his deepest fears with me and withhold anything else. Even when I know he likes what he sees.

Just as I'm about to get dressed and bid my goodbye, he drops his head back with a mumbled curse. He spins on one bare foot and marches right up to me. Pupils dilated and neck pink. His plump lips glisten as he places one hand on my chest.

"I should never have asked you to get naked."

I chuckle as he leans closer. His vanilla scent fills my nose, and I inhale deeply. He always smells so damn delicious.

"And why is that?"

"Because I can't unsee you like this."

"And that's a bad thing?"

"Yep."

I rear my head back. "What the fuck are you trying to say, Roman? Because once again, I'm a little confused about you."

"It's a bad thing because all I can think about is dropping to my knees right here and wrapping my lips around your cock. How will I get any work done now?"

My heart rate kicks into overtime and again Roman teases me. Drifting his fingertips down my chest, he stops and presses his hand against my stomach.

"I'm fucking offended you're thinking of work while I'm standing here naked with a dick that's been waiting for you this whole time." He bites his lip and I push on his shoulders. "It won't take care of itself, Roman. Put those pretty lips around me so I can come down your throat."

He surprises me and does exactly that. Dropping to his knees, he first peers up at me while he licks along my length and I reach a hand out to steady myself, knocking fake Ken off balance before deciding to curl my fingers in Roman's hair.

He moans so loud my eyes widen and he doesn't wait a minute more. Those plump lips wrap about my cock and it's heaven. He sucks me down like he needs cum to survive and I have to tug on his hair for him to slow down before I shoot my load in record time.

"Suck my balls, gorgeous."

He moans again and buries his nose in my sack before taking one in his talented mouth. My fingers grip tighter in his hair and I'm afraid of ripping his hair out. But he seems to like it a little rough.

I can't stop watching him. The way his lips grow more puffy, the bits of drool leaking out the side of his mouth and the down right feral look in his eyes.

"Take your dick out. Show me how much you like this."

My fingers yank on his hair and he gasps.

"You're a bossy prick."

"You seem to like that."

He stands and unzips his pants to reveal a pair of bright blue briefs with a flower pattern. It only takes me a second to figure it out, and I laugh.

"You matched your underwear to your corset? Are those little roses?"

"Get closer and find out."

He licks his swollen lips and slides a finger along the elastic of his underwear.

He doesn't need to ask me twice. I drop to the floor and lay an open kiss on his cloth-covered dick. "I'd say they're more like carnations."

"So you're a master gardener now?"

"No. Just an observation."

"Observations are usually with your eyes. And quiet. Use your mouth for something else for once."

"You're one to talk." But I don't want to fight and yank his pants and flower underwear down so his cock pops free. It's pretty. Of course it is. Why wouldn't it be? Like the rest of Roman, it's worthy of worship, so that's what I do. Licking up his length while staring up at him, I want him to see how worthy he is of this kind of attention, but he doesn't notice. He throws his head back as he loses himself to my touch.

"Look at me, Roman."

He snaps his head forward and tries to focus on me. And it's only then when I swallow his length. Dammit, he feels good on my tongue and I'm compelled to have him come undone for me. I want it all from him.

"I'm gonna come, Perry. You're...fuck you're good at that," he pants and my chest puffs with pride.

He taps me in warning and I grip his ass, pulling him tighter to me.

"Perry...fuck!"

He unloads in my mouth and I can't keep up, letting what I can't swallow leak out the corners of my mouth. Standing, I press him into the wall and seal my mouth on his before kissing a trail down his neck.

"Finish me off like this, gorgeous."

He spits in his hand and, with a wicked grin, he grips me hard before pushing his hips forward. I want him to be marked by me. My mouth. My cum. *Everything*.

"I want to spill all over you. Leave a mark." I bite down below his collar bone this time and suck the skin into my mouth. He cries out. So I do it again because I'm in full on beast mode with this man. Unbridled lust. Primal want. I'm so fucking overloaded with it, I can't help it.

My breath stutters, and my orgasm explodes into his hand.

"Fuck...Roman..."

Dropping my head to his shoulder, I try to catch my breath. He laughs softly.

"Am I too much for you? Can't catch your breath?"

"You will never be too much. More like not enough."

His muscles tense, and he tries to push me away.

"Fuck you for saying that!"

Gripping his chin, I make him focus those eyes on me. We aren't leaving here with a misunderstanding.

"That's not what I meant. I meant having you like this isn't enough. You deserve more, Roman."

"I don't want more," he hisses, but his eyes shift and I don't believe him. "You don't want me like that."

He tries to break free, but I hold him tighter and will him to listen to my words. To know that he's more than a man with a pretty face. That I mean what I say and he's someone I want to be with.

"Don't tell me what I want."

His jaw sets and I step away. The fire to fight flashing in his eyes.

"I'll tell you what you get then. It's this. Quickies when the mood is right. So don't get all moony-eyed and buy me roses." He slips by me to the laundry room and grabs a towel off the floor to clean off his hand.

"I'm going to take a shower."

He's halfway up the stairs before he pauses and throws out. "You looked amazing in that lace, by the way."

Once he's disappeared, I stand there for a few minutes before I set Ken the mannequin right and pat him on the back.

"Ken, I don't know how you work with him all day like that. But good for you. You're a saint. Me...well, I'm willing to play dirty to get what I want." Ken doesn't reply, and that's good, or I'd probably scream like a little girl.

Gathering my clothes in my arms, I head to my room.

I'll let him run for now. But I don't quit until I get what I want.

And Roman will soon find out just how patient I actually am.

Chapter 17
Roman

Sasha shifts his position, camera in hand, and peers at the screen.

"Damn, Ro." He whistles as he scrolls through the photos. "These are going to be amazing. You sure you don't want to go back to modelling full time? You're...fucking hot."

He laughs and walks over to where I'm sprawled across a bright red velvet lounger we rented from a party supplier. I've worked nonstop for two weeks to finish all the pieces for my wedding collections. There are four different ones all together, each one with a variety of colours and slight differences in style for body type. Only photos of me modelling them will be on the site though.

Unless Perry volunteers to pose for a shoot, but I doubt it. And I won't admit that I still think of how sexy he was with a piece of lace around his hips. He wasn't even wearing a finished piece. Just some silk and lace hanging over his groin like he was a damn erotic caveman. And I certainly won't tell him his hard-on gave me the idea for a loincloth-type garment.

Fuck. I should talk to him.

"Ro?"

"Mmm?"

"I asked if you wanted to break for lunch and go through these images before the final set. You sort of spaced out on me."

"Sorry. Just thinking about launch day. It's getting close."

Rising off the lounger, I grab the robe nearby and slip it on as we head up the short flight of stairs to the kitchen.

"I can't believe we've got this much done so soon. Do you want to have a local party or something to celebrate? I could ask Malcolm at the bookstore to advertise, maybe? Oh! And the guy who does wedding cakes from home." Sasha pauses and leans against the counter while I rummage in the fridge for leftovers. "We should've arranged a wedding show to launch this. I wonder if we still should? What do you think?"

Placing all the Chinese food boxes on the counter along with plates, I think about it. It is a groom's wedding attire. Or whatever celebration they want it for. Hell, maybe they just want to wear it at home to feel good. I don't know if I want to just target weddings.

Placing Sasha's plate in the microwave, I sit at the table and study him.

"What do you want to do? It's your business, too. Do you want to do a photo gallery or something? Maybe not make it about weddings, but something else?"

The microwave pings and he switches our plates before sitting across from me.

"Romance? What if we just went with that as the theme? I know it's a small town, but the queer community here is a decent size and they'd support it. Not to mention the contacts we've both made since being here. What about that guy you met at the lodge? Bruce was it? Doesn't he have a big company?"

Sitting across from him with my lunch, I nod as I chew.

"Yeah, he's a buyer for an upscale department store somewhere. I have his card. He told me to call him. I forgot about that."

"So he wasn't that memorable then, huh?"

Sasha pins me with his stare.

"What do you mean?"

"Ro...you went to his room with his fiancé. A threesome doesn't stand out in your memory?"

I laugh out loud. "A threesome? Who told you that? We had wine in the lobby one night. I didn't sleep with him."

His eyes widen, and now I remember.

"Perry thinks I slept with them. He said that to you?"

"He may have mentioned that you were extra cozy with some guests before he got really silent and mad. I assumed." He raises his hands when my expression darkens. "You've hooked up plenty of times. I assumed what he saw was correct, and I didn't question it." He chews his lip and looks away. "I shouldn't have said anything. It was a joke, and it's not funny. I'm sorry."

I shouldn't be mad because Perry came to that conclusion. It's what I wanted him to think! But now... how do I keep making such horrible decisions?

"He saw me drinking with him. Laughing with him and leaving with him. That's it. The rest was his imagination. I haven't been with anyone since I've been here."

"Except Perry," Sasha adds.

"We made out in the kitchen once. Why are we even talking about this? We're supposed to be talking about the launch."

I'm not ready to talk about Perry. I think. Truth is, I should. He's all I can think about, and I've behaved like a royal asshole.

"Right. Romance. That was the theme, and we got sidetracked."

"Your studio is big enough to do an open house, isn't it?"

"Not if we supply some drinks and appetizers. We could rent a room at the art gallery. They have different-sized gathering spaces and even provide catering services. One stop shop."

"I don't know. We have a big enough social media presence and name recognition. Maybe we can have a private celebration with us and close friends of yours?"

I don't know why I'm not willing to commit to an event, but it doesn't feel right to me. Sasha seems to be fine without and shrugs as he scrapes up the last of his rice.

"I can do that, too. Whatever makes you comfortable."

After lunch, we finish the last set of photos, and Sasha leaves me for the evening. He and Leaf had agreed that 6 P.M. each night was a time for the two of them together. Sometimes alone and sometimes with friends, but always no work after 6 P.M.

Which is not how I operate.

With the launch a week away, the only thing I have left to do is load all the photos once Sasha finishes with them. So I'm at a loss. And I'm agitated. I've kept myself busy since Perry was in my workspace in all his naked glory. It was the hottest encounter I've had in a very long time. Just like the kiss in the kitchen, we combust when we come together.

And he wants more. His tender gaze was my undoing, and I ran out before I could let his words stick. Before I could accept that it could be real and more than just sex.

But he's stayed away since I told him I wasn't a more kind of guy. He knows this. And yet... I'm kind of pissed he's stayed away from me. No, it's not logical, but as I pace the basement and tidy up my workspace, the waves of anxiety grow.

I can't interrupt Sasha. I mean, I could, but I won't. And my sister has moved into her '*I'm tired all the time*' stage of pregnancy. But I need to stay occupied and work off whatever this odd, buzzy feeling is.

Perry has baskets of dirty clothes in the laundry room and I put a load in the wash for him. He has work clothes in the dryer, so I fold those and take them upstairs. I know he and Leaf have been working hard on renovating my old suite a second time. Hopefully, with no errors. It should be complete next week and mine to return to if I want.

And now that I have downtime, I know... I *don't* want.

I hate having no work to use as a distraction because now I have to overthink and analyze all these bullshit feelings.

Setting the pile of clean laundry on Perry's dresser, my gaze falls on his rumpled blankets and bed. No. Nope. I'm not thinking about this. Instead, I enter his ensuite bathroom, pick up all the towels he's left everywhere, and throw them down the laundry chute. It's really cool. I only learned about it because I was working downstairs and a giant thump scared the shit out of me. Any clothes sent through the chute drop directly in front of the washing machine. Genius. I bet it was Perry's idea, too.

I don't know when the last time he cleaned his bathroom was, but it's disgusting. Under the sink, I find cleaning supplies and make quick work of polishing his sink, counter and even his toilet. Caught up in the cleaning spree, I even spray his shower and step in to scrub it down.

"Normally, I wouldn't complain about coming home to find a sexy man in my shower. But what the hell are you doing?"

"Ah!"

The shower scrubber flies out of my hand and clatters at my feet. I spin to find Perry, arms crossed in front of his chest, while he leans against the doorframe. Those sinful lips curl into a sexy smile, and I can't help but stare.

"I, uh, just thought I'd do some cleaning for you. You know, you should really think about buying that stuff you spray on shower doors before you get out." I make a motion of spraying the glass with my empty hand. "Game changer."

His smile grows, and I gulp. He has a glorious smile. It's so... warm and genuine. And sexy. I've never met a man who could say so much without his lips moving.

"I'll keep that in mind when I'm shopping next."

He unfastens the buckles on his overalls and then pulls his shirt off over his head, leaving me with a wall of naked man chest. He next lets his overalls drop and now stands in front of me in nothing but his boxers, with one eyebrow arched in question.

"Are you joining me in the shower? I'm game if you are, but since you still have clothes on, it might get awkward."

"You should put the clothes down your laundry chute now. Why leave them in a pile like that?"

He cocks his head and, with a sigh, gathers his clothes and shoves them down the chute.

"Better?"

"Yes."

"So..."

He motions towards the shower, and I remember he asked if I was staying.

"Oh, I...I'll leave you to it."

"Suit yourself."

Perry strips his boxers off before I even leave the room and because I'm weak and a glutton for punishment, I turn to watch him in the shower. He faces forward and lets his head hang. The water runs over his muscled back and I stand there, wishing I might become a stray water droplet on his body. I don't know for how long, but it's enough to question my sanity.

"Offer still stands." Perry's voice carries over the sounds of the shower, and he's not even looking at me. Smug bastard. Assumes I'm still here... correctly.

With a huff, I finally leave the bathroom. And I most certainly don't think about him wet and naked. No, sir.

And to prove he's not currently taking up all my thoughts, I flop on his couch and flick on the TV. There're hundreds of channels but only one I really like to watch.

Wild Discovery.

Yeah, I know I'm as city as they come, but something about these shows sucks me in. The random animal facts are my version of crack and I can't get enough of them.

Pulling the blanket off the back of the couch, I curl my legs under me and snuggle into it while I listen to the narrator talk about moose. I've seen plenty of moose roadside in all my travels but never one close-up on foot. Thank god.

'*A mature moose can stand up to two meters tall at the shoulders.*'

"That's what I'm saying, announcer guy! I don't want to meet that in the wild. No way."

"Who are you talking to out here?"

Perry strides into the room, hair still wet from his shower, and his plaid sleep pants hanging off his waist. One thing about Perry

I've noticed the last few weeks is that he seems to hate wearing shirts around the house. I'm a fan.

He stops and watches the show for a moment and turns to look my way.

"You like this stuff?"

"Just because I hate your rubber boots and loud machines doesn't mean I don't like animals." I jut my chin out, prepared for a battle. "I find it extremely interesting and I like trivia."

He stares at me, absently rubbing his hand across his belly.

"Huh. No shit. Mind if I join you?"

"It's your house."

"Not what I asked."

He waits for my answer, and I pull the blanket closer.

"Sure."

A genuine smile fills his face and it certainly doesn't warm my heart or send my insides tingly.

"I'm going to make myself a drink. Would you like one?"

"What are you having?"

"Well, I found a new tonic water flavour. It's grapefruit. And I have this citrus gin I love. So that's what I'm making."

"That sounds amazing. I love grapefruit."

Perry smiles again before heading into the kitchen to make the drinks. He pulls out a liquor bottle from a small cupboard I've never noticed before and removes the tonic from the fridge.

"Do you like ice in yours?"

"Please. And a lime?"

"It's the only way, gorgeous."

My heart thumps a little more at the way he throws that pet name over his shoulder as he moves. He slices a lime and, if I'm not mistaken, he hums.

He hands me my glass before he sits next to me and he kicks his feet up on the coffee table. I take a small sip of the drink and sigh.

"Oh god, Perry, this is delicious."

"I'm glad you like it. It's one of my guilty pleasures."

"One of? You have more?"

He shrugs, a small smile on his lips. "I might. A gentleman never gives away all his secrets."

I can't help it and snort a laugh. "Gentleman? Pretty sure gentlemen don't wander around shirtless."

Again he shrugs. "Turn up the show if you're gonna snipe at me. I want to hear it."

I roll my eyes and increase the volume, anyway. The ice clinking in our glasses and the television show is the only noise, and it's so fucking domestic I don't know if I love it or hate it.

"I didn't know moose could dive up to 5 meters for food. That's cool. But also creepy. Could you imagine swimming along and kicking a moose?" I shudder. "No, thank you."

Perry's deep laugh shakes the couch. "That would even freak me out. Those things can be mean." He drains his glass and raises it. "Want another one?"

"I'd love one, but I should probably eat or I'll regret it."

"Well...it appears you're about to learn another secret then. Do you have allergies? Are you picky?"

"No allergies, and sometimes I'm picky. I don't like olives."

He takes my glass from me with a sly grin and again my heart dances.

"I promise you'll like this."

Despite not wanting to enjoy myself, I smile back and wonder what other secrets he has.

Chapter 18
Perry

Call me crazy, but I think Roman might actually be open to the idea of liking me. While I offered him his fave drink, it's true, what he doesn't know is that I spent hours searching the internet for facts about Roman.

I like to come to battle prepared.

I scoured interviews or posts on his socials where he gave something personal away. He mentioned grapefruit slices as a child being a favourite and anything grapefruit flavoured. And he also mentioned his fondness for something most people don't like. Spinach dip with pumpernickel bread. It didn't go unnoticed that in a few photos, he was eating pistachios. I'd never tried them before and thankfully I like them.

After all these observations, sleuthing, and strategic questions with Sasha, I have most of his favourite foods to assemble for a couch picnic. They say a way to a man's heart is through his stomach. I'm willing to try anything to get Roman to open up to me again. The last few weeks we've dodged each other, but not without some genuine reasons. I know he's preparing for the business launch and I've been helping Leaf with the renos, so it's not overly disruptive for guests. Once June hits, the lodge will be fully booked and I'll work more to help as he needs me. I desperately want Roman and me to connect again before we get swept up in our busy working lives.

Finding him cleaning my shower tonight, though, was... odd. Maybe he's a neat freak, but I noticed the folded laundry on my dresser and while he could have done that for me out of politeness, the cleaning of my bathroom seemed a bit overboard.

Although so was me getting naked before he even left the room. I'm not opposed to fighting dirty to get what I want. I just hope it worked.

"Wild Discovery is over, but do you like National Geographic? They have a few episodes back-to-back. Oh! The first one is about ostriches!"

I bite my lip to keep the laugh in. I didn't peg Roman as a documentary nerd at all, but I love it. After assembling all my culinary finds on a tray, complete with tiny cheese spreaders and rose-printed napkins, I set the refilled drink glasses on the tray and return to Roman.

He's piled the blanket on the back of the couch and sits like I was with his feet on the table, but takes them down when he notices I have a tray.

"One new gin and tonic—with lime—and snacks, so you don't get tipsy on me."

"Oh, my god. Is that spinach dip? I love that stuff!" He dunks a cube of bread in the dip and closes his eyes as he chews. "That's delicious. Who made it?"

"The deli in the grocery store. They make a great crab dip, too."

His smile grows as he takes in the snacks and I hold my breath.

"These are all my favourites!" He narrows his eyes. "Did you squeeze Sasha for info?"

"Not really. I mean, he confirmed you prefer pistachios out of the shell for me and also as a gelato, but I couldn't find that. The rest I figured out on my own."

His lips part as he stares at me. Blue eyes soft on me as he drops his hands to his lap.

"How?"

Shifting next to him, I figure now's the time to just put it out there. He'll either think I'm a stalker or maybe see that the right person will walk the distance for him.

"Google. I read every interview you've given for at least six years. Then I looked at every photo and scrolled through...god, at least eight million comments on social media posts. I took a bunch of notes and then I asked Sasha a few questions."

"Why would you do that?"

His hands clasp and unclasp in his lap, and he focuses on the tray of snacks. I'd rather he focus on me.

"Roman." He turns to me and those gorgeous eyes I see every time I close my own carry a cautious hope. "Because you deserve it. And you weren't exactly forthcoming with any information on your own." I swallow and reach over to cup his cheek. "Because I want to know you. I actually like you Roman."

"But why? We're nothing but horrible to each other."

"Do you really think that? I don't. We push each other's buttons, but since the first time I kissed you in my kitchen, I knew that couldn't be all I ever have."

He pulls my hand away and slides as far as possible away. Squishing into the corner of the couch, his eyes now accuse me. How does this man flip his emotions so quickly?

"You told Sasha I slept with that couple at the lodge. You assumed it and told your best friend I was easy."

"I never said that! But you said nothing for me to think otherwise, Roman. You left to go to his room with him. Right in front of me."

That was the moment I knew I was in deep. It physically hurt when he turned his back and walked away with another man.

"Not that you need to know, but we talked. He gave me his business card and could help with the company. I didn't sleep with him and his fiancé—even though they wanted to, I might add."

He takes a drink from his glass with a mutter, and my anger grows.

"That's not fair to be mad at me for assuming what you wanted me to! Are you going to tell me the guy in the bathroom that night at the Maple Festival was all a lie, too?"

He says nothing, but I notice the small flinch and his fingers tighten on the glass.

"Why would you mislead me like that? What purpose did it serve trying to make me think the worst of you? Jesus, Roman. That's extreme, even for you."

"Because of this! That's why! I didn't want you to like me!"

I'm so damn confused. Setting my drink down, I reach for his hand, but he jumps up.

"Don't, Perry." His voice drops to a whisper, and I choose to ignore his request. Stepping into his space, I place my hands on his face, forcing him to listen and he doesn't fight, but I know that look in his eyes.

"Why are you so scared? I'm not a bad guy, Roman."

"Because it hurts when you lose people you love and I don't want to do that. I never want to feel that again."

His gorgeous blues well up, but he blinks away the tears.

"Roman...that's no way to live, baby. You're such a beautiful person. You're funny and kind and fucking talented. Anyone you hold close is so lucky to have you." His lip trembles and I stroke it with my thumb. "I'm sorry you lost your parents like that and I'm sorry it's been hard for you to cope all these years. But I can help you. We can help each other."

"I don't know if I can."

"But you've never tried, have you?"

He inhales a shaky breath. "What if you change your mind? Or something happens to you?"

"I won't feed you a bunch of bullshit and promise you that won't happen. Nobody knows what the future brings. Look at my brother. His husband never came home one night, all because of a freak accident like your parents. Yeah, it hurt all of us to lose him but, Roman...we're all so much better having known his affection. Even me."

He stays silent and I'm willing the gods to let me slide through the crack in the door. Just let me get in. I know once he lets himself accept love from a partner, he'll only grow more beautiful. Because he captured my attention the moment I saw him. Even spitting insults at each other, he was still desirable.

From his beautiful eyes and his sexy-as-hell corsets to his verbal sparring. I was falling.

"You even peeled the grapefruit for me." His voice is soft as one hand grips my wrist.

"I'll peel every grapefruit for you if you want me to."

His eyelids flutter closed, and he blows out a long breath.

"If we try this...this thing. Dating. I don't even know what to call it. But if we try this, Perry, I need one promise from you. Well, two actually."

"Name it."

"Don't break my heart."

His words quiver, but his grip on my wrist tightens.

"I'll wrap it in bubble wrap and keep it safe. I don't want it broken. I want it whole."

He swallows and opens his eyes again. This is the look I always want from him. Trust. Desire. Naked vulnerability that I'll never abuse.

"Second, keep walking around here without a shirt on. I think it inspires my best designs."

He smiles as he steps closer to me, and I huff a small laugh. "Am I your muse?"

"I think so."

"Can I start this dating thing off and kiss you?"

"I sure hope you plan to do more than kiss me."

He bites his lip and steps away from me, blue eyes playful, and again I'm captivated by how much he says with a single glance. "If you can catch me!"

The little imp laughs and runs towards my bedroom and the joy I feel for him showing me the real Roman propels me to chase after him. He hasn't made it very far before I wrap my arms around his waist and pull him to a stop against my chest.

"Dammit, I didn't think you'd be that fast." He laughs as I spin us and push him against the wall in the hallway.

"I'm lightning fast when I'm chasing something I want." My lips trail down his neck and he slumps against the wall. "And I want you Roman. All of you."

His hands slide into my hair as I drag my lips up to his.

"Show me how much."

His breathless words caress my skin and if he wants me to show him instead of talking, I hope he's prepared for what comes next.

Bending, I easily scoop him over my shoulder and, making sure I don't bash his head on the wall, I carry him the rest of the way to my bedroom.

I lay him on my bed gently before making quick work of my pants and the sleepwear Roman has on.

"You should really make your bed in the morning."

"Really? That's what's on your mind right now?"

His eyes sparkle and I chuckle. "You're such a shit."

"If you make your bed, you've started your day successfully. You've completed one task. It sets the mood for your day."

"I can't tell if you're serious or yanking my chain right now. I'm literally about to bury my face in your perfect peach of an ass and make you squirm. But you're going on about making my bed every morning."

His entire chest flushes a delightful pink, and he licks his lips.

"Nervous habit. Sorry. Carry on."

Lowering myself over him, I press my lips to his. Fuck, he feels so good against me, all naked and trembling.

"Relax, gorgeous. You asked me to show you how much I want you. Don't be afraid to ask me to stop, or for more, or anything really. I want you so drunk on the pleasure of what it feels like to be with me you can't think about anything else."

"Oh my god." He breathes as I move back to the end of the bed. After propping him on a pillow, I knead his ass with a groan. I can't wait to have Roman finally.

Neither can he. Roman lifts his legs and grips his thighs, allowing me better access.

"Jesus Christ, that's a sight I'll tattoo on my brain."

Keeping my word, I spread him open. Licking and swirling and fucking him with my tongue. He pants and moans underneath me. Pre-cum puddles on his abs and I internally preen over having been responsible for turning him into a needy mess.

"More."

Roman's voice is breathless and sure.

"Yeah?"

"Yeah."

Opening my nightstand drawer, I get what I need and drop the bottle of lube and condoms next to him.

"That kind of more?"

He nods yes and reaches for me, pulling me closer to his lips.

"No one has topped me in a very long time. But yes. That's what I want." He kisses my throat. "From you."

And I'm left speechless for a moment. He's been so hot and cold and it's taken me so long to even get him to be here like this. Or maybe I'm making too big of a deal out of it.

"You don't have to—"

"I know." He caresses my cheek. "I know...I want you to, okay?"

I can't stop kissing him, and he wraps his arms around my neck, pulling me even closer. Our tongues dance together like they've been partners forever. I pull away briefly to reposition next to him and add lube to… well, everywhere. He hisses at the coolness, but it quickly turns to a moan when I push a finger in.

He rocks against my hand and slowly strokes his dick. This is not a rushed fuck me and get it over with. It's exactly what I wanted to do, and it's me giving him pleasure. Worshipping everything about him. He's absolutely stunning like this.

I tease his hardened nipple as I add another finger, and he gasps, the most beautiful sound.

"Oh…oh…"

"Yeah, gorgeous. Just like that. Let me hear how much you love it."

"Perry…god…" He keens as I slip the third one in and I press my mouth to his.

"Feels so good." He mumbles against my lips. "So good."

Our kisses are fevered as he rocks on my fingers. His gasps of pleasure are what I live for, and I want him to make those same sounds when I'm buried inside him.

"I need to be in you, babe."

His hands slap around the bed for the condoms while he chases after my lips.

"Fuck, yes." While I suit up, we share small smiles that say so much. It's trust, desire, and an unspoken feeling that this is just the beginning.

Taking my time, I ease myself into him. Swallowing all his moans and committing every sigh, every touch to memory. By the time I'm all the way seated, it feels like I might explode with the next movement. Roman's hands pull my face to his and he kisses me, but it's different. It's slow and lazy, like he wants to savour this moment just as much as I do. His hands tremble as they slide down my back, and he wraps his lean legs around me.

"Are you okay, baby?"

"I think so." He bites at my lip before mumbling against mine. "I've never felt like this before."

I rock my hips with an ease I don't feel. I want to make him see stars. To bend him over the side of the bed... but I also want to stay here just like this and wish this moment would never end.

His sighs of pleasure keep me moving at the sedate pace. It's like this weird bubble of time where all I see is Roman and what could happen in the future. Everything flashes in front of me. Dancing in the kitchen, modelling for him when he wants, taking him to the lake, and eating spinach dip while watching animal documentaries late into the night. Maybe we'll get a pet. I don't even know if he likes animals. We'll hang out with Leaf and Sasha, and it won't be awkward.

He can be the centre of my entire world.

"Hey, you drifted away there." He pulls me to him, forcing his heels into my thighs with a grin. "Don't make me think I'm a bore in the sheets."

"Sorry. I was just thinking about what happens after this and how I don't want right now to be over."

Roman lets that loaded statement slide and I'm grateful.

"I only want right now to be over because you've edged me too long and I want to come."

He still grips me tight to him and I interpret that as him not wanting to change positions. It makes it difficult to thrust how I want, but he's clearly enjoying it. And to be honest, I am too. I've always enjoyed face-to-face sex because part of my pleasure is watching my partner. And Roman is too beautiful to look away from.

"Just...yeah...that's the spot...fuck..."

Again, his fingers curl into my hair and his breath puffs across my lips with every snap of my hips.

"Come for me, baby. I'm so close."

"Perry...fuck!"

Roman's body arches and then goes boneless as he shoots his load between us. His legs drop away from my waist and I use the moment to push up and take him harder. Those blue eyes snap open and he clutches my wrists as I come with a shaky groan.

God damn.

Easing out, I tie the condom off and I should toss it right away, but I drop it on the floor and pull him to me. Sweat-slicked and covered in cum is a good look for Roman, and I know I could easily make this a nightly habit.

"Since you cleaned my shower so nicely earlier, would you like to join me there?"

"I did a good job, didn't I?" His eyes drop, and he shifts, but I grip him close.

"What's wrong?"

Several moments pass and I think he won't give me a reply, but he does.

And it shocks the fuck out of me.

"You liked this, right? Did you..." He laughs, but it's not humour-filled. "Like...is this how it always is with you?"

"I loved it. I don't know what you have to compare it to, but yeah, I'm always like this. Although I'm not sure what you're getting at."

He laughs and places a kiss on my forehead.

"That's all I need to know. Let's take that shower."

Chapter 19
Roman

"Earth to Roman. Hello?"

Sasha laughs as he waves his hand in front of my face.

"Sorry. I zoned out."

"I know. I was asking if you're happy with the photo setup before we greet the public."

Sasha arranged a launch party for the business in the smallest of time frames, and I'm still in awe. He wasn't even upset that I changed my mind about it and made extra work. After he submitted all the edited images, I got to work uploading everything to the site while he worked magic and called in favours around the globe.

"Yeah, it looks great. I'm not sure how Perry will take this."

After all, it's me splashed around the room in various states of undress and provocative as fuck. Which I'm not ashamed of. It's my job. But we've never discussed it because we've been too busy fucking like rabbits every night when he gets home and sometimes in the morning before he leaves.

"Hmm, when are you going to tell me why you care about his opinion about this?"

Right. That.

"Uh, you probably already guessed, but we're seeing each other. Dating? Is that what it's called still? I've never dated, so I don't really know."

Sasha's eyes twinkle, and he bumps his shoulder to mine.

"I guessed something was up. You two aren't exactly subtle. He almost kissed you goodbye the other morning and don't think I haven't noticed how both of you seem to conveniently be unavailable at the same time."

"Sorry, I didn't tell you right away. It's just fucking odd for me. And it only just occurred to me now we've never really talked about how he feels about me showing myself to the world. Yes, he knows I model, and he's looked me up online himself, but he's never told me how he feels about it."

If he were to say he had an issue with it, I'd have to break my heart myself and let him go. I won't and can't give this part of me up.

"My guess is he's proud as hell to say you're his."

"Do you think so? He's not the jealous type?"

"Perry? No. I mean, he'll stake a claim, I have no doubt, but it's not like he'll be telling you to quit or anything. He'll be your biggest supporter, Ro. I can guarantee it."

"He's not like anyone I've ever met. Or been with."

I've been with many people in a purely sex-only way. There's been no one I've ever shared what I share with Perry. It's a foreign land for me.

"He wears his heart on his sleeve. He won't ever be anything less than honest with you. If he has a problem, he'll tell you."

My lips curl in a smile as I remember how he bitched me out because I cleaned the bathroom for him. Again. He wasn't unhappy. He just doesn't want me to do those things all the time. But then I get to watch him strip and it's kind of win-win.

"I can believe that."

Perry hasn't held back his thoughts at all since I made the choice to try what he said. To let someone love me. Not that Perry loves me yet, but he's so intense I feel like it's just a step away. I don't love him yet either, but what I feel is unlike anything I can describe.

It's as foreign as another language and scary because, like a language, I can get it wrong. I can say the wrong thing and I don't want to be wrong for him.

"You know, I'm going to say this to both of you because it applies. Don't hurt my friend, okay?" Sasha's smile is both happy and wistful. "You're both so much alike in ways you probably can't see yet. I don't want either of you to have a broken heart."

I scoff. "My heart would be the only one at risk. No one is declaring love just yet."

"That's right. *Yet*. It will be, Ro. I know you. And I know Perry. Neither of you can do anything halfway. But this is still new. Especially for you. How are you feeling about it?"

Walking away from Sasha's gaze, I adjust the samples of a lace tankini and boy shorts on the display. How I'm feeling is a heavy question right now.

"Good. I like what we have so far, and the bonus part is we're both sleeping better."

It's hard not to. Having him wrapped around me at night is the best sleep I've ever had. Even better than when I first moved in. And his nightmares have vanished for now, too.

"Well, I won't pry. But I see you both smiling more and that makes me happy." He pulls out his phone from his pocket. "Now, before we go home to get changed, I have a surprise."

He hands me a phone with a video message. It's his favourite band, Wayward Lane, sending their best wishes and all the success in the world. It's actually quite sweet... until they all moon us and tell us they're going commando until they can try a pair of my designs.

It is kind of cool to think famous rock stars want to wear my lingerie, and now I've seen their asses, so that's a bonus.

"You know all the people don't you, Sash?"

He smiles like it's no big deal and laughs.

"I can't wait for you to meet everyone tonight. It's going to be great!"

I've never turned down a party, but this last week with Perry at home with just us... I like it. And it's weird I'm wishing away my launch party in favour of snuggling on a couch eating spinach dip with a man who's increasingly less annoying.

With a sigh, I follow Sasha to his truck and he drops me off at home, wired and babbling the whole time about tonight. His excitement spreads to me and soon I'm just as excited and race into the house to get ready.

Securing the tie of my corset, I smooth the front and gaze in the mirror. Slim fit black dress pants, crisp white dress shirt and a black and white corset with silver accents and buttons. Before I leave, I'll finish it with my black blazer. It's no tux, but in my opinion, it's a million times better.

No shade to tuxes. On the right man, they're killer. But for me, a corset wins every time. I feel my sexiest and most badass when I wear one. Tonight I've even added a black tie with a pattern of silver flowers on it.

My phone chimes as I dab cologne behind my ear.

Perry: I'm running late. I'm so sorry, but I'll be there. Can you get a ride with Sasha?

Roman: If not, I can drive myself. Is everything okay?

Perry: More than okay. Just took longer than I thought. I'll be there soon.

Replying with a heart which is so not like me, I sigh with disappointment. I wanted for us to arrive together. I just wanted to… I don't know, walk in with a handsome man. It's hokey and all kinds of lame for me to even think shit like that, but Perry has made me believe, just a little, that I might like the thought of having a supportive partner.

It's foolish of me. And I should guard myself better, but it's hard to put off Perry. I really fucking like the guy, as much as I hate to admit it.

Texting Sasha, he answers that he and Leaf will pick me up and I wander out to the living room to wait. To stay busy, I tidy up and fluff the cushions on the couch. Perry left his shirt on the floor. With a head shake, I walk into his room and toss it down the laundry chute, all while wearing a smile on my face. A smile that only grows when I notice he made his bed.

Oh no.

My heart sort of thumps and I feel all floaty and... shit. Either I'm about to pass out because I haven't eaten yet today or that was an enormous wave of feelings.

"Ro! We're here!"

"Be right there!"

I'm saved from examining what the hell just happened here, thank god. It's a night of celebration, not of internal examinations on whether it's good or bad to develop feelings.

"Holy fuck, you look amazing." Sasha's gaze roams over me and he smirks. "Bring a stick. Men are gonna fall at your feet tonight for your attention dressed like that."

Grabbing my jacket, I shrug into it and button the single button.

"Well, you know I don't mind the attention. And you look pretty amazing too, Sash. Green is so hot on you."

His forest-green suit fits him like a glove and his eye makeup is gorgeous. In greens and golds to match his suit, he practically glows with happiness.

"Thank you. I couldn't wait to wear this. Almost didn't make it here. Leaf, he ah...you know. He likes it, too."

Sasha blushes with a laugh and again I feel like I'm in an invisible vise being squeezed so hard I just want to scream. But in a good way.

"Um, before we're surrounded by people tonight, Sasha, I just wanted to say thank you for believing in me. For being here..." My voice cracks and I shake my head.

"Don't make me ruin my makeup, Roman. I love you too and there's no one else I'd rather pursue this dream with. We're a great team."

We pull each other into a hug and I'm relieved he took the words out of my mouth.

"Yeah, what you said."

"C'mon. Let's get the party started. Well, it probably already has, but we should make an appearance."

After Leaf parks in the space saved outside the art gallery, he offers an arm to each of us.

"I am the luckiest guy here tonight, entering with you two. I'll be the envy of all the men."

"You already are, baby. The whole town knows how you won me over."

I chuckle as they tease each other back and forth, and I cast a glance behind us. Clouds have moved in and a nasty storm will be on us soon.

"Did Perry say how late he would be to you, Leaf? I thought he was with you today."

"Oh, he was. He, ah, had to leave for some errands, but he said he'd be here."

Leaf forces a smile and opens his mouth, but Sasha smacks a hand over it.

"He knows you're with Perry. Yes, Perry told him, and if he wants to, he'll talk to you again *after* Perry arrives. Right, baby?"

Leaf nods and I raise an eyebrow at Sasha.

"He'll be here. Don't worry."

And there's no more time to think or discuss it because we've arrived at the glass doors to our reception room and it's already full of people. Malcolm from the bookstore sees us and rushes over as we step inside.

"I want to be the first to congratulate you both! Roman, your work is amazing. I've never been into lingerie, but wow...I might change my mind. You two have a lot of handshaking and shmoozing to do." He air kisses both of us and shakes Leaf's hand before he fades into the crowd with a promise to keep things running while we just have fun.

"What the hell did you do, Sasha? I was expecting a few dozen people throughout the evening. There's already at least a hundred here."

Malcolm appears again with a glass for each of us. Mine is grapefruit gin and tonic water with pieces of lime and grapefruit floating and Sasha has champagne.

"I told you. I know people and I invited them."

"I didn't know you had so many connections," I whisper as someone calls for attention and Sasha grabs my hand.

"You're about to find out, Ro."

He pulls me up to the microphone, where Leaf is still speaking, and I survey the crowd. I recognize some of the local business owners, which is nice. A familiar face peeks through the crowd and I shake my head.

"Please give a warm welcome to Sasha and Roman. Stay as long as you like and please enjoy the refreshments."

The crowd erupts with clapping, and I lean over to speak in Sasha's ear.

"You asked Bruce to come?"

"He's a very interested business contact, Ro. And you're friends, aren't you?"

"Yeah, but…"

I don't get to finish the sentence because the first group of well-wishers is in front of us and we're smiling and posing for pictures. Sasha and I are used to this. It's effortless really, just another red carpet walk.

"You came!" He squeals and hands me his empty glass. A group of familiar faces appear and Sasha hugs them all, of course. I didn't recognize them at first without their cowboy hats.

"Ro, you remember Alec and Zane, right?"

The cowboys we spent an eventful weekend with a few years ago. That was a fun time.

"Of course I do. What brings you two here? Surely not just to attend this tiny party."

Alec shakes my hand, his blue eyes bright as he gazes at Zane.

"Well, this one here missed Sasha, and I was down for a fast road trip before the ranch gets too busy." He leans closer. "And Sasha sent me some pics of your stuff. Is there, uh, a way to get some of those in red?"

"Oh yes. Red is a popular colour request. I'll have white, black, red and pink for sure."

"Excellent." He catches Zane's eye again and winks. "I'll tell him. You two enjoy your night and we'll catch up later. Great to see you again, Roman."

Sasha lets go of Zane and allows him to leave with his husband.

"I can't believe they came here. This is exciting! Leaf is fielding questions at the sign-up table. He said someone asked about inviting us to the huge pride festival in Montreal!"

"Wow. This is...more than I expected."

When Leaf appears with fresh drinks for us, I can't help it and tug at his hand.

"Have you heard from Perry?"

He squeezes my arm gently.

"He said he'd be here. Maybe he got stuck in traffic."

"It's a town of 10,000 people. There's no traffic to get stuck in at 7 P.M." Leaf's eyes widen and then it clicks. "Where did he go, Leaf?"

"He'll be here, Roman. I promise. He wouldn't miss this for anything."

Leaf weaves out of the crowd and my mood turns sour. We've been here an hour already, and he promised. He promised! I don't do relationships for this reason. Well, it's one of the reasons. You just get let down.

"Hey," I lean over to Sasha's ear. "I'm going to step out for a break. I'll be back."

"You okay?"

"Yeah, I just need some air."

I walk to the back of the room, where there's a door to a small, covered patio. Since this is the main wedding reception venue in town, the little patio is a perfect cocktail hour gathering place. A light rain patters on the tin roof and I look over the town below.

Now is not a great time for me to unpack the disappointment over Perry being late. I'm not quite ready to accept that it's because I care and there are big feelings growing. Yet here I am, hiding from my party in a mopey mess while it rains. It's a little too cliché, even for me.

Thunder rolls in the distance and serves to match the mess of emotions swirling in me.

The door opens behind me and the chatter from inside spills out into the night quiet.

"I'm fine. Just give me a few more minutes."

"Why would you not be fine?"

Perry's deep, rumbling voice has me spinning around. And then almost fall flat on my face.

My mouth moves, but no words come out and his plush lips tilt in a grin as he watches me.

"You...you're...wow."

He chuckles low and steps closer.

"So, I did good? I'm sorry I was late, but the tux rental place had nothing in my size and if I went to the city, I could pick it up. I wanted this one."

My mouth gapes more. "You went to the city for a tux?"

"Well, I went to the city for you. I wanted to wear something, so I didn't stand out with your crowd. You like it?"

"You look amazing. And you'd stand out no matter what, Perry. It doesn't matter what you wear." I can't take my eyes off him. "You're not wearing any plaid."

He points a shiny black dress shoe forward and pulls up his pant leg to reveal a pair of plaid socks.

"Almost. I couldn't take the whole country boy thing away." He steps closer and places a hand on my hip. "I'm sorry I'm so late. I wanted to be here and walk in with you if you'd let me. But I also didn't want to embarrass you."

"You wouldn't embarrass me. Ever."

He smiles, the mischief twinkling in his eyes. "So it's okay if I get the dress Crocs out of the truck instead?"

"Absolutely not."

He laughs and I've drifted closer on my own. His giant hands hold my hips and mine come up to fiddle with his tie.

"You look absolutely amazing, Roman." One of his hands sneaks under my jacket and slides up my side. "This might be my favourite corset yet."

"Thank you."

And I don't know what else to say. I've run out of snark. I want to melt into a puddle at his feet because he went out of his way to please me. He showed up and all my dark musings disappeared because he was here.

And it all kind of falls into place. Without a doubt, I'm falling in love with Perry.

And I don't know how to handle that.

Chapter 20
Perry

Roman and Sasha network like the professionals they are and I drift to the bar to get us both tonic water. Mine with lime and Roman's with grapefruit. I love his odd quirk for grapefruit pieces in his drink. Nothing common for my Roman.

And that's what he's become to me. Mine. But he's still not completely sold on being called that. Although I think me showing up dressed in a tux and doting on him for the rest of the night has scored me a tonne of points. Even now, when I survey the room, I find him instantly and he looks up. Smiling back at me with a soft gaze that I convince myself has to mean more.

"Hey, there. Fancy seeing you here."

I turn to find the man from the lodge earlier this year. The man who wanted Roman in his bed and turned me into the *Incredible Hulk* with one simple suggestive smile towards Roman.

"What brings you back here?"

The bartender places two shot glasses with red liquid in front of him.

"Nostalgia." He winks with a laugh. "Don't worry. I'm not going near your man unless it's business talk. I like all my limbs attached."

I grunt something that resembles words, and he cocks his head.

"For what it's worth, he only has eyes for you. I knew it then and I know it now." He offers me his hand to shake. "It's Bruce, by the way. And if I do a deal with these two men, you'll be seeing a lot more of me. I hope we can get along."

I take his hand with a gentle squeeze and nod. "We'll get along. And it's Perry. Nice to meet you."

He takes his shooters and I watch as he flits through the room to his partner and hands him one. They laugh and down the shot before kissing, and after a brief conversation, they leave with a much younger man.

With Roman's drink in hand, I cross to where he stands with Sasha and someone I've never met. Roman turns when I'm close, as if he senses me near, and his soft gaze almost makes me drop our drinks.

"Perry! I want you to meet someone." He takes his drink from my hand and leans in to kiss my lips. It's soft and chaste, but it still makes me smile. "This is our friend Lars. We all modelled together and went through some tough shit. He stopped by to tell us he's finally done with this PhD and leading an expedition to the Galapagos Islands for a study with...what was it again, Lars?"

"The mating habits of the marine iguana." He extends a hand and I shake it. "Nice to meet you. Thank you for making an honest man out of Roman. He's a tough nut to crack."

"An honest man? We're not married or anything."

Lars sends a quizzical look to Roman.

"My apologies. He said you lived together, and that's huge for Roman."

"Don't go rushing me down the aisle, Lars. One step at a time, but yes, we live together." He slides his free hand into mine.

"And yes, it is a big deal," Roman whispers as he watches me and everyone else fades away.

Leaning down, I kiss him, soft and with reverence. Doing my best to convey to him how thankful I am that I get to share this with him. This monumental step in not only his professional life but his personal life as well.

He kisses me back, and it takes all my willpower to stop. Kissing his forehead, I whisper, "It's a big deal for me, too."

Lars and Sasha have moved away to talk, and I shake my head.

"How long were we kissing for? Your friends left."

"Do you want to get out of here?"

"You want to leave your party early? Is that a good idea?"

"I don't know, but I want you to take me home."

Roman doesn't need to say why. I feel it too, and against my better judgment, I agree. "At least tell Sasha, and we'll go."

He taps Sasha on the arm, and they whisper together. The two best friends embrace before Roman hugs Lars, and I almost change my mind and tell him he needs to stay and visit with his friends. He needs to meet the people who came here to celebrate him and make contacts to be successful. But I'm selfish. And I want him to myself.

We abandon our drink glasses as we leave, our hands tightly clasped as we make our way to the exit. He's stopped by a few people of course and Roman takes the time to be polite and nothing more before finally we step into the hallway and both of us giggle like school kids and race walk outside.

The rain that was only a light sprinkle when I first arrived has turned into a heavy rain now and I turn to Roman.

"I had to park down the block. Want me to get the truck and come back? I don't want you ruining your clothes."

"It's only water, Perry. I'm not made of sugar, for fuck's sake."

I bark a laugh. "No, you sure aren't." I tug his hand as we step into the pouring rain. "More like salt!"

He laughs as we run down the sidewalk, trying to avoid puddles and failing, splashing each other as we run. The rain sees our fun and falls harder, plastering our hair to our heads and when we finally reach my truck, we're soaked to the bone... and still laughing.

Roman's smiling face is all I focus on and instead of climbing out of the rain, I shove him against my truck. Taking his face in my hands, I devour his mouth. His hands clutch at my waist and pull me closer.

"Perry...I..." He smashes his lips into mine again.

When I pull away, I reach behind and open the door for him.

"Let's get home, baby."

"Home. I like that."

The drive home is slow.

Earlier, the weather issued a warning of dangerous rainfall amounts and the creek in town was already swollen. With twelve more hours of heavy rain in the forecast, flooding was an enormous concern. Our town was in a valley, but both Leaf and I were fortunate to live on high points where floods never reached. Even when my backyard river levels rose, it never put me in danger.

But it was still a danger.

Roman texted Leaf and Sasha to advise them how bad it was getting and, thankfully, the partygoers had cleared out. With a promise to inform us when they get home, we pull into my driveway and I slump in relief.

With all the rescues I've been a part of and the recoveries I've also had to bear witness to, it's always worse when there's someone in your life you care about waiting at home. The pull to do the right thing for the public is always strong, but when I think of leaving Roman behind... it's something I can't do right now.

"Let's get warm and dry."

"You need to do something, don't you?"

Roman's voice is a whisper in the truck cab and I don't need to strain over the pinging of rain on the roof. I know what he means.

"The only thing I want to do now is get you warm and dry and in my bed. That's what I need to do, Roman. The sooner the better."

With a nod, he steps out and we both jog up the front steps and into my house. Once inside, I spin him around, trapping him against the door. His ocean blues swim with a tenderness I hope is real. Because I want nothing more than to have this sometimes prickly man tell me those three words. But until then, I'll do my best to show him what I crave.

"Let me take care of you?" Dragging my lips down his neck, he thumps his head on the door and manages a nod. My fingers fumble with the buttons on his corset and he chuckles.

"Untie the back and pull it off."

"Of course, even taking your clothes off can't be easy, can it?"

Grumbling, I remove his suit jacket and spin him around to find the tie and I listen as he tells me what to do. He's unclasped the front and when I spin him back around, I can finally remove the garment I both love and hate.

"You're sexy as fuck in these things, Roman, but not gonna lie. They're a royal pain to remove and if you weren't soaking wet, I'd not have bothered."

"No? You'd just rip it off me or...?"

He raises an eyebrow as his hands reach for me, working all the buttons and clasps on my tux like a pro.

"Or I'd bend you over half dressed and fuck you to oblivion with it on."

His breath whooshes out like I just punched him.

"Fuck, Perry...you can do that the next time, then."

Our hands keep racing, shoving off the wet clothes with grunts and groans as we refuse to keep our mouths off each other. Somehow we've made it to the hallway of my bedroom and even though we shiver from the wetness, our skin is hot from the fire between us.

"Let me warm up the shower for you," I murmur against his lips and he steps away so I can turn the water on before we step inside.

Roman leans against the vanity and looks one hundred percent at ease as he waits for me to beckon him forward. Together we step under the warm water and, even in this enclosed space, we move in sync. We make it work and with only the sound of the shower, we speak volumes to each other with hungry kisses, teasing touches, and just simply taking turns showing each other care. I wash his hair and he soaps up my body.

We pat each other dry as we somehow walk, tangled together, into my bedroom and tumble on the bed with a laugh.

"How did we get here, Perry?"

"I drove you home and then we used our feet."

He doesn't laugh at my joke, and I immediately tense.

"What's wrong, baby?"

"I just...how did we go from barely being civil to each other, to me living here, to a few make out sessions where I still wasn't sure if I even liked you, to this? How did I start liking you?"

"You like me?" I nip at his shoulder and pull him closer.

"Yeah. By some grace of god, I do."

"Well, I'm pretty irresistible."

He laughs softly and I lift his chin. Those blue eyes stare back at me and they're as naked as we are. My breath catches with hope I'm right at what they say.

"I'll take care of you, Roman. Always. I don't know how we got here either, but I've never been happier to fuck up a plumbing job in my life." He laughs freely at that one and I'm glad. "And if you repeat that, I'll deny it."

"I just...it's a big step for me and...shit. When you showed up in that tuxedo? And you were late because you drove two hours each way to make it happen just for me? That's a pretty big deal to me. You might think it's shallow for me to be happy you did that, but I was. Not because you looked hotter than a burning building, but because you cared so much about 'fitting into my crowd,' as you put it. You could have showed up in sweatpants and a T-shirt, and I still would've been happy to see you there."

"I wanted it to be the best day for you, Roman. I wanted to blend in with you."

He pushes me over and climbs on top of me. His blond hair still drips and a water droplet runs down his cheek. I wipe it away and he leans down, pressing his lips to mine and taking my breath away with one kiss.

"Thank you." He whispers across my lips. "Let me show you how much I appreciate you."

He moves down my body, my legs still dangle off the side of the bed and he slides to the floor. He tugs on my legs to move me closer, and I slide down.

"This is perfect." He purrs before swiping his tongue across my balls.

"God...Roman...what are you—"

And just like that, *poof*, the inability to speak has disappeared because Roman is feasting on me like a starving man. Propping myself up with my elbows, I stare down at the sight.

I can't see his face because it's buried in my ass but his blond head is there and when he pulls away, the blue eyes I get lost in stare up at me, just as wrecked as I feel.

"Why'd you stop?" My hoarse voice sounds foreign.

"I want to be in you. Fuck...I need to."

He hurries up my body and presses his lips to mine. "I want to lose myself in you. I want to feel you from the inside when you come."

"God...yes."

We reposition ourselves up on the bed and my heart feels like it might shatter against my ribs. He grabs the lube and condoms from the drawer and pauses.

"This isn't your first time, is it? Being topped? Is this okay?"

"Not my first time. But like you…it's been a long time." I reach over and stroke his cock. He closes his eyes with a hiss. "I prefer not to, but for you? Anything. I want you to mark me on this inside. Would you do that?"

He swallows hard, throat bobbing as he pins me with a tender gaze.

"You want it bare?"

How can I tell him I want him and all the most intimate things he can offer me without telling him I'm so fucking in love with him that my heart leaves my body every time we part? I want this pure and unfiltered Roman. And I want him to have me.

"Yeah. I have no reason to use protection. There's nobody else."

He runs a trembling hand through his hair.

"I've not been with anyone since I moved here. I've never… I'm always…"

"I trust you, Roman. Please?"

"What are you doing to me, Perry?" Draping himself over me, he nudges his nose next to mine and trails his lips down my jaw. "I don't do this kind of thing and you have me all…I'm…fucking gone for you."

And that's pretty close to being in love. Arching my back, I invite him to take it all from me. To hold nothing back and know that I feel the same way.

Every inch of my skin he covers in kisses so tender I quiver. The cap of the lube clicks and he coats my aching dick. Slow and measured, he strokes me while I only want him to get lost in me.

"Roman…."

I'm so breathless I should worry about passing out, but I don't care.

Everything is so much. The thunder picks up outside and I'm reminded briefly there's a storm. My body is limp as his fingers work magic until I'm a whimpering mess.

"I got you. Shh..."

He kisses my lips before the head of his cock breaches me, and I hiss at the sensation. But he waits and twists his hand around my dick again in the slow, slippery way I love. And bit by bit I relax until Roman's lips are on mine again and his balls touch my ass.

"You feel fucking amazing, Perry. I can't...wow."

"Make me yours."

His eyes close as he rocks his hips at a gentle pace, and I cling to him. Every muscle in his back pops with the strain and his breath, ragged pants, crosses my skin and leaves shivers in its wake.

"I'm already close. Fuck, Perry. This is..."

He pushes up on his knees and adjusts to rock harder into me, and I cry out.

"Just like that. *Yesss...*"

My balls tighten, and I lock my gaze on Roman. His focus is gone and the ultimate bliss on his face is breathtaking. It's my undoing.

"Roman!"

God, it just comes out of nowhere. My orgasm isn't just a runaway train. It's a nuclear blast. Roman's thrusts stutter and he readjusts to lie over me again.

"Fuck, fuck..."

He kisses me wildly. Like it's his last night on earth and pumps through his orgasm. All finesse is gone as the act of claiming takes over. Finally, he stills and wraps his arms around me.

Our laboured breathing struggles to be heard over the thunder booming outside. Roman rests his forehead against mine and I press a kiss to his lips.

"Perry, I...I think I—"

With a thunderous crack, the power goes out.

Chapter 21
Roman

The storm still rages after the power went out. I stand in the kitchen looking out the window into the darkened night. I almost told Perry I loved him.

After cleaning ourselves again, he fell into a deep sleep. For the first time since moving into his house, I can't sleep. The restlessness I always fight is worse now. Before he drifted off, he mentioned the town will probably need help if the river rises too quickly and it shouldn't bother me this much.

He's a rescuer. It's what he does. But all I keep seeing is the police officer at our door telling my aunt they found my parents' bodies and I don't know if I can survive that a second time.

It's 3 A.M. and I know she'll rip me a new one, but Josie will understand.

I hit dial as I walk back to my room, thankful for the flashlight Perry keeps in his bedroom. Oddly enough, in the same drawer as the lube and condoms. That's Perry, always prepared.

"Ro? Is everything okay?"

Relief washes over me as I close the bedroom door.

"Hey, Jos. I'm fine, but I'm sorry for waking you. I just need to talk to someone."

"I was awake anyway. This baby likes to kick their mama."

My heart squeezes. "Hopefully that's all the kicking they do."

"What happened?"

My sister was never one to beat around the bush. Just right to the point.

"Wait! Before that, was your launch party a success? I heard a girl at work mention your website is on fire."

"It was excellent. But to be honest, it was hard to focus on because...well, you remember I told you about Perry?"

"The guy who wears Crocs and plaid, pushes all your buttons, but is a good kisser and learned all your favourite foods? That guy?"

She says it with a chuckle, and I shake my head with a smile. Fucking sisters.

"Yeah, that one. He ah, showed up with a tuxedo he drove two hours in one direction to get especially for this event and he looked fucking killer, Jos. Like, swallow my tongue. And he just...I don't...he..."

"Take a breath, Roman."

I do and another one.

"Without giving me the dirty details, what's got you so shook up? Anytime you've talked about him, he seemed like he was a nice guy. And if I'm not mistaken, he seems into you."

"Yeah, he's into me. He brought me home tonight and I... we... Jos... I think I'm in love with him and I'm shit damn scared."

The silence lasts so long that I make sure we're still connected. "Jos?"

"Still here. I'm just shocked." She laughs softly. "But why are you scared? Love isn't supposed to be like that."

"Lots of reasons, but mostly the thought of him not coming home one night. Like mom and dad."

"Mom and Dad were a freak accident. I know it's the source of your anxiety and why you keep people at a distance, but you need to let love in if it finds you. You'll be happier."

"There's a storm here right now. Severe rainfall and flood warning are in effect. Before he fell asleep, he mentioned he'd likely volunteer if the town needed help. He'd willingly go out in this to help people, Jos. That's what scares the fuck out of me. I just figured out I have big feelings and he might not come back home!"

Pacing the small room, I feel the tightness in my chest build and my sister knows exactly what I'm doing. She talks me through breathing and calms be back down before she continues.

"He sounds like a man with so much room in his heart to help people like that, Ro. Perry sounds amazing. Nothing you've told me makes me think he doesn't feel the same way as you do."

"I think he does, but he knows if he says it, I might run."

"Will you?"

"I've thought about it."

"But have you thought about the future and what it might be like to have someone like Perry share it with you? To always watch those dumb animal shows with you? To cheer you on with the business like Leaf does for Sasha?"

"Probably too much, to be honest. And they aren't dumb shows."

My sister laughs and apologizes for mocking my favourite programs.

"Roman, there's never a guarantee in life or love. Does he make you happy?"

"Mostly, yeah."

She laughs. "Mostly. That's a ringing endorsement. Why are you calling me at 3 A.M., brother?"

"For advice, duh. What am I supposed to do?"

"Well, you could start by having an adult conversation and telling him you love him. Ask him what he wants if you were to have a relationship."

"You're always so fucking logical."

"That's why you call me, though."

"So I should tell him how I feel and we should take it a day at a time?"

"Pretty much."

"I'll try. Hey...thanks for listening like always. I love you and I can't wait to be an uncle."

"I can't wait to see you holding a baby. Good night, Ro. Let me know how it works out."

Ending the call, I creep back to the kitchen and a weather alert pops up on my phone.

Flooding imminent in Maple. Please seek higher ground immediately. Obey evacuation orders when given.

Oh god. Perry's going to go out in this.

When I enter his bedroom, he's already sitting up and squinting at his phone.

"Hey. Where did you disappear to?"

He pats the spot next to him on the bed and I eagerly squirm up to him and curl into his side.

"I couldn't sleep."

"Oh? Anything I can do to help?"

He kisses the top of my head and hugs me close.

"How come you're awake?"

"Oh. The fire department called me and asked if I was available to help. Sounds like they might need to do some evacuations, so I'm on standby."

"Standby to go out and rescue people from the water."

Damn the tremble in my voice that gives me away.

"Yeah, babe." He kisses me again to soften the blow. "If they call me, I'll do whatever they need to help. You know this."

His phone rings, and my heart drops as he listens and nods.

"I'll be there as soon as I can."

He tosses the phone on the nightstand and forces my chin up to look at him.

"I want nothing more than to spend this day holding you and having so much sex my dick chafes. But it's in my blood, Roman. I help people. I'm trained for it and this town needs me. People need help."

His lips take mine and I feel the regret there. He really wishes he could stay and I get it.

"Would I be of help?"

He startles and searches my face.

"You want to come help? For real?"

"I mean, I'm nervous, but if it means that much to you, then yeah...for real. What can I do?"

This time he kisses me hard, and the pride in his gaze is unmissable.

"Get dressed and come with me. Even if you're making coffee for the workers, there will be something you can do."

Nodding, I leave his arms to head to my room.

He yells out after me.

"Make sure you have your boots and coat I bought you! Yellow looks good on you! Thank me later, gorgeous!"

I don't know why, but remembering the day he took me out to get the horribly coloured gear I need to live here makes my heart beat faster.

And it actually makes me smile.

My heart is in my throat as Perry's truck nears the fire station in town. The station is on elevated ground and in no danger, but the river that runs along the far side of town is already creeping over the banks and towards businesses.

The rain hasn't let up either and the wipers on Perry's truck struggle to keep up. He reaches a hand over the middle console, palm up, and I grasp it like I'm someone adrift he may rescue today.

"Would it ease your mind to know that every time I've assisted with this kind of evacuation, no one has died?"

"It should. But right now I'm scared and a little in awe that you do this kind of thing without a second thought."

He says nothing, but he squeezes my hand and I keep staring out the window.

When he finally brings the truck to a stop, it's ironically at the same place we were last night. The art gallery.

"This is the volunteer command centre and a place where displaced people will stay temporarily. I bet you won't even recognize the place from last night."

"Um, okay. Do I just go in?"

"I'll introduce you and then I'm off to the station to go where they need me." He leans over to kiss me in the truck cab. The rain still pours down in sheets. "I'll come back to pick you up. Don't even try to leave here without me."

We exit the truck and dash into the art gallery. He's right. I don't recognize the place. Tables filled with bottled water and small food boxes line the hallway. At the end is a giant coffee machine with paper cups, sugar, and creamers. People walk with purpose, phones pressed to their ears or clipboards in front of them.

An older man approaches us. Grey flecks his hair and mustache and smiling blue eyes behind a pair of black frames.

"Mr. Attwater! Nice to see you again. Although I wish it was under better circumstances."

Perry greets the man with a hug, and I don't miss the fondness in Perry's eyes for the man.

"I wish it was under other circumstances, Leo. But I bring another set of hands to help." He grasps my hand with a tug. "This is Roman. Roman, meet Leo."

Leo bypasses my hand and hugs me so hard I think he cracked a rib.

"Roman! Thank you so much for volunteering. I'll give you a tour and a job. Then I'll feed you lunch, too."

"Oh, ah, that sounds great. Just tell me where you need me."

Before I can follow Leo, Perry grabs me and pulls me back. His large palm cups my cheek and he places a soft kiss on my lips.

"Thank you for doing this. Listen to Leo, and I promise I'll be back for you."

"Please be careful." I kiss him again, this time lingering a little longer. "I'll wait for you."

Wordlessly, he turns and leaves and I watch his neon yellow back exit. I should have told him. What if that was my only chance to say I love him and I missed it?

"He's a good man."

Leo's voice startles me back to the present, and he lays a comforting hand on my shoulder. "He's good at what he does. I won't tell you not to worry because if we could all turn that off on a whim, it would make life easy, wouldn't it?"

"It sure would. He promised he'd be back, so I'm holding him to it."

"I would too. How long have you been dating? I didn't know Perry was seeing anyone."

"Oh, we're not dating. He's a...friend."

Leo raises a single bushy eyebrow and I smile a crooked smile.

"You're right. That sounded lame, and I'm still used to denying it. But it's still new."

"That I can believe. It's hard the first time you admit you care about someone."

Leo leads me into the gallery where our event was just last night, and I can't believe what I'm seeing. Rows of cots have been set up and there's a stack of blankets and pillows nearby.

"A part of our town is an island. There aren't a lot of houses on it, but there are a few elderly couples there that I know of and one younger family that I'm sure will need to stay here for a few days. Perry will make sure they get here."

"Does he know them?"

Leo smiles. "He knows one of the children. He taught him how to swim when he helped at the school."

Is there anything he doesn't do? How do I not know this?

"What did he do at the school? Are you a teacher?"

"I was. I'm retired now. But I had Perry come to my kindergarten class and teach them about water safety. When he learned a lot of the kids had no experience around water, he gave them swimming lessons. It was up at his brother's lodge in the lake, mind you, but it was important to him. Do you know his brother as well?"

"I do. Sasha is my best friend. I've only been here since February so we could launch our business."

Leo grins as he spreads a blanket on a cot.

"You're kidding! Sasha is a good friend of my son Caleb. He and my husband run the coffee shop, Ragged Chutes. I've heard all about you, but didn't put the pieces together." He hands me a stack of blankets. "Could you finish setting all these up and add a pillow to each one? I'm going to check on the kitchen and I'll be back in a bit."

It seems like something so minuscule compared to what Perry must be doing. He's risking his life to get families to safety. I don't even know how they'd do that. Meanwhile, I'm spreading blankets on cots for people who will arrive wet and cold.

And he taught kids to swim? He volunteered at the school? I feel like such an asshole for being so rude to him. No wonder he thought I was a spoiled city kid when we first met. My idea of volunteering was writing a check for a cause until I met Perry.

He volunteers himself, his time, and his knowledge to help others.

My sister was right. Perry's heart is bigger than I imagined. And there's a lot more to him I don't know.

As promised, Leo kept me busy. After making the cots up, he led me to the kitchen, where I helped make sandwiches for lunch and prepared a hot supper.

Several families arrived on their own. They loaded their prized possessions into their vehicles and drove here before being forced from their homes.

But one particular family drew my attention. A young couple with four small children under the age of ten. Despite being in a shelter, they still seemed happy. One of the little boys clutched a puppy to his chest and gushed about how his friend carried him through the water.

"Hi. I'm Roman. What's your puppy's name?"

"Mortimer. We call him Morty for short, though. Wanna pet him?"

"Of course I do. What's your name?"

I let the puppy lick my hand and watch its tiny tail wag. Mortimer squirms and jumps into my arms.

"Oh, he likes you! I'm Ethan. Our basement is full of water and the firemen came to get us out. I got to ride in a big rubber boat and my friend Perry carried me because I'm so short."

My heart hitches at the mention of Perry's name and Ethan babbles on like we're old friends.

"It's so cool! He has a special suit. He brought it to school once when I was in kindergarten to show us. I think I want to be like him when I grow up."

"And what would that be? A person with a cool suit?"

Ethan smiles a gap-toothed grin. "No silly. An emergency person. Like a superhero, but you're real."

Ethan switches gears, telling me about the puppy and his parents smile apologetically at his motor mouth tendencies. I wave them off and listen raptly. He tells me about Morty's fear of pooping alone, how he only likes sandwiches with peanut butter on one side of the bread and jam on the other, not both on the same slice of bread. Oh, and he's relieved he has his favourite yellow boots.

For a kid displaced from his home for an undetermined amount of time, his positive outlook is commendable. And I could learn a thing or two from this chatty six-year-old.

As the hours tick by and the night grows closer, a gnawing in my chest grows. Perry never gave me a timeline. He just told me to wait here for him.

The longer he's out there in danger, the more agitated I become.

A murmur among the volunteers sends my pulse racing.

"I heard the building caved, and a rescuer is still inside."

Leo is in the group and notices me approaching.

"Is that true? What happened?"

Leo speaks in a hushed tone so only I can hear.

"We don't know if anything happened yet. I'm waiting to hear from the command post." He grips my shoulders and forces me to make eye contact. "Don't panic."

Too late.

Chapter 22
Perry

I couldn't just leave the poor cat there.

It was wet and scared and should have been an easy grab. Our crew was on the way back to base. Everyone from the island was out safely, but we thought we should give the abandoned warehouse in the valley a pass since it was a known area for the few homeless people and often some transients on their way across the provincial border.

And the odd time it held teenagers making poor decisions.

The area was clear, thank god, and we were making our way back towards town. We travelled using zodiac boats as the water was now too deep, and the strength of the current was building.

But I heard the meow for help and saw a young cat perched at the edge of a broken window.

"Eddie, hold up. There's a cat."

Our crew leader surveyed the area and pointed to the powerful current pulling a nearby tree.

"Perry, the currents are strong. That tree is leaning and I'm worried it might fall into this house any minute. It's too risky."

But I shook him off. "Three minutes. I'll swim over, drop it in the basket and get right back."

"I don't feel good about it, Perry."

"I can't leave it!"

The moment Eddie reconsiders, I'm in the water before he can change his mind. The rescue tube with a mesh bottom trails behind me as I swim up to the building and find a safe place to grab onto.

"Hey, fella. I'll get you."

The cat makes a pitiful cry that tugs my heart and leaps into my arms.

"Good boy. Now you just need to sit in this biscuit thing and I'll get you back safe, okay?"

Reeling in the tow rope, I place the cat in the basket and swim back to the boat.

I'm only fifty feet from the zodiac when the guys on board shout and a loud boom sounds behind me. The tree has fallen and caught a part of the abandoned warehouse, but now the tree is heading right for me.

With no scuba gear on, I hold my breath and duck under the surface in a move to evade the tree faster underwater. When I surface, I think I'm in the clear until I'm yanked backward and away from the zodiac coming toward me.

A branch of the tree latched onto the tow rope and my rescue cat howls as we float down the river a little too quickly for my liking.

Eddie's boat is gaining on me, and I pull the knife from my belt to cut us free.

"Just hang in there, little dude. I'll get us out of here."

The thunder of blood rushing in my ears makes my hands shake, but I'm not fucking leaving this world today. Not now. Not after finally finding what makes me happy.

The knife cuts the rope, and after jamming it back in my belt, I swim with one hand over to the waiting lifesaver tube. My team reels me in and Eddie orders the boats back to the marina ASAP. After taking the cat, I haul myself in the boat. The team is quiet, concern etched across their brows.

"You said I could go, Eddie."

My team leader nods, his jaw set as he tips his chin towards the water.

"Look behind you, Perry."

Rolling over to survey the area I was in only moments ago, the bottom of my stomach sinks. The building is folding in and the damage the tree did was enough to send it crashing. The wall where the cat was sitting is bowed out and ready to float down the river, creating a chilling sight.

If I'd been there even thirty seconds later, this might have ended differently.

The boats take a wide berth around the tree and building and head towards the marina.

"I'm sorry, Eddie. I should've listened."

"Don't apologize. I'm the one who didn't stand firm. I'm the one who put you in danger."

"It won't happen again, Eddie."

He claps a hand on my shoulder with a curt nod. The silent understanding that we both dodged a bullet and he won't let it happen again.

The rest of the journey is in silence, except for the howls of a wet and scared cat who I tuck against me to shield from the wind as best as I can. When we arrive at the marina, the water completely submerges the docks. Some have dislodged and are now hazards, floating freely anywhere the water takes them. It's dicey to land safely. But we manage because we're professionals and that's what we do.

"What the hell? Why is someone here past the scene tape?"

Looking across the lot, an unmistakable lemon yellow coat and giant green boots call like my own personal lighthouse. With a touch of frustration that he came looking for me when I told him to stay put, I turn to the man beside me.

"Mitch, take the cat for a minute. I got this." Shoving the cat into the man's arms, I jog over through the calf deep water over towards Roman.

He remains still as I lumber towards him. His blue eyes are wide under his yellow hood and his lower lip trembles.

"What are you doing down here, baby? It's not safe to pass the yellow tape. I told you to wait for me."

His hands clench at his sides before he shoves them in his pockets.

"I did! I was! And...and... there was talk about a building collapsing and...and..."

Roman gulps in air before swiping at the wetness on his face. I'm positive those are tears and not raindrops. But we can talk about that later.

"You should've stayed put! Don't you ever come out and put yourself in danger. The water is rising all over and it's not safe. Don't ever risk your life for me like this."

His blue eyes flash, and he stomps closer, sending water flying. One small fist thumps on my chest.

"If I can't risk my life for you, what's the purpose of loving you? Isn't that the point? To search for the people we care about when they're in trouble? To make sure they come home safe even when they spent the day saving others?" He sobs and collapses against me. "I didn't tell you I loved you before you left and I thought I might have missed my chance. I'm sorry."

I'm too stunned to process all that, and this is definitely not the hallmark moment I pictured. There're no hearts and flowers and the glow of candles. No tender kisses and caresses.

But it's gut wrenching just the same as I hold him tight and take a moment to let the words sink in. Leave it to Roman to make a declaration of love confrontational.

"I love you too, Roman."

"I know!" He sobs and I can't help but laugh.

"Okay, Han Solo. Let's get everyone out of here safely and talk about this at home, okay?"

My team member, Mitch, hovers nearby. He hands me the cat when I motion it over and I push the wet and scared animal into Roman's arms.

"Hold this while I help with the boats. And keep standing right here, understand?"

He nods and hugs the cat close.

"I'll wait for you. I promise."

And the conviction in his voice almost breaks me.

After checking in at the shelter and updating everyone that nobody was trapped or injured, I brought Roman and our new furry friend home.

Leo was relieved by someone else to run the shelter overnight and when he hugged me goodbye, he whispered something that made me rethink a lot of things.

Once we got home, our power was back on. Roman silently went to work drying off the cat and finding a can of tuna it could eat. After filling its belly, the cat curled up on the end of the sofa to sleep like it's always lived here.

Roman's face is still pale and without the cat to distract him, he finally gives me his attention. But I know that's how he is. When big things, emotional things especially, need to be dealt with, Roman needs time and space to process. He may randomly blurt out thoughts and feelings sometimes, but he's anything but random.

He plans and overthinks. But I love him like that and I understand why.

"Where do we start with all this, Perry? I don't know what to do here."

He pulls his knees to his chest and leans into me on the couch.

"Well, can we start with you telling me you love me again? I'd really like to hear it without being calf deep in sludgy river water."

A small smile appears, and he laughs softly.

"You know, my sisters always tell me I'm dramatic. There was never anything boring or plain about me. I guess that's really true now, huh?"

"I wouldn't want you any other way."

He nods his head before uncurling his legs and turning to face me.

"I think I've had feelings for a while, but I wasn't sure until...." He bites his lip before huffing a breath. "Until last night. Before we even had sex. When you weren't at the party on time and I saw Leaf with Sasha, it just sort of slammed into me. That I wanted you there so badly my chest ached. And I missed you."

"Aww, you missed me?"

I bump his shoulder with a playful grin, and he shakes his head.

"Yes I did, asshole. I'm baring my heart to you like you asked. Don't make it worse."

"Sorry. Go on."

He winks at me, gaining his confidence to speak about his feelings, and my stomach swoops. How does he always do that to me?

"Against my better judgment, yes, I missed you. And even when we came home, and you took care of me, I...I don't know how to explain it except there was a voice inside me screaming that you were special and I need to look past your obsession with plaid—"

"You'll wear it one day. You'll love it."

"Do you want me to tell you I love you or not?"

"You just did."

He huffs a laugh while his hands twist themselves in his lap.

"Will you promise to always be a bit of an asshole sometimes? I think that's what I love most about you."

"Only sometimes?"

I can't keep my hands to myself any longer and reach over to calm his fidgeting. He stares at my hand on his, giant and rough to his, smooth and small, before raising one to his lips.

"Yes, only sometimes. Because sometimes I need you to put me in my place." He focuses on me, still clutching my hand. "And sometimes I need you to leave me peeled grapefruit in the kitchen and hold me while I sleep."

My eyelids fall closed as I puff a breath. This was not what I expected today, but I can't say I'm not happy about it.

"So when I'm not asshole I'm to be what?"

Roman swallows before kissing the palm of my hand. God. The strength he needs to say all this knocks the breath from me.

"Be the amazing man you are." He leans forward and places a kiss on my cheek. "Because you are and I'm sorry it took me so long to tell you."

"It's not easy to always say the way we feel." My palm slides along his cheek, still pale, but still so beautiful. Always beautiful. "If we're agreeing to do this...this thing, to be something for each other, I need to tell you something."

"If you tell me you're about to move and take a job in Alaska, I'll fucking scream. But I'd pack my bags to follow you after."

"Really?"

"Yeah. I mean, I wouldn't like all the snow and darkness, but they have cool animals there. Wait, no, some are dangerous. Okay, I'd not like that part after all. But you're there and I'd be happy."

Roman just says all that with a certainty that wraps around my heart and catches me off guard.

"Wow. That's...you're serious about this, aren't you?"

"Yeah, Perry. I mean, Sasha is different. He's my best friend. I followed him because I can't live without him in my life. But it's a different love. With you...I can't breathe without knowing you'll still be there. I've never felt that before." He leans in to kiss my lips. "I'm either in love with you or I need to see a doctor."

"Fuck...Ro..."

My voice cracks as I stare at him. He's thrown me so many crumbs over the past few months, and I've waited for this conversation. It almost feels surreal.

"My previous serious relationships couldn't handle the nature of my job. You know, sometimes I was away for three weeks at a time, only to come home for two days and be gone another week." Those were days I don't miss. Losing people I loved while I tried to make a living at a job I loved was a hard pill to swallow. "The last one was especially hard because she cheated on me with another cop. One who didn't travel all the time and was home most nights."

That was my lowest point. I felt like such a failure.

"That's their loss, Perry. My gain, I suppose. But you're retired now, right?"

"I am. Sort of. It's not like I draw a pension yet. I'm only forty-one, but I saved well and made some good investment choices. Mom and Dad left us their estate, too. I work for Leaf when needed, mostly to keep busy. Sometimes I help my friend with his construction business if I need to do something else. But..."

Searching his face, he's just listening to me and taking it all in. There's no dramatics right now, but what about the next time I need to join a rescue effort?

"I still do things you need to be okay with. Like today. I'm a volunteer firefighter and I *will* be called to a scene. I offer to help in any crisis and that might sometimes mean putting myself in danger. It's who I am, Roman. I can't just turn it off."

He nods but stays silent, and I tilt his chin back up.

"I need to know you're not gonna run on me if something comes up again. If I'm away for an extended time, or—"

"No. I won't and I'll tell you why." He climbs onto my lap and places his hands on my shoulders before sliding them up to hold my cheeks. "I may be skittish of relationships because of how I lost my parents, but one thing I never acknowledge is how grateful I am that someone like you gave our family closure." He swallows and brings his forehead to mine. "I...fuck, Perry...if something happened to you, I'd be a wreck. But if you provided that same thing for a family? I'd be so proud that I once called you mine and knew you in a way nobody else does."

His voice cracks, and he sniffles.

"Look what you've done to me already. And it's only the beginning. I don't cry and do all this...this...kind of shit."

This is as romantic as Roman is likely ever going to get. And I love it because I know even this *kind of shit* is from the heart.

"That's right, gorgeous. It is the beginning. Buckle up."

"Buckle u—"

I stand with my hands firmly on his ass as he laughs in surprise.

"Buckle up because the ride is about to start."

"I hope you mean your dick is the ride. I like that kind of ride." He nibbles my ear and I almost drop him as I stride to the bedroom. "I didn't know sex could be so good when I let someone else take over."

"Sex with me will always be good." I drop him on the bed with a smirk. "No matter who is in charge."

"You're such an arrogant ass." He laughs as he rips off his shirt and reaches for me.

"And you're a judgemental prick."

He barks another laugh, and his lips smile against mine as I crash my lips to his.

It's not much different from any other time we've made out and pawed at each other like needy animals, but there's this simmering layer of something else now. Like the last barrier he had up has toppled, and he's giving me all of him.

His fears, his snark, his body... his heart. The one thing I've been wishing for is finally mine.

And to have it all unlocks this fucking feral animal in me.

"Come into the shower with me." I pull away and he whines, honest to god whines, and I can't fight the smile.

"Babe...I want you to fuck me." He rubs his bulge through his pants, and I pull him by the ankles down the bed. He squeaks and glares at me.

"I will and you're coming in the shower with me."

I shuck the rest of my clothes and make sure he has a good view of my cock before turning into the bathroom. He'll follow me. I know he will. After I turn the shower on, I rummage in a vanity drawer for what I want. As my hands close on the waterproof lube and plug I hoped I still had his arms wrap around me from behind.

"I hate that I'm so fucking into you I listen so easily."

Turning in his arms, I plant a kiss on his lips and he squeezes me tighter, not letting me pull away.

"I love it when you listen. When you argue." I kiss him slow, deep and he sighs against me. "Right now, I hope you'll listen." I tap the plug against his ass cheek.

"Mr. Attwater, have you been hiding things from me?"

He grabs my hand to see what it is and raises an eyebrow.

"Sometimes I liked to play a little. I was never into bottoming like many are, but now and then I liked to—"

"Stuff yourself up?"

"Yeah. I guess."

"That's so hot. I want to see that."

"Another time, if you ask nicely. Tonight it's you. If that's okay?"

Again he stares at me with those fucking blue eyes of heaven and I'm truly and utterly shocked this man is so different from the one I first met.

"It's more than okay."

Leading him into the shower, I crowd him against the wall and kiss him until I need to stop and gulp in air. "I was going to take this all slow and sensual, but I can't. Turn around."

Roman does immediately, and I coat the plug and my fingers with lube. I press one into him and he arches his back, pressing his ass back into my hand. It's not a huge plug, maybe a medium size, and it's been so long since I felt the desire to use it. It's black with a giant flat crystal on the end and I know it will look so hot against his creamy skin.

He rocks back and moans for more, and I drizzle more lube into his crack. Blocking the shower spray so it doesn't wash it off, I drag the plug through it and press it to his pretty pucker.

"My dick is bigger than this, gorgeous. Breathe. I want to see you take it."

Roman hangs his head and the moment he relaxes, the plug pushes past his rim and he gasps while reaching for his cock. I press it all the way in and he exhales raggedly as he adjusts to it.

I was right. It looks incredible nestled in his cheeks and I wonder if he'd think the same for me?

Stepping to the side, the water now hits his back, and he turns to me, cheeks flushed and eyes glazed, his damp blonde hair sticking to his forehead. Pulling him forward, I make him stand under the water as I hurriedly wash him. I had grand plans of edging him in here, worshipping him and driving him out of his mind before taking him to my bed.

But all those plans are out the window because I'm too fucking horny to care about anything sweet and sentimental. I want to fuck him. Hard and against the damn shower wall.

Tapping at the plug, I whisper those thoughts in his ear.

"I can't wait." I pull it and twist it a little and he moans. It's low, but so damn loud within the confines of the shower.

"Me neither."

Growling, I fucking spin him and press him into the glass before playing with the toy a few more times to make him squirm.

"Perry…" His breathless plea sets me off and I remove the plug, barely giving him time to adjust to it missing before pushing my cock into him.

"That's it, baby. Relax and breathe. You've done it before. Take my cock, Roman."

His breathing picks up as he struggles to focus and I push more, unwilling to wait. My arm snakes around his waist to stroke his dick. He wiggles and squirms, and bucks his ass back on me, burying me inside of him. We both gasp and his hands slap against the shower glass. He looks over his shoulder at me.

"Jesus, Perry. Don't just stand there. Fuck m—"

I snap my hips, and the words die on his tongue as bliss washes over his face.

"Oh, fuck...you're gonna come inside me, right? I fucking want that. Please, please."

He's begging me now? Dear god, I'm glad we're in the shower because that's a direct line to my balls and I'm going to erupt.

"Yes." I bite his earlobe and he moans. "I'm gonna fill you. You want me to plug it back up, gorgeous? Do you want to keep that cum in there longer?"

"*Fuck*!"

Roman drops his head against the shower doors with a thud. He groans again and shoots his load, coating my hand and the shower glass as he impales himself on my dick. If I thought I was in control here, I got it all wrong. He's braced himself and rides me like he didn't just come all over the shower wall. Like he's still chasing an orgasm and I'm honestly not sure if he's chasing mine or trying to come again himself.

And it just hits me. My balls don't even let me think about it. Just *kaboom*! It's the orgasm to end all orgasms and I'm emptying into Roman, gripping his hips so hard it's likely to leave bruises.

"Yes, yes...Perry...shit."

Finally, both of us stop moving and I ease out of him. Pulling his back to my front, he leans back for a kiss, resting his head on my shoulder.

"You okay?" I reach for the soap to clean us both up before the hot water runs out.

He nods as I soap his body, and take care when washing his ass. Even this soon after a rough and dirty fuck, he's pushing back for me like he's needy for more. I gently dip a finger inside and he releases a low hum.

"Perry?"

"Yeah."

"I need some rest and you can keep doing that later."

Laughing softly against his neck, I let him rinse his body while I hurry to do the same.

After drying each other and exchanging lazy kisses, we finally agree to crawl into bed.

"You've got to be kidding."

He doesn't sound impressed and when I look to see what has him in such a snit, I laugh out loud.

The kitten has curled up on his pillow.

Chapter 23
Roman

My classical music plays softly, the perfect accompaniment to the constant whirring of my sewing machine. My lingerie is a hit, and for the last two months, all I've been doing is sewing. And cutting. And more sewing.

Sasha kept up on the email enquiries and organizing the orders so I could do what I needed and Perry, well... he's just about the most helpful boyfriend on the planet. I knew the way I wanted to run this business would be an immense strain on my time, and he understood.

He asked how he could help and ran packages to the courier for me. I even showed him how to press the fine laces and silks. Thankfully, he's an excellent student, and he became invaluable to me more than he already was.

And he reminded me when I needed to eat and sleep. Which I sort of forgot about the first week and when I almost blacked out in the kitchen one day, he went all stern daddy on me. While I hated him scolding me like a child and yelled back at him like one, he just stepped up. And again, I hated it, but it also made my heart so full for him to just do this for me. He took care of me whether or not I wanted him to. I hate asking for help. Perry doesn't wait for me to ask. He just does it and I couldn't be more grateful.

"Ouch! What the fuck!"

Abandoning the sewing, I push back to stare at the offending source of pain.

Duke, the kitten Perry saved during the flood, sits under my sewing machine, proud as hell that he attacked my toes. Honestly, the cat wasn't even supposed to be here still. After he slept on my pillow and my side of the bed that night, I knew Perry wouldn't go through with it and adopt him out. He's too much of a softie.

But right now Duke is a pain in the... well, in the foot, and he should be upstairs.

"Come here, mister. I have deadlines and you're not helping."

He tries to bat at my hand and run away, but I'm too fast for him and scoop him into my arms. Marching up the stairs, I find Perry in the kitchen and pause for a moment to stare at this man who holds my heart.

In a pair of plaid lounge pants and those hideous Crocs he wears inside, he sings along to the music playing on his phone. About beautiful things and never letting them go. And my heart lodges in my throat.

He grabs a wooden spoon from the holder on the counter and uses it as a microphone, no longer singing, but lip-synching and god... I love him. Outrageous fashion choices and all. When he finally notices me standing there, he blushes and drops the spoon to the counter.

"Hey, how long have you been watching?"

"Right before the spoon microphone kitchen rockstar bit." I thrust Duke into his arms and the cat snuggles into him. I can't blame him. "You need to keep him up here today. He bit my foot while I was sewing."

He frowns at Duke, who does his best innocent kitten face.

"I can't believe something this cute would be a pain in the ass, Roman. Look at him!"

He scratches Duke's chin with a huge dopey grin on his face and I swear if I had ovaries, they'd be bursting right now.

"I *am* looking and he's a devil with me. Just keep him here or I'm shutting him in the spare room."

He gasps at the cat before snuggling him closer. "Don't listen to your other daddy. You don't have to go into the room. Just hang out with me and be good."

Other daddy.

Jesus. My heart can't take this man.

He smiles at me and I kiss him softly. Why do I have so much work when this man is on the floor above me, acting like a domestic god?

"There's a snack for you in the fridge. I was just about to bring it down."

"Oh?" Opening the fridge, I can't miss it. Slices of grapefruit, pretzel crackers, and a tiny bit of goat cheese. He arranged the grapefruit slices in a smiley face, and while the pretzels are the hair, I'm not sure what the cheese is supposed to be.

"I like your artistic presentation. What's the cheese supposed to be?"

He pours a mountain of cat treats on the floor and Duke immediately chows down.

"Jizz."

I cough. "Um...what?"

"I don't have white crackers for hair and pretzels are your favourite, so it doesn't even look like you."

"I doubt white crackers would have helped with that." I deadpan and his eyes drop to my lips.

"But the little pieces of goat cheese I imagined painting your face with my cum while you smile."

Honestly. Goat cheese and cum shouldn't be in the same sentence together, but Perry makes it work.

"Jesus, Perry. You can't...fuck...how am I supposed to work when you say shit like that?" He presses me into the fridge and rocks his hips into mine.

"You're a professional. You can do it. And now you have something to look forward to when you're done." His fingers flex at my hip and I bare my throat to him. He dips lower, knowing I love his marks, but not always visible, and he sucks a red spot above my right nipple.

"You should work naked, not just shirtless."

Laughing, I gently extract myself from his hold, and he adjusts himself.

"A dick out where there are tonnes of pins and needles is not a smart idea, babe."

"Oh! That reminds me. Neither are bare feet." He raises a serious eyebrow. "I worry about you stepping on them. I got you something."

He rushes to the hall closet and pulls out a brown paper shopping bag. There's a glint in his eye as he hands it to me. I look inside and immediately shake my head.

"No, fucking way am I wearing those."

"Roman, don't be so snotty. You shouldn't be barefoot with all that stuff."

"Then I'll wear a pair of stilettos!"

Perry pauses. "Do you have those? Cuz that would be hot: heels and your corset with the roses." He bites his lip and his gaze is like a brand on my skin, drawing a flush without trying.

"I do, and that's not the point. I'm not wearing—" I pull out one of the black Crocs. The hideous footwear I despise and I'm about to launch into a million reasons why I won't wear them when I look closer. There are those stupid Croc charm things on the front, and the one I focus on has me clamping my teeth together.

It's a sparkling charm. Likely those rhinestone abominations, but a sparkle dots the eye in the word boyfriend. I fish out the other Croc and it reads 'I love'. So if I wear them, it says 'I love my boyfriend' with a tiny pink rhinestone and I'd be the biggest dick in the world if I didn't wear them.

"You need to stop doing these sweet things for me." I sniff and drop the shoes on the floor. Sliding my feet in them, I find him watching with a crooked smile and I wag a finger at him. "No pictures."

"Too late." He snaps his phone off the counter and clicks. "I'm only sending it to Sasha."

Grumbling, I take my snacks and give him the finger as I head backstairs. And once I'm out of sight, I set the plate down and test the Crocs. And they're actually pretty comfortable, but it's the charms that make me smile.

With Duke out of the way and a snack in my belly, I power through two more orders before my phone lights up with a call from my sister.

"Hey, Josie! How's the—"

"It's me, Ro. She's in labour."

My sister-in-law Violet's voice quivers and I'm in immediate panic mode.

"Is everything okay? It's only two weeks early, and that's okay, right?"

"Yeah, that's okay, but the baby was breech at her last ultrasound and that was only a few days ago and…It'll still be fine, but it might not be, you know?"

"I'm coming home."

"Roman you don't need—"

"I do *need*, Vi. She's like my mother most days, but if there's…I'm gonna be an uncle and I want to be there. Keep me posted, please, and I'll let you know when I'll be there."

We had planned to drive up in two more weeks. The busy time at the lodge would be over and Sasha was going to come along, too. I wanted my sisters to meet Perry and him to meet the new baby. But now the baby is premature and possibly in danger.

I make a note of the order I'm working on and leave it on the machine. After shutting everything down and double-checking there's nothing for Duke to destroy, I race up the stairs.

Duke is asleep on his cat tree and Perry flips through the channels while reclining on the sofa. When he sees me, the smile drops and he's at my side.

"What happened?"

"The baby is coming. My sister. It might be breech, and I really need to get there."

Perry nods, calm and oblivious to me spiralling.

"I'll arrange a cat sitter and let Leaf know. You call Sasha so he can do whatever you need for the business." He kisses me on the forehead. "Then we'll pack and I'll drive you there."

"It's...I can't ask you to do that. I can get a flight."

"You're not asking me, love. I'm telling you. Go make your call and we'll get this done."

He picks up his phone from the coffee table and, after he puts it to his ear, he cocks his head while I still stand there.

"Roman. Call Sasha."

"Right."

Putting my phone on speaker, I head back to the spare room. Which is technically still my room. I sleep with Perry every night, but all my clothes are still here. It's a little odd, but there's still one part of me keeping a separate space as a 'just in case.' Of what, I'm not entirely sure. Thankfully, Perry doesn't question it and calls it my dressing room.

"Hey, Ro!"

"Sasha, Josie is in labour and I have to go."

"Shit. That's early. Is it okay that she's early?"

"Vi says it is, but they're worried the baby is breech and I'm...mildly freaking out."

"What do you need me to do?"

"I don't know how long I'll be gone. I finished a few orders today, and they need to be packaged and shipped. Could you drop by and do that? Oh, and could you pause orders online so I don't get swamped?"

"Of course I can. Perry is going with you, right?"

"I told him I could fly, but he said no."

"Roman. That man would do anything for you. Don't you dare be an asshole right now."

"I'm not! I wore the damn Crocs he bought me."

"He gave them to you already? Awww, he was supposed to wait for me."

Rolling my eyes, I pull out a small suitcase and toss it on the bed.

"Was it your idea too?"

"Not even a little. So when are you leaving?"

"He's getting someone to watch Duke and we're packing and heading out. I hope this doesn't cause too much trouble with the lodge. I know you're about to have a busy few weeks and we weren't supposed to leave until after. And now you'll have to visit another time."

"We'll take care of it, Ro. I'm sad I'll miss out. Don't forget to take the gift with you and let me know when you're there."

"She would've loved to see you. Next time then."

After a bit more chatter with Sasha over business plans and the baby, I end the call with a promise to keep him in the loop.

I'm not that good at packing on short notice. My brain keeps going to scary thoughts and when Perry comes to check on me, all I've accomplished is a pile of clothing on the bed.

"Hey, do you...Roman? What's wrong?"

My chest feels tight and maybe I might want to throw up and I can't breathe.

Sinking to the floor, I struggle to draw in breaths and fight the urge to scream.

Perry drops beside me, his large hand on my back.

"In through your nose, babe. Great job, and out through your mouth. Let's do that some more."

His gentle murmurs near my ear are more help than the breathing I think.

"I haven't had a panic attack for years. Years. Like…I think I was still in high school the last time."

"They can sneak up on you. But you recognized it and you dealt with it." His hand still smooths circles on my back and I inhale more deep breaths, feeling the grip of the anxiety seep away. "Be proud of yourself for recognizing it."

I smile. "Leave it to you to find something positive about me having a meltdown."

"Roman," He chastises, but his voice is like a hug and I turn to let him give me a real one. "You work so hard and so much. Don't be like that. You're human, and we all have tipping points." He kisses the top of my head and holds me closer. "You never let people help, I noticed. Maybe it's time to allow people to help you more."

"I let you help."

"You do, and I always will. But…"

Pulling away, I look up into his concerned face. "But?"

"It's nothing bad, but once we get back, I'd like for us to talk about how we can make your life easier."

I place a soft kiss on his lips.

"You're amazing, you know that? And sometimes I think you're far too good for me."

"I could say the same about you." He taps me to stand and after I'm up, he follows me.

"Let's get packed and on the road." He surveys the mess on the bed and tries not to smile. "If you need help with choosing, I can pick your outfits."

He plucks a pair of silk lounge pants off the pile. "These are my favourite when you wear one of my T-shirts with it." He holds up a pair of black dress pants. "These make your ass look so good and when you roll up your sleeves?" He bites his lip. "Damn."

"That's, uh, helpful. Thank you."

"You're welcome. Now finish up so we can get on the road and stop at that burger joint I love on the highway before they close."

Perry smacks me on the ass with a grin and leaves me to the task. But I take several minutes to compose myself.

But he's right. Maybe I should make my life easier.

Chapter 24
Perry

You'd think they'd make a more comfortable hospital chair after all these years. But nope. Still those shitty cracked pleather ones.

Roman paces and more than once expresses his displeasure at not being allowed to go into the room when his sister specifically asked if he could. But I understand his frustration. It's his family. They're extremely close.

The prickly man I met six months ago has almost faded away. Almost.

He still likes to argue and pick fights when he can, but mostly he's not like that. He's warm and funny and so fucking talented with his artistic visions. And he's so kind. Behind that icy stare and cut cheekbones is the biggest of hearts—one he lets no one but his closest circle see.

"Babe, come here."

He huffs and glares at me, but I chuckle. "Please?"

Once he's in reach, I fold him into my arms. Inhaling the vanilla-scented shampoo he likes. I hold him until his shoulders droop, and then I hold him some more.

"If anything was wrong, they'd have let us know by now."

"I know. I just…I want to fucking see my sister." He buries his head into my shoulder and I squeeze him closer.

"I know you do and—"

"Roman Auclair?"

He bolts at his name and runs to the nurse. "That's him. I mean I'm me. I'm Roman."

"Follow me."

He casts a glance over his shoulder at me, and I give him a thumbs-up to go. He mouths an 'I love you' and I feel my heart leap out of my chest to follow him. Jesus.

I've had several relationships over the years. I was even engaged to a woman for a brief time. None of those relationships compare at all to how I feel for Roman. Now that someone has taken him back to see his sister, I step out into the late August afternoon for some fresh air. And to call my brother.

"Any baby yet?"

"No, but he just got to go back to see her. My gut says she's opting for a c-section and about to tell him that. The last update Vi gave us was that the baby wasn't turned, and with the contractions growing stronger, they'd have to make that choice soon."

"As long as baby and mom come out of it okay. How's he holding up?"

I huff a laugh. "He's a basket case. Pacing the floor like he's a dad from the 50s."

Leaf laughs along with me, but his tone softens. "And you? Are you okay?"

There's a tiny garden at the corner of the hospital and I plop my weary body onto a bench there. Butterflies dance from one flower to the next as I consider my words.

"I'm okay, but I...this...fuck..." I laugh at myself. I've never been at a loss for words before, but Roman seems to have that effect on me.

"Ah, yes. I know the feeling." Leaf chuckles. "It's how I feel about Sasha. I get it."

"I want to ask him to marry me."

Leaf hums and I can picture his sly smile as he does, knowing far sooner than I did that this is where I was heading.

"Do you think he'll say yes?"

"God. I hope so. But I don't want to keep waiting, Leaf. He's not like anyone I've ever been with, and I don't want him to ever leave my life."

"I think you should tell him that, then."

"Yeah. Maybe not while we celebrate the baby. But soon. Is Sasha with you?"

"No, he went to the studio and then he was going by your place for some packages or something. He said he'd check on Duke while he was there."

"Good. I'll give him a shout too. And I think we need to plan a party after the last guests are gone. Anybody booked in near the end of September?"

"I'll check and get back to you."

Before I call Sasha, I wander back into the waiting room in case Roman comes looking for me and my ass barely hits the chair before a nurse calls my name.

"Yeah, that's me."

She smiles at me and I can't help but return it.

"I've been asked to bring you back. It's quite the party this baby is having."

"Is the baby here!? Oh my god."

I can't help the goofy grin I know must be on my face. It's like bubbles cover my skin and I'm just plain giddy.

The nurse stops at a room and waves me inside and I'm only two steps in before my breath catches and I freeze.

Roman is standing beside his sister's bed holding a tiny bundle and the pure happiness on his face as he holds the baby is breathtaking.

"You must be Perry." A small woman on the other side of the bed holds out her hand. "I'm Violet, Josie's wife and Roman's sister-in-law." She gestures to her wife, whose gaze is locked on Roman just like mine. "We would've had him come in sooner, but just as we started prepping for the cesarean, the baby's heart rate dropped, so it became an emergency."

"Is Josie okay? And the baby?"

"Right as rain. Other than being scared for a bit, we're all okay."

"I'm sorry. I forgot my manners." Leaning down, I hug her. "Congratulations. Thank you for having me here on such an intimate day."

She cocks her head. "Why wouldn't we? You're Roman's boyfriend and by the way he talks about you, you'd think you've been married for a century."

My gaze finds Roman again, and this time I step closer. His eyes lift for a second to see me before going back to the tiny bundle.

"Babe. Meet my nephew. He's perfect."

Peering over his shoulder, I take in the little pink blob of baby. Chubby baby cheeks and a mass of dark hair with a squished button nose. And the cutest little pursed lips that remind me of Roman's. Now I know how some people get baby fever.

"Oh, Roman. He's gorgeous. Just like his uncle."

His body rocks gently as he stares at the tiny thing and my hand rests on his hip. Roman is in his element and he doesn't even know it.

"I'm Josie." His sister says with a laugh and I feel myself flush.

"I'm so sorry. I should have said hello first."

She raises her arms to invite me for a hug and I do awkwardly around all her monitors and IV lines.

"It's okay. My brother holding a baby is quite the sight. I'll allow you to be smitten with the image."

"Violet filled me in. He was pacing a hole in the floor."

"Probably best he didn't know ahead of time. He would've been a sobbing mess with worry."

"I'm right here, you know. I can hear you."

"Good. Because we didn't tell you his name. You just grabbed him like a baby snatcher."

Roman looks up at me. "Do you want to hold him?"

"Heck ya."

I make grabby hands and he chuckles before passing him off to me. The baby looks so tiny against my giant arm.

"We wanted to name him something with meaning." Josie reaches out her hand and Roman takes it. "His name is Alexander Roman. Two men who will forever mean the world to us. It's a big name to live up to, but you and Dad are two of the best men I've ever known."

Roman's shoulders shake, and I wrap my free arm around him. Instead of hugging his sister, he turns his face into me as he quietly sobs. Violet notices my dilemma and quietly takes baby Alexander from me so I can hold Roman properly.

"What can I do, Ro?"

He shakes his head before wiping at his tears and finally crushing his sister in a hug.

I've heard a lot about this family. First from Sasha, since he's known them for many years as he and Roman modelled and grew up together. Then from Roman, as he opened up more and more. After telling me about his parents' untimely death, he never lacked things to say about his sisters and Violet.

His other sister Camryn was away at a conference in Europe and would get here as soon as she could. Leaf and I had a great family life. Our parents were older when they had us and they died of natural things. They loved us, but there was no significance to our names. I'm pretty sure Mom named Leaf that because she read a book about Vikings before she went into labour. My name, I'm not sure of, but I'd be willing to bet it was a random name from a baby book.

But Roman's family has a rich story. A legacy they want to keep alive not just through genetics but with names. It says a lot about the importance of the family to them. I know how Josie raised Roman and how much he loves both of his sisters. It's a rare bond and I'm privileged to be here and maybe one day, even be a part of it.

Little Alexander fusses and when it's time for the whole breastfeeding thing to happen, I excuse myself and step into the hall. My heart thumps out of whack and I briefly wonder if I drank too much caffeine to make it go this crazy.

Then Roman shows up and I know it's not the caffeine.

His beautiful face glows with happiness, even with the puffy eyes from crying. His shirt has wrinkles, and he's not as fully put together as he usually is. But he's just so... pure. So fucking him and I can't help it when I reach for him and pull him closer.

"I love you." I press my lips to his in a gentle kiss and he stares up at me. "What?"

"Let's go to our hotel and rest up. We can come back tomorrow." He bites at his lip. "Are you...is everything okay?"

"More than okay, babe. Let's say goodbye and get some rest, like you suggested."

"Are you just freaked out with the breastfeeding stuff?"

I huff a laugh. "No. But Violet and Josie would probably like some time alone as parents, too."

"You're right. She's probably exhausted, and we'll be here for a week. We should all rest." He kisses me again, lingering there before pulling away. "I love you, too."

After a prolonged goodbye and a few more tears from Roman and Josie, we exit the hospital to his car.

As we pull out of the lot, Roman reaches over and leaves his hand, palm up, on my thigh.

I slide my fingers through his and squeeze tight.

Chapter 25
Roman

"**A**re you sure you don't want to stay longer? I can fly home and come back for you later."

Turning into Perry's chest, I snuggle into him and slide a leg through his.

"I don't want you to leave without me. That would be too hard. But I'll make plans to come back here soon."

Josie's early labour threw a wrench into my plans, but we'll see her again this morning now that she and baby Alex are being discharged. I'll make sure they're settled at home and then we'll get back to our life. Even Duke. Who I actually kind of miss.

Along with the routine that Perry and I had gotten into. The couple-y, domestic stuff from watching TV on the couch together to cleaning the kitchen up side by side. The things I said I'd never do are now small things I crave. And apparently miss even above spending time with my new nephew, who bears my name.

"Perry." I kiss his neck and watch a bit of this lip curl into a sleepy smile. "I miss you."

"What do you mean? I'm right here."

"I miss us. Home. I miss the damn cat."

His body shakes with laughter, and he rolls over, pinning me to the bed. No longer a sleepy smile, but one that's just for me all the same.

"You hate the cat."

"I don't hate him! He's okay when he's not stealing my spot next to you or biting my feet. I miss home. *Our* home."

He leans in and kisses me. Slow and deep, our tongues sliding next to each other's, and it's overwhelming in the best way.

"You referred to my house as your home. You know you never have before."

"I haven't?"

"No. You always call it Perry's place or my place. You've never called it home."

I brush my palm over his cheek and run my fingers through his short beard.

"That means a lot to you?"

"Yes. I want it to be yours. I want you to...to always come back to it."

His blue eyes swim with so much emotion, I pull him back to me and press my mouth to his. "I'll always come back to you," I whisper across his lips.

We get lost in one of my favourite morning activities: slow sex. Perry is the most sensual in the morning and I love that about him. Not that I don't love it when he gets all bossy on me and our sex is a battle of wills.

But him like this, all tender with both of us just letting hands and lips wander to make each other feel good, is fucking amazing. Perry is the most thoughtful lover I've been with. So much so that

I trust him with anything. I give up control for him and I don't even mind.

Perry's rough palm grips my morning wood with a squeeze before he slides down my body. His beard scratches my skin as his lips nip and caress down my body and I lose myself to his hands on me. His mouth. His fucking everything. Every inch of him brings me pleasure, and when his tongue laps at my hole, the garbled sounds from my mouth don't even sound human.

"Perry...come...come back here. I want to kiss you."

He doesn't even hesitate. He just slides back up my body with no complaints and kisses me.

"What else do you want, gorgeous?" He trails his lips back to my neck. "How do you want it?"

His breath, warm and silky, makes me shiver.

"I want...I want to kiss you. I want to feel your cum on me."

Perry rolls us on our sides to face each other and presses close so our cocks touch. He rolls his thumb across the head of mine, gathering the leakage and drawing a sigh from me.

"Want lube?"

"No." My voice is already raspy as I stare into his eyes and kiss him again. "Just like this."

I don't know how we seem to work so well together, but we do. Our hips move and our hands stroke. Our mouths never leave each other. I could drown in his kisses; they've become one of my favourite things. Perry kisses me with so much passion it makes my head spin.

"I'm close, baby."

"Yeah?" I speed up my hand and bite his lip. "Make sure you do that sexy groan when you come. I love that."

"I didn't know I had one."

His hand on my cock slows and he tenses. The low groan as he comes has me chasing his lips again. "That's the one." The splash on my abs as his orgasm runs through him is heady. Again, something I never knew I liked. Until Perry did it. It's like he brands me as his every time he comes on my skin or leaves a bite mark. And I love it.

Perry knows this, and he runs his hand through the mess, smearing it across my belly and onto my swollen dick.

"I like you all painted like this. You do too." He dips his head to suck an area of skin on my chest. "I love making you mine over and over."

"Fuck. Yes...Perry..."

That sweet feeling of bliss floods over me as I come over his hand. I'm spent. More from the enormity of feelings swelling in me than from the physical exertion. There's been so many ups and downs since we got here, it feels like it's finally catching up to me.

"Shower with me. I'll run to the corner for coffee and that muffin you like while you do the packing."

"Yeah. Okay."

He tips my chin with his spunk-covered fingers, and I don't even mind.

"Are you okay?"

"Very okay. Just a little twisted up, but I'm okay."

"I trust you to tell me if you're not."

"I will. Now get off me so we can get the day started."

He pushes off, laughing, and I lie there for a moment longer to calm my emotions.

And think about home.

My old childhood home, now Josie and Violet's, along with my new nephew Alexander, explodes with baby stuff. So much so that it's hard to recognize what was supposed to be the living room.

"This outfit you made Alexander is perfect, Roman. We love it. You're so talented."

"Isn't he?" Perry chimes in as he carries grocery bags into the kitchen for Violet. My cheeks heat as my sister smirks.

"What's that look for?"

"Love looks good on you, little brother. He's wonderful."

Perry smiles into the living room again as he goes outside to reload. After arriving at the hospital with the baby outfit and filling my phone with a jabillion pics of the little dude in it, Perry offered to do a grocery run when Violet tried to offer us a drink and found the fridge incredibly bare.

This is the first real alone time I've had with Josie all week. Not that I'm complaining. The baby comes first. And Violet. But I miss her and our talks fiercely. The last month was so busy with my sewing and her nesting, we haven't talked as much.

"He's amazing, Jos. So fucking amazing." Alex snuffles and squirms in her arms and I smile. "He might want to take this little guy fishing or hiking or any number of outdoor things I'm not keen on. Just to be prepared for that, I couldn't help myself and I bought something at the mall yesterday."

Handing her a tiny shoe box, she shakes her head.

"Accessorizing him already?"

"Damn right. He doesn't need the hideous boots I wear."

"Hey!" Perry calls from the doorway. "I heard that, and they aren't hideous. They are functional and exactly what you need in the springtime."

Laughing, I shoo him off and he heads to the kitchen to help Violet put groceries away.

Josie opens the box to find a tiny pair of red *Hunter*-brand rubber boots. He'll likely never wear them, but I couldn't resist the cuteness.

"These are too cute, Ro. Thank you. I never thought you'd dress my kid in plaid and rubber boots. You've changed."

I huff a small laugh. "I have. But not every part. I'm still an obnoxious asshole. Perry will confirm that if you need it. But I saw this kid at the lodge and as much as I hate how much they wear plaid like a religion in that town, the kid looked so cute in this tiny little plaid coat. And Perry always wears these plaid lounge pants I love and…"

My sister listens with a soft smile, and I give her the finger.

"Shut your mouth, Jos."

"I didn't say anything!" she chortles, and I'm self-conscious for the first time in forever.

"You're about to. I was preemptively telling you to shut up."

"I love that you're happy, Roman. It's all I ever wished for you. You've spent too long closed off to a real life."

"Just because I never wanted love doesn't mean my life was empty. I have no regrets about it."

"No, it wasn't an empty life. You did well and kept doing well. But there was always something missing with you. You're thriving now. He pushes you out of all your preconceived boxes."

"He does. Surprisingly, I don't even hate it. Most days."

We both laugh again and Perry comes in. He sets a glass of water next to Josie and smiles at Alex before passing me a glass. The citrus aroma has me sip to confirm before turning to Perry. "You got me the lime tonic?"

He nods and I press a kiss to his cheek. "Thank you."

"I had an ulterior motive."

"And what might that be? There's not much I don't give you without plying me with my favourite drink first."

He grins. "That's true. But I wasn't sure about this one."

Perry watches Alex sleeping with a fond smile.

"Where did you get the plaid from to make his outfit?"

Damn. I was hoping he wouldn't notice.

"If you're asking me, you already know the answer."

"Well, I don't," Josie adds. "I'd like to know what this is about."

I was honestly hoping Perry wouldn't notice. Stupid me for thinking he'd ever forget one article of plaid clothing in his wardrobe big enough for a small army.

"I wanted a unisex outfit since we didn't know if it was a boy or girl. And it's for a baby, so I wouldn't use the most expensive lace I had either. Plus, that stuff is hard to work with sometimes, because...uh..."

Perry has the grace to laugh and blush a little. "Yeah, I get it."

"So I raided your closet and picked a shirt that looked like you hadn't worn it in a long time. It's a flannel and babies like soft stuff. It's like a hug, really. And you give good hugs. And it's the plaid I hate the least since it's kind of Christmas-like? So, I guess the answer is I stole it from your closet."

"Aw, Roman, that's the sweetest thing ever." Josie mists up as she gazes at Alex in his plaid-trimmed onesie. It's not entirely plaid but the feet are and there are ruffles on the bum along with plaid cuffs and half the body. The other half is plain white cotton.

When I made it, I was only thinking about it being something to keep to remember where I was and what I was doing when I made it. Gifting my first niece or nephew with high-class Italian lace underwear didn't seem like the best choice, so plaid was the winner.

"You could have just bought some, though. Why mine?"

"Because..." Swallowing, I glance at Josie, who will never give us privacy right now. Perry waits, still gazing at Alex and I figure, fuck it. "Because I know this baby will always be a part of my life. Just in case you and I parted ways, or worse, I wanted a piece of you to be with him. Just like a piece of you will always be with me."

"Oh my god, Roman." Josie sobs. "Don't say shit like that in front of the postpartum woman!"

She wipes at her eyes and finally grabs a nearby baby blanket to dab at her face. Perry says nothing. His throat bobs and he runs a hand down his face before finally turning to me. Our gazes lock and he lifts a hand to my cheek.

"Thank you."

I want to say something back, but Alex chooses that moment to cry, and the moment is lost. Violet comes to take him to be changed and Josie excuses herself.

"Sorry I stole your shirt."

"I don't mind one bit. We should probably get going, though."

"Yeah, we should. I want to go home."

His face fills with a giant smile that takes my breath away.

"Me too."

Chapter 26
Perry

Since visiting and meeting most of Roman's family—his other sister didn't get back while we were there—we've been exceptionally close. He's extra touchy and I'm hyperemotional to the point I don't want to leave the house without him.

But I do because our routine is important; which is why I'm currently having lunch with my brother at the Log Jam on a Wednesday afternoon in late September. Our tradition for when he decides the lodge is officially in its downtime.

"So what do you have coming up?" I ask as I remove the tomato from my sandwich.

"Normally nothing." He laughs. "But Sasha had another idea for a fall leaf viewing thing. He's renting a horse and wagon for the sugar shack and, if it doesn't rain, taking people on a tour, along with this camera. To take family portraits or some shit like that." He squirts a giant puddle of ketchup on his plate. "He arranged it all and filled the eight rooms I gave him to use at the lodge. So I guess it's a success."

"That sounds like fun, actually. Great idea."

"What about you? Any side jobs with Ted coming up?"

Ted knows I like to be busy and usually offers me odd projects on his construction sites. It's not for the money, but for me to keep busy. I can only take so much sitting around. But this time I have something else I want to do.

"Nothing with Ted. But I have something I want to talk to you about."

"Okay. Go for it."

He pops a fry in his mouth and waits.

"I went to see my financial planner last week and changed the beneficiary on my life insurance. I put Roman on." I pause for the next bit. "I also updated my will."

"To Roman?"

Clearing my throat, I nod. "Yeah. Because, usually, you have your spouse as a beneficiary."

Leaf coughs and chokes and reaches for his water glass.

"Uh...did I miss something?"

"Not yet. I mean, I think he'll say yes, but I didn't want to wait to get all this stuff in place. With his new nephew and things with his business, I just want to...I want him taken care of."

"I understand. Connor did the same thing when we were together. Before we were even married, he did that. When are you, I mean, do you plan to propose soon?"

"Well, that's why I asked if the lodge was empty this weekend. If it is, I'm gonna need Sasha's help and probably yours, too."

Leaf's smile is easy. "My little brother is gonna get hitched. Should we hug now?"

"Oh, fuck off." I laugh and steal a fry from his plate. "I've never loved anyone like I do him. He's a prickly bear some days, but he's also so warm and kind. He's like nobody I've ever met. And so fucking hot. How do you not like him in a corset? I didn't even know I liked that until he showed up."

Leaf makes a gagging sound and laughs.

"Can you not be all lovey while we're eating?"

"Says the guy who had to show me when he learned what sexting was."

He laughs, unashamed.

"Okay, that's fair. But I *really* wanted to make sure you knew how fun it could be."

"I taught you how to use the phone, genius. I think I'm aware."

Leaf just laughs again. Like he didn't traumatize me when he showed me a picture of his dick. Thank god that's all I saw.

"So why the lodge and is Roman on to you?"

"Because it's where we met. A lot of big things happened for us at the lodge. It seems fitting to clear all the negatives with a positive. And I want my romantic confession of love, dammit."

"I didn't know you were just as into that shit as Sasha. I thought you read those books for the sexy parts only."

"In the beginning I did." Some of that shit was spank material. "But I really like how people fall in love and make all these gestures. I want to tell him I love him with some enormous display, like candles and rose petals."

"Gross. Really?"

"Oh shut up, Mr. I-made-a-batch-of-maple-syrup-and-name-it-*Sasha's-Sweetness*. That's more gross."

Leaf laughs and has the decency to be embarrassed.

"He went bananas over that."

"I know. One of his best friends here, remember? Sometimes I hear things about my brother that I *really* don't want to. So cut me some slack."

Sasha sometimes over shares and forgets I'm Leaf's brother. Which is... disturbing at best.

"So what is it you have to make up for?"

"Well, he told me he loved me first. While standing in calf-deep muddy river water in his raincoat and boats while I was in my wet suit with a scared kitten in my hands. It wasn't exactly romance novel material. I want something more. Something epic."

And by the time I finish laying out my plan to Leaf, he's a little misty-eyed. But he's on board.

Operation Secret Proposal is a go.

Now to get Roman there without figuring it out.

"You swear he'll like this? I don't want to fuck this up."

Sasha may have been Roman's best friend longer than he's been mine, but I trust him to guide me.

"Perry, you chose well. He loves roses. He also loves that gross citrus water you both drink. And there's nothing more romantic than an I love you under the stars." He sighs and stares dreamily outside.

"Is the suit too much? Should I tone it down?"

Sasha shakes his head.

"No. He'll love it. It's hanging upstairs at our place. You can go up and get ready while I finish up the decorations here. You can play the bonfire by ear. Sometimes he gets all pissy about his clothes smelling like campfire."

Sasha rolls his eyes and I grab him for a hug.

"Thank you for your help. I just hope he says yes."

"He's a moron if he doesn't."

I leave Sasha decorating the common area of the lodge. He strings the same twinkle lights around the room that I used for his welcome home party. Two huge floor-standing vases I rented from a local wedding decorator sit under the archway. They're overflowing with a metric tonne of blue and white roses. It cost me a small fortune, but his blue rose corset is my favourite and I hope he wears it tonight.

Millie baked his favourite gingersnaps, and Sasha made a punch with the citrus water we both like. It's by no means an extra elaborate display, but once all the battery-powered candles are in place and the timer goes off, there's no way he won't swoon.

And there's no way he'll say no.

Chapter 27
Roman

Stretching out my back, I walk the final custom order of lace underwear over to my packaging table.

Since the return from my sister's, I've worked non-stop to finish them. Some were for weddings and anniversaries and needed to be there for particular dates. Not wanting to disappoint anyone, I finished the most urgent ones.

Never in my wildest dreams did I think I'd sew four hundred and seventy-three custom-made lace pieces in three months. If I didn't have the help of Sasha and Perry, I would never have been able to do it.

Duke meows at my feet and bites one Croc-covered foot.

"If you bite through that or steal my charms, I'll leave you outside for good." He cocks his head and I nod. "That's right. I mean business, you little shithead."

Scooping up the cat, he purrs while I carry him upstairs. Perry should have been back hours ago, but when I check my phone, there isn't a message from him.

Plopping Duke at his dish, I feed him dinner before heading to our bathroom for a shower. After we came home, I made it official and moved my clothes to his room and all my things to his ensuite.

Now it feels like we do actually live together and it's not just me sleeping in his bed.

It's our bedroom now.

Our shared home.

Peeling off my clothes, I shove them down the laundry chute before stepping into the shower. I know we have plans with Leaf and Sasha tonight, but part of me wants to cancel and just spend the night curled up watching the documentary series about ducks. I'd even let Duke share Perry's lap.

And the more I think about it, the more I want to do it. Except I have to find Perry first.

With a towel around my waist, I choose a pair of jeans and, in a last-second decision, I steal a T-shirt from his drawer and one of his long-sleeve plaid button-up shirts. It's super soft. Inhaling, I close my eyes. It smells like him, too.

It's like he's hugging me and he's not even here.

My phone chimes with his tone, and I trip over my feet, running to it.

Perry: I'm still at the lodge. Would you mind just meeting me here?

Well, so much for me convincing him to stay home if he's already there.

Roman: Of course. But can we leave early? I wanted to stay in tonight. That duck show is on.

Perry: I'm sorry, babe. I totally forgot about the ducks. But yes, we can leave early. Are you on your way?

I send him a kiss emoji and as I walk out of the bedroom, I bump the dresser, sending a stack of paper fluttering to the ground.

"Why can't this man just put shit away instead of piling it all over?"

I grab all the loose papers and, as I set them back to where they were, I pause. I shouldn't look, but that's my name.

The beneficiary of your term life policy has been successfully updated to Roman Auclair. Please keep this paper in a safe place and inform the beneficiary of your change.

He put me on his life insurance policy? Oh god, is he sick? My heart pounds and my skin goes clammy. He sounded fine on the phone.

Not wasting a minute more, I grab my keys and rush out the door.

Perry's truck is parked next to Leaf's on the side of the lodge with Leaf's private entrance. Pulling up behind it, I throw my car in park, and after two steps when I still hear the engine running, I go back to turn it off.

The entire drive here I've been creating all kinds of what-if scenarios and none of them good. Without knocking, I let myself in and run up the flight of stairs.

"Perry? Leaf?"

The apartment is empty and quiet. There's no sign of a dinner on the go like we planned. Maybe dinner is in the lodge kitchen?

Flinging the door down to the lodge open, I fly down the stairwell and burst into... another empty kitchen.

What the fuck? Where is everyone?

When I step into the main lodge, it's dimly lit with twinkle lights. Sasha is staring out a side window, and it's Leaf who notices me.

"Roman! Uh...how come you didn't come in through the main door?"

"Where's Perry? Is he okay?"

"He's fine?"

"Roman." Perry steps out of the office and strides towards me. Dressed in a dark navy fitted suit, I furrow my brows.

"Why are you wearing a suit? I thought we were having dinner here and why didn't you tell me you're sick!?"

My voice quivers, and Perry rushes forward.

"Sick? I'm not sick. What are you talking about?"

Pulling the paper from my pocket, I shove it at him. "This fell to the floor when I was leaving. Please tell me there's nothing wrong. I only just found you. I can't lose you already."

"Babe. Whoa. I'm not sick. I just changed the beneficiary on my life insurance policy. It already existed."

Ok, this is good.

"Why are you wearing that?"

Sasha raises his camera and clicks away.

"Is that my shirt?" Perry's fingers caress the edge.

"Yeah. I…I had it on before I saw that. But why are you in a suit? Aren't we eating here? And why make me a beneficiary?"

Perry's head hangs with a chuckle. "Because that's what people do. They make their spouses beneficiaries. Look around, Roman."

He motions to the side where two giant vases of roses stand. They're stunning. And the twinkle lights. Sasha loves those. They're beautiful.

My best friend circles me and Perry, snapping away the whole time, and I search Perry's face.

"Is this a surprise?"

"I was hoping it would be a romantic surprise, yes."

"To tell me you're not sick?"

Perry rubs his forehead with a sigh.

"Oh, for…Roman…to ask you to be my husband. I want to ask you to be my husband."

"Are you asking right now?"

In the background, Leaf snorts, and Perry sighs again.

"Roman Auclair, from the moment I saw you in this very lodge kitchen, I knew you were someone I'd like to know. You constantly tested my patience—"

"I probably still do, to be fair."

"You do. But when you finally accepted I'm not that bad of a guy and we got to know each other, I fell for you. So hard, babe, that I worried you'd never feel the same. I wanted to tell you I loved you so many times, but each time I didn't because I knew you were so scared of what we were building."

"I was. That's true. But I told you I loved you."

Perry smiles and takes my hands in his.

"You did, and I wished we had this big romantic declaration. I wanted...romance."

"Like your books?"

"Exactly like that. So I thought Id propose memorably. I'll make it romantic and then you went and came into the building from the wrong side."

"Well, you said we were going to Leaf and Sasha's. That's an oversight on your part."

"I suppose it is."

Perry pulls a box from his coat pocket and my chest squeezes.

"Oh my god. This is real? You're actually asking me to marry you?"

"Well, I would if you'd stop interrupting."

"I would have dressed better if I'd have known!"

With another sigh, his free hand reaches out to grab my hip, and he steps closer to me, resting his forehead on mine.

"Will you marry me, Roman? And tell me yes so I can please have the romantic moment I missed before to say I love you."

He steps back and opens the box for me. I want to reach for it, but I'm overcome with a *Pretty Woman* moment and don't.

"Yes."

"Really?"

I laugh now. "Why do you sound shocked? There's no one I want more than you." Bringing my hands to his face, I pull him close for a soft kiss. "If you don't let me see that ring, I'll change my mind. But yes, all the fucking yes. I want to be your husband."

"Oh, thank fuck." He grabs my hand and jams the ring on before crashing his lips to mine. "I love you. You still drive me impossibly crazy some days, but I love you."

My whole body shakes once the enormity of what happened hits me and I look around to notice the effort Perry put into this with fresh eyes.

My favourite flowers in my favourite colours. The romantic lights. And as I turn around the room, dozens of candles are lit up. They're on the tables, in the flowers and around the punch bowl. They flicker in the dimly lit room and I turn my attention back to Perry.

"This suit is fire. The room is gorgeous." I look down at the ring on my finger. A plain platinum band with a row of five small diamonds. "This ring is...hard to take in. It's romantic. I'm sorry I ruined your plans."

"I should have known you wouldn't come in on this side. I told you we were going to Leaf's, and I was too excited to think about that, I guess."

Sasha interrupts us. "Can I pose you both now? I have enough candids."

"Of course." Perry's hand on my back leads me next to the display of roses.

"Wait. Sasha, come here."

My best friend waits and I step over to him. "I'm gonna get married. I know you're aware since you helped plan all this," I say as the shock dissolves and excitement takes its place. "But I had to tell my best friend first that I'm engaged."

He does a little jump wiggle before throwing his arms around me.

"I'm so happy for you both. And I'm so happy you finally let love in, Ro."

"Me too. Thank you for being my friend. For being a great business partner and for being there for me and putting up with all my shit."

"I'd do it all over again, too." He pushes me away and points at my feet. "You were in such a rush to get here you didn't change your shoes."

Staring down at my feet, the Crocs mock me, and I can't help laughing.

"I think this is a statement about how much I love you, Perry."

"Because you left the house in Crocs?"

"And your plaid shirt. Two things I despise and would never be caught wearing. Yet here I am. Captured in photographs forever, too. All because I had to race here to see you and make sure you were okay."

"I think there's a compliment in there somewhere."

Turning to Perry, I smile and wrap my arms around his neck.

"There was, but you deserve better than that for your romantic moment." Kissing him softly, I slide my nose along his. "Perry Attwater, you are the most amazing person I've ever met. You're patient and kind and have a heart so big I wonder how it stays in your body. You've made me a better person, for real. I know that sounds all kinds of cliché, but you have."

"Sometimes we just find the right people to make us whole. That's you, Roman. You just slid right into this space in my life like I'd been waiting for you forever. You weren't what I expected, but I'm so fucking happy you're exactly what I needed. Don't ever change."

"Don't expect me to wear these clothes longer than the next hour."

I smile big and kiss him again as he huffs in annoyance. "I know you meant me, and I have no plans to stop annoying you for the rest of our lives."

He chuckles before kissing me.

"I love you. I might regret it, but I love you."

Sasha finally gets us to pose and shows me the pics while Leaf and Perry do the brotherly sharing bit.

"You know, there's not a single professional photo of you where you look this good, Ro. Not even the lingerie ones for the website. Look how damn happy you are. This one is my favourite, I think."

He passes the camera to me and my breath hitches.

"Remember when I left Leaf that scrapbook after we met? I had that one selfie together where Leaf looked at me just like that. That's when I knew I had to make it work out."

"I remember." It was adorable, and I remember the pang of sadness I felt. I was happy for Sasha, but I allowed myself a moment to wonder if I would ever meet someone who looked at me the same way. "I asked you if he had a brother." Laughing, I recall the conversation. "Pretty sure you said yes, but I wouldn't like him."

Sasha grins. "Well, initially you didn't. So I wasn't wrong."

"Hey, babe. You ready to go?"

"Yeah. Can we still watch the duck show?"

Perry softens, and it's that look right there that stops my heart every fucking time. Like there's nothing else in the world he'd rather do, as long as it's with me.

"We can, but I need to show you something first."

After saying our goodbyes, Perry steers us towards the path to the cabins at the lodge. He takes my hand as we walk and I enjoy the night quiet. Sasha told me it was a different type of noise out here once. I think I finally get what he meant.

The lap of water on the shore, trills of bullfrogs and tree frogs, and rustles of animals along the ground. And the muted silence of darkness. It's peaceful in a way I've never experienced.

We step off the path and onto the beach of pebbles and sand. Perry stops us just before it turns to real sand.

"When the moon is high, and the night is clear, it reflects on the lake's surface like tonight. It's so bright it's like someone shines a flashlight just for you to find your way."

The moon is indeed high and shining a runway across the lake's smooth surface. No matter where you stand, it's like it shines only for you.

"It's gorgeous, Perry."

I have to admit I'm kicking myself for not making the time earlier to experience this. I'm not big on outdoor stuff and whenever Sasha invited me I begged off, certain it wasn't as great as he hyped it up to be. I was wrong.

"That's how it felt when I knew I loved you. You were so bright it made me see what I was missing." His eyes are shiny as he strokes the back of his hand over my cheek. "This is what you do to me. You bring light to my life, to my heart, to everything. When things are dark, you're my moon on the water."

He presses a kiss on my forehead.

"This is the moment I wanted. Not everything inside the lodge. Not even seeing my ring on your finger. Just you and me, out here with the moon and stars and me telling you I love you."

"It's perfect." My voice wavers, but I shake it off. "You're perfect. Thank you."

We wrap our arms around each other's waist, and I rest my head on his shoulder. When I shiver, he wordlessly removes his suit jacket and holds it out for me. I slip into it and we return to our position, neither of us wanting the moment to end.

But there's only so much romance I can take.

"Perry?"

"Yeah?"

"Can we go home so I can show you a real moon?" I can't stay serious and snort a laugh.

Thankfully, he laughs too and turns us back to the path, but I pull on him to wait.

"This is the most beautiful thing anyone has ever said or done for me. I'll never forget it. Thank you for once again giving me something I didn't know I wanted. Romance isn't my strong point, but I'll do my best for you."

I kiss him once more before we return to the truck and steal one more glance at the moonlit water.

"I'll always be your moon, Perry. For as long as you have me."

"That's forever."

And that sounds perfect to me.

Chapter 28
Epilogue

Three years later

Perry

Rolling over, I find the other side of the bed empty and sit up. Right. We have a house guest and he likes to be awake at night. I swear that kid is part owl.

Pulling on my lounge pants that sit on the floor, I shuffle out to the living room. Sun pours in through the window and I shield my eyes. Cartoons play on the TV and I follow my husband's voice down the other hall.

"Alex, you said you had to pee."

A giggle follows, and I bite my lip at the tired sigh from Roman.

"If you pee, we can go back to the cartoons. When Uncle Perry wakes up, we'll go outside, okay?"

I lean against the wall, listening to the mini version of Roman sass back at his uncle. There's probably karma involved somewhere in all this.

"I peed!" little Alex shouts, and Roman hoots with joy. I listen as Roman reminds him to flush and helps him wash his hands.

"Unckey Perry!" Alex flies into the hallway when he sees me poke my head in and I scoop him up. He laughs as I raspberry his neck.

"Are you giving Uncle Roman a hard time this morning?"

Alex babbles his answer as my gaze finds Roman. The dark circles under his eyes tell me all I need to know about how much he was up last night with our little nephew. But the fond smile on his face also tells me he doesn't regret a thing.

Setting Alex down, I tell him to go watch his cartoons and I'll make some of his favourite bacon in a few minutes.

"Was he up all night?"

Roman steps into my arms with a sigh.

"Almost every two hours. He's too excited to be here. It's cute and endearing the first few times. Then it just gets on my nerves and I want him to sleep." He kisses me and I hum against his lips.

"You were cute and endearing the first time you came here too, if I recall."

"Don't be an ass and rub it in. I don't know how my sister does it 24/7. It's only been two nights and I feel like a zombie. I always forget how busy he is."

He's not the only one, but we love him. Even though Roman complains, he loves having this one-on-one time with Alex.

"I know we never really talked about it, but...did you want kids? Seems like we should've had this conversation before we said I do."

Roman snorts.

"We did. At his first birthday party, when he was so excited, he threw up all over the cake table. I said, lord remind me I don't want to be a parent."

He tilts his head at me. "Did you ever want kids? You're so much better with him than me. He wants you to show him how to fish, by the way. He couldn't stop talking about it at 2 A.M., so thank you for that."

"I did once, but I also had a job that took me away too much. If I had kids, I wanted to be there for them every day. I wouldn't have been able to leave for a week at a time."

"You're such a softie that way."

"It's why you love me."

His hand drifts down my chest and ends with cupping my balls over my pants.

"It's only one reason. I like you hard, too."

I laugh and kiss him, pressing him back into the wall. "You're so cheesy."

"I'm horny. I love the little dude, but Jesus, Perry, I didn't think he'd never sleep a wink at night. I miss our morning wake-ups."

Shoving my leg between his thighs, I press into him. He whines and rocks his hips.

"A quickie at nap time?" I trail my lips down his neck. "Will he sleep for seven minutes?"

"Unkey Ro! Look it!"

I step away from Roman and adjust myself. But there's no need because my erection deflates like a balloon left in the cold.

"Oh god. Alex, give that to me. You've been bad. That's not a toy."

Roman throws a panicked look my way, and I shrug.

"If he was in our bathroom, he saw it. And it's a fun, cool blue colour."

Alex waves the silicone dildo in the air and laughs while Roman chases after him.

"Stop laughing and help me!"

I know I should, but I can't. Until Roman calls from our bedroom.

"Perry! Oh lord…"

Alex stands in our bedroom with a quivering lip, and I rush to scoop him up.

"Hey, don't cry. We can fix it."

Roman drops his head back with a groan. Peering into our bathroom, I join him.

Alex was out of sight for maybe five minutes. During that time, he found the dildo on the counter, emptied the shaving cream in the sink and sprayed it on the shower doors. My *Gold Bond* powder floats in the toilet, the empty container on the floor.

"Are we supposed to punish him? I don't know how this works."

Which is true. Do three olds understand? Is it like animals and you need to catch them in the act?

"I don't know!" Roman throws his hands in the air. "Technically, it's our fault for not watching him." He still holds the blue dildo in his hand and it wiggles as he rants over the mess he has to clean up, but not once does he yell at Alex or even take his frustration out on me.

"Go make him the bacon he loves and I'll clean this up. Chalk it up to another life lesson."

"And what's that?"

"I don't want kids." He laughs and tickles Alex in my arms. "But I'll be an uncle every day of the week. Just promise Uncle Ro you'll never come in here again."

Alex nods. "Prawmiss, Unkey Ro. Love yous."

Roman rustles his blond hair, so much like his own. "I love you, too. Go eat bacon."

He squirms out of my arms and tears off to the kitchen.

"If you need a nap, just lay down when you're done. I'll keep him amused."

"Save me some bacon."

Another year later

Roman

"You're sure this won't fly away and we'll be alone out here?"

Leaf brushes off his hands with a smile.

"Nothing will fly away and there're no guests scheduled." He roots in his coat pocket. "Here's the key to cabin three if you decide to stay longer and need to get warm or whatnot. Just in case."

"Oh, good thinking. Thank you for your help."

"Anytime, Roman. Thank you for making my brother so happy. You two are good for each other."

"Thank you. I think you're right about that."

Leaf and I chat some more before he leaves me, and I check my phone. Perry finally read my message and I hope he can make it. My text was only a little cryptic, but he's smart.

Perry: I'm on my way.

I send him a heart and wait. I shouldn't be nervous. He'll eat this up with a spoon, but other than laying in bed decked out in lace, I've done nothing purely romantic for him. Nothing grand, like organizing a surprise proposal that I fucked up.

My business took off, and I spent my days scaling and managing it. We visited my sister and nephew as often as possible. And Perry often got called out on fire calls as a volunteer firefighter. Those were the hardest for me. Knowing he was off and possibly in danger for hours at a time with no communication.

It was hard fighting off the anxiety of those nights and the fear of him never coming back, but it was getting a little easier. It's always there, but my coping has improved thanks to Perry.

But he deserves more from me. To give him what he secretly wishes for.

And it's time for me to show him I listen. He talks about his book club meetings with me often. It makes me laugh. The book club is still just him and Sasha, but he enjoys it. And I've been taking notes.

The crunch of footsteps draws my attention to the path and I wait for Perry to step into the beach clearing. When he does, my god, I wish I had done this sooner. His face fills with a joyous smile as he quickens his step over to me.

"What's all this?"

He cups my face and leans in for a kiss, the smile never leaving his face.

"This is our spot. Where you told me you loved me, and I was your moon in the darkness." I kiss the shell of his ear. "On this exact day four years ago. I hope you remember."

"Of course I do. The best night of my life. Next to marrying you, that is."

"Instead of rushing off, we can get comfortable and watch the moon and stars." I slide my hands around his waist and into the back pockets of his jeans. "I also have a special surprise for you."

He grins even bigger.

"Do we get to fuck under the stars? Please say yes."

Laughing, his eternal happiness rubbing off on me, I kiss him again.

"Well, yeah, that was part of the surprise, but I have something else for you. Come on."

We leave our shoes outside the tent Leaf set up for me. The whole top of the tent is a screen so we can still see the moon and stars, and I arranged the door to face the moon. Inside is only a thin foam mattress and a few blankets, but it will do the job.

He lies on his back with a sigh and looks out the top.

"This is amazing, Roman."

"You're amazing," I whisper across his lips before crawling over him. "I didn't think it was possible to love you more, but I do. You make me do mushy, romantic things."

His body shakes with laughter under me.

"To be fair, I gave you the idea since I brought you here first."

"True. But I remembered and..." I roll off him and find the gift. "I wrote a book about it."

His smile falters briefly before noticing I'm telling the truth.

"For real?"

He takes the package from my hand with a raised brow.

"Just open it, Perry."

His fingers gently rip open the paper to find a hardcover photo book. The photo on the front is what we see right now. This very moon and this very lake. The title is simple: You're my Moon.

I watch as he opens it and reads each page, his smile never dropping, but he blinks faster and wipes at his cheeks.

"Don't tear stain the paper, baby."

"I can't believe you did this. You put our life into a book. You made our romance into a fucking book." He shakes his head with a shaky breath and the last page is a photo of our wedding. It's our favourite because it wasn't even a professional photo. A friend snapped it while we shared a quiet moment together at the reception. Our expressions leave nothing unsaid. My fingers curl around his tie and one of his hands grips my chin. What came after that photo was mostly x-rated because our love isn't just grapefruit pieces in the fridge and muscular arms to hold during nightmares.

We're passionate and equals.

Each other's rock.

Messy and somehow imperfectly perfect.

"I love you, Perry. I tell you that all the time, but I wanted you to know there's no one else in this world I want to spend my days with. You, too, shine your light on me when things are dark. You're my moon, too."

He wipes at his cheeks and sets the book aside.

"Get naked."

Laughing, I crawl on him again and cover his face with kisses.

"A well-spoken man. I love it."

"I'm gonna show you how much I love this, and you. Because there're no words for it, Roman. Thank you isn't enough."

"Well then, not that I was looking for *that* kind of thanks, but I'll take it."

"You're a rotten liar. You're a horny bastard on every day that ends in y." He smiles big as I laugh again. He's not wrong.

And if you told me five years ago when I moved here to follow my best friend that I'd fall in love, get married, enjoy plaid—in moderation—and have sex in a tent, I'd have told you to seek therapy.

Yet here I am. Proving that love really changes a person.

And I wouldn't have it any other way.

Thank you for reading!
If you want to know how Sasha and Leaf got together, their story is Beauty and the Beard.
If cowboys are more your thing, and you want to meet Sasha before he falls in love, he and Roman first appear in Alec.

Acknowledgements

Thank you so much for reading Roman and Perry's story. They were so much fun to write. I initially planned for them to be enemies to lovers, but Perry's heart was much too squishy for that. He wanted romance. All the hearts and flowers and the poor guy had to fall for the one guy who wasn't into romance even when he's in love.

After Leaf's book and the grief I carried, Roman was a lift I needed to follow my groove again and I will always love him for bursting into my head and demanding I tell his story next. Which is exactly what happened and why this book is out seven months ahead of plan. Yep, Roman was that chatty and I couldn't say no.

You might have noticed a few cameos in this one. I couldn't resist having Alec and Zane back. And if you read the short story Take the Shot in the Truth or Dare anthology, there were likely a few familiar names as well. If you missed that short story, keep watching my website. I'll have it for sale directly in the future.

I had so much fun writing this, it's hard to say goodbye. But maybe they'll be back somewhere else one day. Whose to say?

Every book has its team to thank, and this one is no different.

Thank you, Kathleen and Kristen for the early feedback. I appreciate the extra time you gave me to read their story. First times are always nerve-wracking, lol. You both set me at ease.

Jenn, as always, thank you for making everything better. Your emoji strings and crazy outbursts in the middle of editing always make me smile. You're my rockstar. Not quite Benson Boone, but you'll do.

Several author friends listened during my struggle over dropping one project to write this one instead. I can't thank you all enough for easing my mind and cheerleading me on. There's far too many of you to list, but you know who you are. I cherish your friendship and encouragement. Thank you for being there.

Finally you, dear reader. I truly appreciate your support in any manner you provide. Without you, there are no stories. Your reviews, ratings, recommendations and presence in my online social communities aren't taken for granted. Thank you for being there and giving me the confidence to keep going. You make all this happen, so thank you.

Much love,

RM

Also By

Want to read more by me?

Scan the code to find my back list.

www.ingramcontent.com/pod-product-compliance
Lightning Source LLC
Chambersburg PA
CBHW072055190726
48294CB00005B/1531